THEN
YOU
HIDE

THE CRITICS LOVE

ROXANNE ST. CLAIRE

AND

THE BULLET CATCHERS

"Roxanne St. Claire leaves us wanting just one thing—more Bullet Catchers."

—Romance Novel TV

"Sexy, smart, and suspenseful."
—Mariah Stewart, *New York Times* bestselling author

"When it comes to dishing up great romantic suspense, St. Claire is the author you want."

—*Romantic Times*

NOW YOU DIE

"The incredibly talented Ms. St. Claire . . . keeps the audience on tenterhooks with her clever ruses, while the love scenes pulsate with sensuality and an exquisite tenderness that zeroes in on the heart."

—*The Winter Haven News Chief* (FL)

"Top-notch suspense."

—*Romantic Times*

"A non-stop thrill ride of mayhem that leaves you breathless."

—Simply Romance Reviews

Also by Roxanne St. Claire

Now You Die

Then You Hide

First You Run

What You Can't See
with Allison Brennan, et al.

Take Me Tonight

I'll Be Home for Christmas
with Linda Lael Miller, et al.

Thrill Me to Death

Kill Me Twice

Killer Curves

French Twist

Tropical Getaway

Hit Reply

And coming soon from Pocket Star Books

Hunt Her Down
in September 2009
and

Make Her Pay
in October 2009

ROXANNE ST. CLAIRE

THEN YOU HIDE

POCKET STAR BOOKS
New York London Toronto Sydney

Pocket Star Books
A Division of Simon & Schuster, Inc.
1230 Avenue of the Americas
New York, NY 10020

This book is a work of fiction. Names, characters, places, and incidents either are products of the author's imagination or are used fictitiously. Any resemblance to actual events or locales or persons, living or dead, is entirely coincidental.

This Pocket Star Books paperback edition June 2009

POCKET STAR and colophon are registered trademarks of Simon & Schuster, Inc.

For information about special discounts for bulk purchases, please contact Simon & Schuster Special Sales at 1-866-506-1949 or business@simonandschuster.com

The Simon & Schuster Speakers Bureau can bring authors to your live event. For more information or to book an event contact the Simon & Schuster Speakers Bureau at 1-866-248-3049 or visit our website at www.simonspeakers.com.

Cover Design by Carl Galian

Manufactured in the United States of America

10 9 8 7 6 5 4 3 2 1

ISBN: 978-1-4391-4946-1

For Kern Walsh Zink, a woman of wisdom, a lover of life, a compassionate sister who completed our family when she married into it and left a hole in our hearts when she departed. She is missed and loved by many.

ACKNOWLEDGMENTS

I NEVER TRAVEL alone. This trip to the Caribbean was made possible and more accurate by some generous and helpful sources and I thank them all. In particular . . .

Down in the islands, mon, there are amazing people. They include the informative and helpful staff of the Villas Caribe, who guided me through the steep curves and even steeper costs of island vacation rentals; the angels who run a piece of paradise on earth known as the Four Seasons Resort in Nevis; and the supremely knowledgeable public relations department of the Star Clippers, who, for the second time in my career, let me make waves on one of their ships. Also a nod to good friends Christie Locke and Tammy Strickland, who shared their Nevis experiences with me.

The investment geniuses at The Blackstone Group and Pope Financial (thank you, Marcel!) provided insights into the world of Wall Street, hedge fund management, and the life and times and mind-set of an asset manager.

Roger Cannon, my go-to source for anything that

shoots a bullet; he is truly Bullet Catcher material for his patience, humor, determination, and dedication to the truth. And he's kinda hot, too!

My team of experts in the publishing world: Micki Nuding, a visionary editor with a magic pencil and perfect touch; and my agent, Kim Whalen of Trident Media Group, who always has my back—usually to catch me when I'm about to fall.

Although they were not part of my research, there was a team of heroes who took over my world while writing this book, so I have to give a shout and a box of the finest chocolate to the nurses and staff of the Holmes Regional Heart Center. Most of all, I would like to acknowledge the skill and brilliance of Dr. Michael Greene, a surgeon, an artist, a healer, a gentleman. In his gifted hands, I trusted the heart that matters most to me, the one I married. My deepest gratitude to the entire team of cardio superstars who have the courage and capability to save lives, fix broken hearts, and create medical miracles every single day.

And because of those miracle makers, the husband whom I depend upon is strong, happy, and healthy enough to let me hide in my hole and write. As always, I am profoundly grateful for the love and support that carries me through every day. Thank you, Rich, for being an exemplary heart patient and an even better husband. And finally, a lifetime of love and gratitude to my children, Dante and Mia, who amaze me every time they define grace under pressure. You three are why I live, love, write, and breathe.

THEN YOU HIDE

PROLOGUE

Charleston, South Carolina, 1978

"WELL, LOOK WHAT we have here. The prettiest little suspect in Charleston County." The fluorescent lights cast a sick, yellow shadow on the cheeks of the man who'd just entered the interrogation room.

Eileen Stafford straightened in the uncomfortable wooden chair and met his gaze. "Where's my lawyer?"

"He's comin', sweetheart. He's comin'. Mind if I sit down?" Across the table, he yanked out the other chair, flipped it around, and spread his legs around the back. "You remember me, don't you?"

As if she could forget the man who'd tried to blind her with a flashlight, cut her with handcuffs, and insult her from the front seat of his squad car.

She sat silent. Because *anything you say can and will be used against you in a court of law.*

"We met the other night out on Ashley Bridge." He

lifted thick black eyebrows and crinkled his forehead, all friendly and social.

She glared back at him. "Pretty convenient, you and your partner just cruising along looking for people driving away from crime scenes."

"Oh, now, honey, you know what happened. Someone saw you running and called the cops. While we were following you lead-footin' out of Charleston, Ms. Sloane's body was found." He held out his hands to imply that this happened all the time to a good cop.

Or a very bad one.

Didn't he realize this case was so flimsy you could see through it? She'd seen the murder; she'd witnessed it! She knew who did it, yet she sat here, sweating, waiting for a lawyer who was supposed to be here hours ago. When he came, she could tell him who pulled the trigger and who put that gun on the passenger seat of her car—a gun she'd never touched.

But would she have the nerve to tell the truth? To take on the most powerful man in the county? The thought made her stomach roll.

"Why'd you do it, Miss Stafford?"

She bit her lip to keep from saying a word.

"It *is* miss, isn't it?" Hazel eyes dropped to her chest. "Sure it is. I've seen you around the courthouse. You're a flirty little thing. Real friendly with all the lawyers and judges. You're a legal secretary. Just like . . . the deceased."

"Which makes me smart enough to know I get a lawyer before I talk to anybody."

He chuckled, propping his elbows on the table and locking his hands into a little shelf for his chin. "And smart enough to know that the South Carolina legal system don't always work as right as it should."

She fought a quiver, unwilling to let him see her fear. "I'm not going to talk to you, Officer."

"Then how 'bout you *listen* to me . . . Leenie."

Oh, God—only one person on earth called her that. Which meant whatever this cop was about to say was a direct message from *him*.

"Listen real careful, okay?" His look made her heart wallop against her ribs. "I'm gonna offer you a fine deal."

"A deal?" Or her worst nightmare? The man who had destroyed her happiness, forcing her to make a decision she would regret until the day she died—that man could do anything. He could lie, cheat, steal, and, oh, Godamighty, he could kill.

"Real simple, this deal. You tell your lawyer exactly how you killed Wanda, how you were hidin' right there in that alley, just waitin' to pounce on the gal who'd taken your place as the prettiest legal secretary in the courthouse, and—"

"I wasn't waiting for—"

"—and we'll make sure you don't have to sit in the hot seat." One corner of his thin-lipped mouth slid up. "You know what I mean by the hot seat, don't you, Leenie?"

"There hasn't been an electrocution in this state since 1962."

"Capital punishment is alive and well in the state of

South Carolina, darlin'. In the hands of"—he bared straight, shiny teeth—"the right judge."

Eileen closed her eyes. She'd known this was coming. Ever since she'd hidden behind that brick wall in Philadelphia Alley and watched her former lover put a bullet into Wanda Sloane, she'd known she couldn't run far, and she couldn't hide for long. Not from him.

"It's a simple deal. You tell the lawyer just what happened, Leenie. And in exchange . . ." He shrugged, as if the rest were obvious.

"Say it," she insisted hoarsely. "You have to say it."

He leaned close. "Sign the piece of paper pleading guilty . . . and nothing will happen to your baby."

She *knew* it.

"I don't have a baby."

That statement would be the truth in a deposition. She didn't have *a* baby. She'd had three. But he didn't know that. No one in Charleston knew that.

"You have a child," he said in a patronizing tone. " 'Course, you sold the poor li'l fatherless bastard. But anyone can be . . ." He took out a handkerchief, blew his nose, let the unfinished sentence hang in the air. ". . . found with the right people pulling the strings."

She stared at him.

He folded his hanky and stuffed it into a breast pocket. "And you know, sweetheart, those black-market babies are not always the healthiest. They've been known to just die in their li'l cribs."

That murdering, lying son of a bitch. Would he kill his own daughter?

Of course he would. He was capable of anything.

He bought cops like this sleazebucket, bought juries, bought witnesses, bought loyalty. Hell, he'd bought her.

But he only knew she'd gone to the farmhouse on Sapphire Trail to have a baby. No one except the nurse, the lady who owned the place, and one of the sets of adoptive parents knew she'd had triplets that night eight months ago.

Three tiny, helpless baby girls who were all sold to strangers. He only knew of one, but she didn't know *which* one. Any of those tiny babies could be his victim, unless she . . .

"Make this deal." Impatience edged his voice. "Or she dies."

Right now, her daughters were safe and loved. And marked. If they ever found one another, would that tell them the story of what their mother did and why? All that mattered was that they lived. Her life was worthless without them, anyway.

"Okay," she said in defeat.

He pushed away from the table and sauntered to the door with a lazy, cocky grin. "I heard you were a very smart girl, Leenie. Guess it's true." He pulled the door open, and she heard him say, "The suspect is ready to bargain."

Eileen dropped her head into her hands. Maybe someday, her babies would forgive her for selling them to strangers. And if they ever discovered who gave them birth, maybe they'd understand why, eight months after they were born, she'd shouldered the blame for a crime she didn't commit.

CHAPTER
ONE

Astor Cove, New York
The Hudson River Valley
Summer 2008

"I'M NOT IN the business of killing people anymore." Wade Cordell slid the contract across Lucy Sharpe's writing table, his defined jaw and steel-blue eyes hard in contrast to his soft Southern drawl.

"Bullet Catchers don't kill people, Wade. We protect them. If pushed to the absolute limit and forced to save the life of a principal, we do what needs to be done. And we do it better than any other security and investigation firm in the world." She slid the paper right back and tapped the signature line with one red nail. "That's why I want you on my staff full-time."

"Call it what you like, ma'am, but killing is killing, and I have murdered my last person."

"It's not *murder* when the world is a better, safer place and thousands of people are alive because of your skills."

He shifted his muscular frame in the antique chair and nailed her with his deadly sniper's gaze. "I had no problems pulling that trigger as a Marine, Lucy. It was my job, it was war, and it was right. But those other times . . ."

"Special assignments for the CIA are as much an act of war as anything you did in Iraq, and you know that."

"Spoken like a true former spook."

She acknowledged her background with a nod. "But you aren't in the CIA, you're a free agent. And I want you as a Bullet Catcher. Not because you're the best damn sharpshooter the Marines ever produced but because your overall instincts are masterful."

He snorted softly. "Yeah, that last kill was pure genius."

"You did what had to be done. I heard the details from the top of the agency, and you may think it was a mess, but—"

"It *was* a mess."

"They were pleased with the outcome. But not so pleased that you've refused every assignment since. I, however"—she picked up the pen and offered it to him—"am thrilled."

He leaned back and stretched out his long legs. "I like consulting occasionally for you, Luce. It suits me to drop in quickly, then disappear. I don't want to get too . . . close to anything." He treated her to a grin as sweet as pecan pie. "That's just the hunter in me, I guess."

"That's just your inability to commit to anything but a clean shot," she replied, instantly erasing his smile. "You need to commit to an organization. This one."

He pushed himself up to amble over to the window and studied the summer green hills of the Hudson River Valley for a long time. Finally, he turned back to her. "You have any assassins on your payroll, Luce?"

"Wade, you are not an assassin. You are a man with an extraordinary sniper's skill, a hunter's eye, and a powerful sense of duty. You briefly combined those abilities to rid the world of a few evil beasts. It didn't work out for you, and now it's time to do something else." She tapped the contract. "Be a Bullet Catcher."

"I've been one," he replied.

"You've done special projects for the last five months, and you've been brilliant. Now it's time to belong."

He returned to the view, undoubtedly thinking and deliberating, as he always did before making any decision.

"Bullet Catchers' clients are some mighty high-profile people," he finally said.

"They can be. Some are just enormously wealthy."

"I imagine they want to know exactly who is protecting them."

"They aren't privy to the backgrounds of my specialists and bodyguards, Wade. And believe me, not every Bullet Catcher can wear a halo, including me."

He turned to give her a slight smile. "Yet what could be more on the side of the angels than this operation?"

"Which is exactly why I want you." Lucy waited a beat. "I run a tight group, and a sense of community and trust is critical to our success on every assignment. As the owner of this business, I prefer full-time staff to consultants."

"Because you can't control consultants."

True. "I want you full-time, committed to the job and the company. You'll make an outstanding Bullet Catcher, and you'll get tremendous satisfaction from the work." She folded her arms and leaned back in her chair. "But I'm not going to push anymore. The decision is yours."

He strolled back to the desk. "I need some more time."

"To do what?" she challenged. "Beat yourself up for what happened in Budapest?"

"I shot a man in the face from two feet away, Lucy. I watched his skull crack. He looked me in the eye as he died." He dropped into the chair, his wide shoulders slumping. "That's a whole lot different from taking a shot from fifteen hundred yards, peering through a rifle sight. And I doubt you can promise that I'd never have to do that again, as somone's paid protector."

"I won't lie to you, Wade. You might have to kill someone again in the line of duty. But most of the time, you'll be saving lives and protecting people. You may be looking for missing persons, and hunting is another of your proficiencies—along with a keen mind and a steady hand. Honestly, what else are you going to do with your life?"

He lifted one impressive shoulder. "I haven't figured that out yet, but I will. I like to take my time and plan things."

"All right." Disappointed, she was sliding the unsigned contract back into his file when her fingers grazed the paperwork for her next meeting . . . and lightning struck. She plucked the folder out and held it to her chest, regarding him. "I was going to send Donovan Rush on this case as his first official assignment, since it's a gimme."

"An assignment so cushy they should pay you to take it?"

"Precisely." She handed him the file. "My gift to you. Go take a few days in paradise, and find a woman."

Humor glinted like ice in his eyes. "So everything your men say is true."

"That I have a kind, understanding heart, and I'm a goddess to work for?"

He laughed at her sarcasm. "That you have elevated manipulation to an art form and don't take no for an answer."

"Oh, that. But I'm not manipulating you. I'm giving you time and a lovely place to think and plan. You'll never have to touch your Smith and Wesson. The only talent you'll use is charm," she added with a wink.

Wade opened the folder and glanced at the top

page. "Who is Vanessa Porter, and what sins has she committed?"

"Nothing but being born and adopted on the black market. We need to find her."

He glanced up. "I thought that case was closed after Adrien Fletcher located Miranda Lang out in California a few months ago. I did some backup for him on the takedown. The cult leader who was terrorizing Miranda Lang was turned over to the FBI."

"Yes, and Miranda went with Fletch to South Carolina and met the birth mother, who, as you may recall, is in jail for murder."

He nodded, returning to the file. "The mother needs a bone-marrow transplant to live, right?"

"Correct. But Miranda isn't a match. We hope Vanessa Porter is."

He studied the photo clipped to the file, intrigued. "How's that?"

"She's Miranda's sister. Eileen Stafford, the birth mother, revealed that Miranda was one of triplet girls sold through the Sapphire Trail operation. Vanessa Porter is another of the three."

Wade looked at the photo of an impeccably dressed blonde striding down Wall Street, a cell phone pressed to her ear, a sleek briefcase clutched in her other hand, no-nonsense black glasses completing the look. He skimmed through a few more pages, which described a single, workaholic money manager living in Manhattan.

"According to your men in California, Jack Culver thinks this Eileen Stafford might be innocent."

"Jack is not one of my men," Lucy said coolly. "He's simply a PI who initially launched this investigation on behalf of Eileen Stafford. Her guilt or innocence isn't my concern." Nothing that involved former Bullet Catcher Jack Culver was her concern. "I promised to locate Vanessa Porter, and I have. She's a passenger on a Utopia Cruise Line sailing clipper, currently cruising the Leeward Islands. The next stop is St. Kitts. I'm offering you a few days in the islands, a pretty blonde to persuade to meet her birth mother, and a chance to think about what you want to do with your life."

He glanced at the pages again, returning to the photo. "How much time do I have?"

"Not much. Stafford is in a coma and fading fast. If we're going to reunite her with her daughters and try to find a bone-marrow match, we have to move quickly. There may not be time for Vanessa to finish her Caribbean cruise—which could be a sticking point, since she evidently hasn't taken a day off in six years."

"What if she doesn't believe me? A financial wizard will probably demand irrefutable proof. We have, what . . ." He pulled a paper out. "A list of babies born in this farmhouse and sold sometime in the summer of 1977. No birth certificate? No legal docs?"

"We have something." She touched her nape. "Under her hair, there should be a small tattoo. Evidently, all three girls got them at birth. Once she hears the story, her sister Miranda is hoping she'll have a soft heart."

"This Wall Street high roller doesn't look like she has a soft anything."

"You'll never know until you find her."

He closed the file and stood. "All right. I'm in. Tell Donovan I'm sorry I stole his gimme job, and thanks for the R-and-R."

Lucy stood to shake hands. "Thank you, Wade. Sage will arrange for the Bullet Catchers jet to get you down there, and she'll hook you up with an international phone and a password for our locator system to track you. She'll also have all the necessary paperwork for you and a bodyguard's license to carry concealed anywhere in the world."

There was skepticism in his smile. "And here I thought I'd never have to touch my S-and-W."

She came around her desk and gave him a friendly pat on the shoulder. "Only in extreme situations."

"Exactly what I'm trying to avoid."

After Wade left, Lucy reread the confidential report on Budapest she'd managed to get from the agency. It *had* been a wreck, but they still believed in Wade Cordell, and so did she. This trip to the French West Indies was a brilliant way to remind him of how great the Bullet Catchers job could be. Then he'd sign, and they'd both be happier.

If not, she'd still be looking for a fearless, intelligent security professional with unparalleled sharpshooting skills for her staff. And Wade Cordell, a man she admired and respected, would still be trying to make peace with the fact that his greatest talent was killing people.

Vanessa Porter was *not* his type.

Not that Wade didn't appreciate a tall, sexy blonde

as much as the next male, especially when her black tank top and white shorts hugged some sweet curves. But something about her irritated him—even from fifty feet away with clusters of tourists separating them across Port Zante.

The horn-rimmed glasses? A power play. The speed of her trajectory? That screamed Yankee to him. The little left-right sway in her backside that grabbed the eye of every man she passed? He despised women who drew attention to themselves. Her generous breasts were more than the requisite handful, her hair needed a six-inch trim and something to keep it from flying all over the place, and those thighs? They didn't quite touch at the top, as if there were room for . . . someone else in there.

She was plenty womanly, all right, but not *feminine*. He liked a sweet, tender peach, all squeezably soft and fresh. Vanessa Porter was no peach.

She was a tart.

And just for the record, this tart was *not* on vacation. He didn't have to scope her for ten minutes to figure that out. She'd disembarked a water taxi from a sailing ship anchored a half-mile away and held a brief conversation with an older woman who wore a ridiculous orange sun hat and a matching muumuu. Discussing an itinerary or shopping and lunch plans? But then she took off at the speed of light, leaving the big orange hat looking vaguely disappointed.

Wade followed her, easily matching her speed and agility but marveling at it.

She navigated packs of tourists on the promenade, sidestepping street vendors who hawked their wares, heading straight into the crowded streets and clogged sidewalks of Basseterre. Carrying only a huge handbag, her flip-flops snapping on the pavement, she moved like a heat-seeking missile with no camera or guidebook in sight. She was on a mission, all right, and it wasn't to sightsee in the capital of St. Kitts.

But whatever she had on her agenda, Wade was about to change it.

He planned to get the adoption-and-dying-mother announcement over with as quickly and cleanly as possible. Find the target, scope out the situation, take a clean shot, be done.

If he got lucky, she'd take the Bullet Catchers plane to South Carolina all by herself, and he could hang around the tropics with no shirt, no shoes, no problems.

Watching her buzz through Basseterre, that fantasy faded fast. Everything about her body language was uninviting and closed. Her delicate jaw was set in the direction she strode, her left arm clutching her bag like a warrior's shield, her right hand pressed protectively to her side as she barreled along. What was so dang important?

Maybe that was just the walk of a New Yorker, as observed by a man who grew up fifty miles south of Alabama. Still, he followed her easily, his interest notching up. After years of stealthily tailing targets, Wade had gotten very good at surmising what someone was up to.

And Vanessa Porter, thirty-one-year-old Wall Street high flyer who hadn't taken a vacation in six years and pulled in a quarter-mil a year—base pay—as vice president and director of mergers and acquisitions at Razor Partners LLC, was definitely up to *something*.

Every few minutes, she whipped out a handheld device and angled it to the sun, touching the screen and muttering to herself. Once, just for fun, he circled around and brushed by her and heard what his mama called the "dirtiest of dirty words" when she didn't get whatever she wanted from the little computer.

She'd glanced up and met his gaze, holding it longer than any Southern girl who'd been schooled in the art of averting her eyes. She gave him a thorough checking-out before she zoomed on. She didn't pause to admire the landmark tower, inhale the sweetness of the frangipani that hung over the whole island, or toss some change to the herds of barefoot children pleading for pennies on every corner. She sailed right past candy-colored buildings and marched over cobblestones and bricks with the focus of a woman who knew exactly where she was going and why.

Wade stayed right on her tail and watched those white shorts hitch left, right, left, like her own military march.

Not far from the Circus clock she slowed her step, glanced up and down the busy intersection of Fort and Banks Street, then crossed to enter the Ballahoo Restaurant. The tables were outdoor, under umbrellas, mostly peppered with the early lunch crowd, and she snaked through them straight to the bar, where she levered herself into an empty stool and whipped out that handheld again.

Wade followed, murmuring some "Excuse me's" she'd no doubt skipped, and stood close enough to her to hear but not draw attention.

The bartender placed an empty cocktail napkin in front of her. "CSR and Tang? It's the official drink of St. Kitts, you know."

"No, thank you." She slid something across the bar. "Have you seen this man in here in the past few weeks?"

So *that's* what she was up to. On the hunt for the one that got away.

The bartender raised his brows a little, glanced at the picture, then at Vanessa. "No, sorry."

Wade saw her shoulders sag in frustration. She pushed the picture forward again. "Are you sure?"

The man's smile faded. "I'm sure. And if you're going to sit here, you need to buy a drink."

"Are you absolutely positive?"

The bartender glowered at her. To be fair, the man had barely looked at the picture, and Wade would have wondered the same thing. Only he'd have taken the time to get friendly first, to make a connection with the potential informant and probably get a better response.

"Listen." She leaned closer and reached for the bartender's hand. "I know about this place."

Wade glanced around the bamboo bar and its higher-end clientele. What about the place?

The bartender's black eyes narrowed. "I have never seen your man in here. Sorry." He turned away.

She stared at him for a second, then turned in her stool to survey the patrons. She lingered over a table of four young men, tanned, toned, and dressed in the tourists' uniform of khakis, T-shirts, and flip-flops. One of them said something; they all laughed and toasted frosty mugs of beer.

She watched for another few seconds, gathered her giant bag, her phone, and her picture, and headed straight for the table. The laughter died down when she reached them, changing to a look of surprised interest.

If she was out to get lucky, maybe she didn't realize she'd gone to the wrong side of the street. That group was more interested in one another than in a woman in short shorts and a tight top.

Wade moved to the other end of the bar and leaned against the last stool. He couldn't hear the conversation, but he had a direct view of the table and their interaction.

Out came the picture again, passed from man to man. The first three shook their heads. The last one studied it and said something, eliciting laughter from the others.

Except for Vanessa, who gave them a tight, impatient smile. Then she crouched down and spoke again, her mouth moving as fast as her feet had, and whatever she said definitely held the men's attention. One nodded. Another put a sympathetic hand on her arm.

"Buy you a drink?"

Wade turned from the scene to an older man who stood next to him, quickly taking in an impression of wealth and confidence.

"Unless you're more interested in that table of play-boys you're ogling," the man added.

His target had led him right into a gay bar.

"No, thanks," he said, but the other man eased into the next barstool, forcing Wade to move his arm.

"You on vacation?"

"Business." Wade turned away, just in time to catch one of the men at the table write something on a paper napkin and hand it to Vanessa.

"What business are you in? Modeling? You've got the build for it."

She said good-bye and whisked her way toward the street.

"'Scuse me." Wade pushed off the stool and fol-lowed, staying about twenty steps behind. She paused at the entrance, reread the napkin, and crunched it into a ball before tossing it onto a table that hadn't been bussed.

Wade grabbed the discarded napkin just as a large group of tourists entered, blocking him long enough for her to dash across the street and get into a taxi. He uncrumpled the paper.

Bartholomew Nine. Gideon Bones.

"You won't do any better there."

Wade drew back at the intrusion, meeting the gaze of the guy who'd tried to pick him up at the bar. "How's that?"

He cocked his head and gave him a get-real look. "More babies at Bonesy's place. No *real* men."

Wade held up the napkin. "Is this another bar?"

That was met with a snort. "That's a whorehouse for fags. Men like me wouldn't be caught dead there." With a disdainful shrug, he walked away.

Wade stuffed the napkin into his pocket, crossed the street to the taxi stand, and got into the first cab.

"Bartholomew Nine," he ordered.

"In Monkey Hill?" Black eyes met his in the rearview mirror. "You looking for a mon to fuck?"

"Actually, I'm looking for a woman."

The driver shook his head and bared spaces where his two front teeth should have been. "Not at Bonesy's house. For twenty dollars, I take you to a woman."

"I'll give you fifty if you take me to Bartholomew Nine and wait."

The cabbie flipped the meter. "No problem, mon. But you don't find no woman up dere."

Wade had a feeling that he most certainly would. "Just hurry, please." Because that woman moved fast.

CHAPTER
TWO

VANESSA TAPPED. EVERYTHING. She tapped her foot on the scarred wood floor. Tapped her fingers against her thigh and her tongue against the roof of her mouth in a *tsk* of impatience.

How long would she have to wait in this cigar-stinky parlor for a "madame" named Gideon? She'd been here ten minutes, and except for the creepy little guy who'd opened the door, she hadn't seen anyone or heard anything. She smelled plenty, though. Stale cigar smoke, dank air, a litter box in the near vicinity.

She rubbed her bare arms against that creepy sensation she'd had ever since she'd gotten off the boat. As if someone were watching her. It didn't help that the cabbie refused to stay in spite of the twenty she offered, leaving her in front of a two-story house at the edge of the mountain rain forest.

She whipped off her glasses to wipe some perspiration from her face, then looked at her watch for the six-millionth time. It was still early in the day in New York, but near the close of the London Stock Exchange, and most of her Hong Kong clients were asleep. Everywhere on the globe, deals were going down, money was being made, and investments were changing hands.

While she was on some godforsaken pile of sand doing . . .

The right thing.

That's what she had to keep reminding herself. She flipped out her iPhone—no signal, of course—then cursed the only man she loved enough to put herself willingly through this torture. The son of a bitch was *so* going to pay for this. As soon as she found him, got him on his meds, and dragged his sorry ass back where he belonged, Clive Easterbrook would pay.

He'd pay for lunch every day for a year, drinks on Friday after the closing bell, and possibly half the commissions she was missing while she pulled Good Samaritan duty.

Eight excruciating minutes later, the floorboards of the hallway stairs squawked with heavy footsteps, and she reached into the side pocket of her tote bag to dig for the picture, pulling it out as a shadow darkened the parlor.

He filled the doorway. Then he filled the room. Literally.

A huge three-hundred-pound man with ebony skin, India-ink eyes, midnight dreadlocks, and dark clothing that made him look like a big black Mack truck.

And from the look on his face, Vanessa was about to be roadkill.

"Mr. . . . Gideon?"

"They call me Bones."

Then they clearly had a sense of humor.

He walked past her, around her, made her turn to follow him and the heavy, vile stench of a stogie that clung to him.

"What do you want?" His voice didn't match his body. He had a British accent with a little island lilt.

She held out her hand to shake his. "I'm Vanessa Porter, from New York."

He didn't move, didn't blink, and forget any glimmer of a smile. His eyelids were no more than folds of flesh, his cheeks wide, puffy, and shiny. If he had teeth, he wasn't showing them. She dropped her hand.

"What do you want?" he repeated.

She raised the picture, but he didn't reach for that, either. "I'm looking for a friend of mine."

He just stared her down with a crushing glare, the only sound the rhythmic clicking of the inefficient overhead fan.

"I think he's been here recently."

His nostrils widened like a dragon, and she half expected a shower of flames. "I cannot help you. Please leave."

"You don't even know what I want yet," she shot back, indignation straightening her back. "I'm trying to find a friend. This man. Here." She fluttered the picture at his face. "About a month ago, he came down her on vaca—"

"Go away."

"Won't you just look at the picture?" Her voice rose, exactly as she didn't want it to. She cleared her throat and looked him in the beady eyes. Far badder badasses than Gideon Bones had tried to spook her in M&A negotiations, and every single time, the bastards failed. And so would this freak. "His name is Clive Easter—"

"No."

"—brook," she finished, her jaw clenching. "Clive Easterbrook. He's my friend. Won't you even look at this picture, Mr. Bones?"

"No."

Her hand hit her thigh with a thud. "Look. I'm not with the media or the police or anything. Clive is a really good friend of mine who—"

"No."

Shit. "—went on vacation a month ago and decided not to come home. I'm worried about him."

His eyes turned to thin black slits. "Why?"

"Because he's . . ." Would she have to reveal Clive's secret to get some help? She hated to be a rat.

"He's gay?" he said, raising his eyebrows in challenge.

"Yes, but that's not why I'm worried about him. Clive is my closest friend and colleague at work, and he's also . . . moody." Bipolar was more like it. "I think he might be depressed."

Drunk, high, and suicidal, too.

"No."

The single syllable irked. "No what? No, he's not

depressed, or no, you won't help me, or no, you don't know him?" Her voice tightened with frustration. "No *what*, Mr. Bones?"

"No, I will not discuss visitors to my home. You can leave now."

She exhaled with a curse of frustration. It'd been like this since she'd arrived in the Caribbean.

"I understand your position, Mr. Bones. I have clients of my own, and I respect confidentiality. But I'm worried that my friend's sick or hurt or spiraling into depression, because he's prone to that, and—"

She froze as something hard and round stabbed her in the back. Whoever it was had entered without creaking a single floorboard. Despite the hellish heat, chills rose.

Bones just stared at her, not acknowledging whoever was behind her.

"You talk too much," he said.

Her whole body went rigid, her knees locked, her neck stiff. She wasn't afraid of too many things . . . except guns.

Guns killed people. She knew that better than anyone.

"Leave, Miss Porter."

"Fine." She automatically raised her hands, as if there was a snowball's chance in the Caribbean that she was armed. "I'm going to step away now, okay?" *Please don't shoot.*

She kept her gaze straight ahead, unwilling to make eye contact with whoever held a gun to her back.

"I, um, I let the cab go." Or, rather, it bolted, leaving her in the Armed House-o-Male Prostitution in a skanky part of town, up a deserted dirt road and a good mile from what passed for civilization. Clive was *so* dead for doing this to her.

If she didn't die first.

"Go."

She heard the gun cock, felt it shift against her back, and slowly walked toward the front screen door, where sunlight poured in, along with freedom and safety.

She glanced over her shoulder at Bones, who looked at whoever was behind her and nodded. *Oh, Jesus.* What did that mean? *Go ahead and shoot her?*

She dove for the screen door and thwacked it open so hard it hit the house. Just as she stepped outside, a bright yellow cab screamed around the corner, coming to a gravel-spitting stop in front.

"I'll take that!" Clive was right—the cab gods *were* freakishly good to her.

The cab door flung open just as the screen door slammed, making her jump.

"Go!" Gideon lumbered onto the wooden porch, the boards groaning under his enormous weight. Then he looked over her shoulder, and a huge smile broke across his face. "Oh, hel*lo*."

Vanessa whipped around. Speaking of the gods, this one had dropped down from Olympus to deliver her cab in person. Six seriously solid feet of . . . gold. Close-cropped sun-kissed hair, tanned, chiseled, square features, broad shoulders in buttery yellow cotton, and eyes the precise color of the sea and sky behind him.

A customer, no doubt. Wait till she told Clive about this. *You guys get all the good ones.*

She pointed to the cab. "I'm taking that back into town." She practically leaped off the wooden porch to the dirt drive.

The man merely stepped aside, then held the door for her with a quiet "Ma'am."

She muttered thanks and dove in, dragging her bag across the seat. "To Basseterre, please," she said to the cabbie. "Really fast."

Golden Boy slid right in next to her.

"I'm sorry." She added a smile, just tight enough to let him know she'd fight for the cab if she had to. "I have an emergency, and I need to take this cab to town."

He nodded to the driver. "Take us to town, please."

"But . . ." She glanced at the house. "I'm sure he'll get you another cab when you're, uh, done."

"I'm done." He settled into the seat and calmly rested his arm across the back, giving her a look that was as reassuring as it was sexy. "I'm going where you go."

Through the dirty cab window, she saw black eyes bore a hole through her from the porch.

"Thanks a lot. He didn't like me before, and now he really hates me."

"Why's that?" He stretched out long legs, drawing her gaze to the muscular thigh covered in crisp khaki pants.

"Because I asked questions he didn't want to answer, made him mad enough to sic his hit man on me, and now I'm taking his hot new john away." She tapped the driver's seat. "I'm really in a hurry, if you don't mind. Basseterre. Stat."

"I'm not a customer," he said.

"You were sightseeing up a deserted hill and just happened to cruise by the best li'l gay whorehouse in St. Kitts? Sorry, don't buy it."

"I came up here for you."

For a split second, she hesitated, drinking in the sexy way that line was delivered and the glint in his eyes. Nice. "Excellent pickup line, and if I weren't running for my life at the moment, you might have a chance." She nudged the seat in front of her. "The Ballahoo Restaurant, please. *Now!*"

Finally, the cab took off, kicking a few stones at Bones to seal her fate as his lifelong enemy. She looked out the back window to see him on a cell phone. God, did everyone on this stupid rock get service but her?

"Did you find whatever it is you're looking so hard for?"

His question threw her almost as much as the sharp downhill curve. She hung on to the cracked vinyl seat to keep her balance, the picture of Clive still clutched in her other hand.

How did he know she was looking for something?

"No," she said. "I was too busy pissing off the madam."

"I saw that."

Something in his voice sent a little shiver over her skin. Smooth and sweet and from way below the

Mason-Dixon Line, and a little too damn sure of himself.

"Yeah? Did you catch that 'I'm gonna kill you' look?" she asked.

"No, I caught the barrel of a Walther 99 in the second-floor window pointing right at your head."

"And that's why you got into the cab?" He was either extremely chivalrous or as scared as she was of guns. Her eyes took a quick trip over his rock-solid shoulders, his corded neck, his washboard-flat stomach. She'd bet on chivalry, 'cause this dude wasn't scared of anything. "Well, thank you, but I don't need an escort."

"I didn't join you to be an *escort*." He added a killer smile, which under any other circumstances would be returned.

Whatever he was doing at Bartholomew Nine, he wasn't gay. No way. This guy drank testosterone for breakfast, chewed nails for lunch, and then made a meal out of whatever lucky lady offered herself up on a plate for dinner.

Then what was he . . . *Clive!*

She shoved Clive's picture at him. "You know him, don't you?"

He took it, long, strong fingers brushing hers and sending a tingle straight up her arm. Unlike everyone else she'd shown the picture to, he didn't just glance at it and shake his head. He angled it to the sun and truly studied the picture, taken in April when she'd gone with Clive to the Boston Marathon.

He frowned, looking up at her. "I'm sorry, ma'am, I can't help you."

Disappointment stabbed, familiar and sharp.

"I take it he's . . ."

"A friend," she said. "He came down to the islands on vacation a month ago and never came home."

His eyes widened in surprise. "Have you contacted the authorities?"

"No." Although after what just happened at Big Bad Bones's house, she probably should. "He's not in any danger. He just . . . dropped out. You've probably heard of people who go to the islands and decide to stay to find themselves, even though they're already the best damn hedge-fund manager in New York City." Bitterness darkened her tone.

"Are you sure that's what he did?"

She pushed her hair off her face, hooking it behind her ears. "Yes. My boss talked to him, and I saw the letter of resignation, and I know his signature, or I wouldn't have believed it, either. And he called his mother and left a message."

"But you've never actually spoken to him?"

"I've had text messages." Terse and weird but nothing to merit the look that said she was a complete idiot for not calling the island police.

"And you're here to, what, fetch him back home?"

She smiled at the antiquated verb and the drawl it came with. "Yeah, I'm fetching him. Or, at least, I'm going to talk some sense into him. He's given to mood swings. So for the last three days, I've been running around the islands trying to track him down."

"Literally running."

She shrugged. "That's how I roll. Fast."

"I noticed."

Noticed? Was he some kind of stalker? "When?" she asked sharply.

"About two minutes after you got off the boat."

Her stomach did a funny little flip. "You followed me here? Why?"

"You're Vanessa Porter, right?"

Apprehension pushed her away, into the door. She could jump out if she had to; they weren't going very fast.

"How do you know my name?"

He reached out a hand to shake hers. "Let's make it official, ma'am. My name is Wade Cordell, and I'm in St. Kitts to find you."

She didn't know whether to laugh or pop the door handle. Was he *serious*? Maybe he'd been on the cruise. Or maybe someone from work had sent him? Did this have to do with Clive?

"You are Vanessa Porter, right?" he asked when she didn't respond.

Instead of taking his hand, she put her fingers to her temples to quiet the sound of her rushing blood, but her ears still vibrated and buzzed. "Yes."

"I thought so. I've been—" He glanced at her bag. "Do you want to get that?"

"Get what?"

"Isn't that your phone?"

Instantly, she dived for the clip on her bag. "It's been so long since I heard it . . ." She touched the screen, and the vibration stopped. "Text message." The name of the sender took a moment to appear, so she glanced at the man who'd gone from stone-cold sexy to slightly scary in less than a minute. "How do you know who I am?"

"Because I've been sent to find you." Each vowel was drawn out like hot caramel over ice cream.

This *had* to be because she'd questioned dozens of people and waved Clive's picture all over the Caribbean. The iPhone vibrated again, reminding her of the text. She glanced down and almost cried out with joy. A message from Clive!

watch ur back

She lifted the device and shaded the sun to read it again.

watch ur back

Three weeks without a word from him, and she got *this*? It was an inside joke as old as their friendship, a private reference to the sharks that trolled Wall Street looking for prey.

Why? What did he mean by that?

She dropped her hands onto her lap with a thump, holding the phone as she studied the man in the cab, questions bombarding her. She went with the ones this stranger could answer. "Who are you, and why are you following me?"

"I plan to tell you outright, ma'am, but I'll warn you, it might be a little upsetting."

What could he possibly tell her that could make her day any suckier?

"Hit me, pal. I'm in a hurry."

"All right." He straightened and turned to look directly at her. "I'm here on behalf of a woman named Eileen Stafford."

White lights flashed behind her eyes as if she'd been punched in the head.

Eileen Stafford.

Oh, yeah. Her day just got seriously worse.

CHAPTER
THREE

WADE KNEW THAT look so well. That blood-draining, eye-popping realization that distorted a target's face the millisecond they realized they'd been shot. Instinct made him reach a reassuring hand to Vanessa, but she snapped her arm back, clutching the phone to her chest, speechless.

"You know Eileen Stafford," he said.

It wasn't a question, because that wasn't the blankness of confusion that paled her creamy complexion. That was raw horror and a shell-shocked brain that hadn't quite engaged yet.

She flipped the metal handle and threw the car door open. Wade lunged and managed to snag a handful of her shirt before she leaped.

"Hey!" the cabbie yelled, slamming on his brakes.

She jerked away, and cloth tore as Wade yanked her back.

"Stop the cab!" she hollered, throwing him a venomous look as he managed to pull her back safely and the cab squealed to the curb.

He let go of the shirt, his whole hand circling her slender but solid bicep. "I'm not going to hurt you."

She shook her arm hard. "You *are* hurting me."

He loosened but didn't release. "Please listen to me."

Her eyes blazed. "No. I know who Eileen Stafford is, and I know what she is." She tried to shake him off again, clenching her teeth when she failed. "Whatever you're selling, buddy, I'm not buying."

"Just stop moving long enough to listen to me."

Her eyes turned to slits behind her glasses. "I don't need to listen. I know what you're going to say. She's my birth mother. I'm adopted. She's rotting in jail for murder. I've known for years."

He opened his mouth to speak, and she held her hand up.

"Stop." She wrenched her arm free. "I am not even remotely interested in hearing anything about her. I don't care if she died and left me a stash of gold bullion. She doesn't exist. This is nonnegotiable."

"I haven't had a chance to say my piece, ma'am."

"No you haven't, *bubba*. Don't you know the meaning of nonnegotiable?"

He took his shot. "She's dying."

"Oh, Jesus Chri—hey!" She yelped as he squeezed her arm again. "I don't *care*. Not my problem. I don't . . ." She dropped her head back, closed her eyes, and exhaled in pure surrender. "Of what?"

"Leukemia. She needs a bone-marrow transplant from a relative."

She choked. "Oh, that's great." She shot forward again, fingers stabbing through her cornsilk hair, color flooding back to her sculpted cheeks. "The woman sells me—*sells me*—to a total stranger, shoots a hole through some poor woman, then writes me off for thirty years. Now she wants me. Now she *needs* me. Oh, that's just rich. And who are you, the warden?"

"I work for a security and investigation firm that's attempting to locate the—"

"Not that I'm sorry she sold me." She cut him off. "My dad was great, and I wouldn't trade him for anything in the world. Especially because I probably would've ended up in some orphanage, since she was a *killer*. Did you know that about her?"

"I know she's in jail and has been accused of murder."

She snorted. "And you say that like she might not be guilty. Have you read about her case?" She angled her hands like a book. "Open and—" *Crack*. She slapped her palms closed. "Premeditated first-degree murder." Drawing out the last two syllables with total repugnance, she shook her head. "And now she needs my bone marrow? I don't believe this."

He remained still, letting her blow it all out. She opened her mouth to say something, then suddenly stared at the phone as if it held an answer.

"Clive sent me a text message sometime in the last hour. 'Watch your back,' he said. I thought maybe he meant you, but if you're telling the truth . . ."

"I never lie."

She finally pulled the cab door closed. "Well, good for you. I wish you were lying now. I wish you weren't the emissary of My Mother the Murderer." She leaned forward and spoke to the cabbie. "Sorry about all that. I still want to go to Basseterre. Can we go there now, please?"

Her hands were still shaky as she reread the message on her phone. "Naturally, there's no satellite service now."

"Sounds like your friend might be in some trouble," Wade suggested, letting her get a little more calm before he dropped the next bomb. "Does he normally send that kind of message?"

"No. I've heard from him only three times since he left, including this one."

"So why exactly is his disappearance your problem?" he asked.

"Because A, he's my friend, and B, he left a mess at work, and C . . ." She shrugged. "He's my friend. That's all that matters. Don't you have friends you care about so much that you'd put your ass on a plane and fly to hell in July to find them?"

"As a matter of fact, that's exactly why I'm here."

"You're helping a friend?"

"I'm working for a friend."

She looked skeptical. "That woman in jail. Is she your friend?"

"No. I've never met her."

"Then who sent you here?"

"My friend owns a security and investigation firm, and she's launched this search."

"Well, search is over, hon." She dipped down to peer out the windshield. "How far are we from the Ballahoo?"

"So, you're going to keep looking for this friend of yours? Even though he sent you a warning?"

"That wasn't necessarily a warning. 'Watch your back' is a private joke with us."

"Not a very funny one."

She shot him a look. "Right here is fine," she told the driver. "What do I owe you?"

Wade put a hand on her arm. "I'll pay for this."

She produced a wallet, hesitated, then tossed it back into the abyss of her bag. "Fine."

"And I'd like to come with you," he said, handing a bill over the front seat.

"As much as you'd be very nice gay-boy bait, I'm sorry, I have my own agenda, and you're not on it."

"I'm actually quite good at finding people."

"So you've demonstrated." She whipped the car door open and climbed out to the sidewalk.

Wade got out on the street side, sauntered toward the back, and blocked her. "I'm not done."

She glared at him. "Sorry, but you are *so* done. You have my answer, I'm tired of this conversation, and I have more important things to do. Good-bye."

She moved to the side, but he blocked her again. "I have access to tremendous resources that could help you find your friend. Like tracing that text message, the satellite it came from, and what island he's on. I can help you."

"That's very impressive, but I'm pretty good at

getting information myself," she said impatiently. "I found my own birth mother years ago."

"I'm just offering to help you."

"And what's the exchange rate? I have to fly to the Big House, visit Mom, and suck out some marrow for her? I don't think so."

She managed to get by and sprinted into the street, barely avoiding an oncoming cab.

"Sheez," he blew out, charging after her. The woman was like a human tornado. He reached her in four long strides and got hold of her elbow.

"Then maybe you'd do it for a chance to meet one of your sisters."

She froze, then slowly turned to him, her eyes narrowed in disbelief. "What?"

"As I mentioned, we have impressive resources. We've been able to locate one of your sisters."

"One of my *what*?" It was barely a whisper.

"I thought you were so good at finding information? Evidently, you didn't find it all. You were one of triplets given away by Eileen Stafford in July 1977."

Once again, she wore the expression of someone who'd just taken a bullet to the heart. He used the rare moment of speechlessness to guide her back up to the sidewalk.

Gideon Bones took a long, deep drag on a Los Bancos Robosto Criolla and cursed Vanessa Porter and her nonstop mouth. Although, truth be told, whatever she'd just been told had shut her up good and fast.

If it weren't for her untimely arrival, he'd be sitting

on his roof deck, staring up at the cloud-fringed crater of Mount Liamuiga, enjoying the Dominican roll he'd saved in a humidor for this afternoon's smoke.

But she'd interrupted that peaceful pleasure, and now he was in the backseat of his Porsche Cayenne, watching her swoon in the arms of a thoroughly and unfortunately straight stunna who must have something good on the mouthy Miss Porter.

Did the man know Clive? Or, worse, did he know Clive's enemies?

Bones didn't have all that worked out yet, but he would. He'd figure out who was the threat, and then he'd eliminate it. Clive might swear his fag hag was harmless, doing exactly what she said she was doing, but Bones trusted no one.

There was no such thing as harmless in this situation, and Clive would be wise to remember that. At the very least, she was a magnet, attracting attention they didn't want or need.

So Bones watched. And smoked. And admired the man who, based on the posture, the alertness, the subtle command in his body, was probably ex-military. Certainly armed, because he had that cool confidence that came with carrying.

What did he want with Vanessa, other than the obvious?

He tried to see her as a straight man might. Nice pouty lips, even if they did move too much for his taste, and the black-rimmed glasses against the platinum locks might appeal to a man with hot-for-teacher fantasies. She had a decent body, with nice cans that jostled around as if they were real and a tight ass, but so did half the trollops who climbed off those cruise ships looking for available players. Would that hottie boy endure all that chatter just to get laid?

No. This wasn't a mating dance; this was more like a battle royale. There might be attraction, there might even be some electricity, but it wasn't welcome, he could tell.

So what was the man up to?

Bones knew men well. He worshipped them and had spent his life learning how to spot types. He could psych out an artist, a warrior, a leader, a thrill seeker, a competitor, a thief, a cheat, or a spy. He'd made a fortune by understanding the male species, and he'd bet a box of Los Bancos that those baby-blue eyes were trained to hunt, and those strong hands were able to kill.

So, what was he hunting, and who was he killing, and how did it involve Vanessa Porter?

He flipped the butt out the window. "Raoul!"

The driver turned, training a bloodshot gaze on his boss. Raoul had been smoking again, and not a Criollo. "Yeah, mon?"

"Did she see you when she came to the house?"

"No. I was upstairs."

"Are you sure?"

Red-rimmed eyes turned to insulted slits. "I am sure."

"Good." Bones dug in the seat pocket for the notebook and pen that he kept there in case an idea came to him while he was being driven. Sometimes it was a line of poetry, sometimes an observation on the foibles of humanity, sometimes a game of hangman.

He flipped to a clean page. "I want you to deliver a message to her. And I don't want him to know about it. Can you do that?"

"I can do that."

He scratched the words and folded the paper. "Here. Don't screw up."

The only way to stop a hunter was to deflect him. He would start by sending the prey on a hunt of his making, one that would lead her to a controlled environment. A small place where he could watch her and move her around like a pawn on his chessboard. It was a little risky, but he didn't think she could outsmart him. Hell, she might give up her search and get naked with the stud.

But just in case that stud was hunting something Bones didn't want him to find, and just in case Vanessa Porter was truly as relentless as she appeared to be . . . then this plan ought to shut him down and shut her up.

If not, there were other, less civilized ways to accomplish that goal.

CHAPTER
FOUR

TRIPLETS. *TRIPLETS?* FOR the second time in one day—hell, in one hour—Vanessa was dumbfounded. "Nobody even *had* triplets thirty years ago, did they?"

He laughed softly. "They had them, it was just a surprise on delivery day."

"How could I not know this?" After all the research she and her father had done, it didn't seem possible that a fact as monumental as *there are two sisters* slipped by some of the best adoption investigators Daddy's money could buy.

"Very few people do know about this," he said.

"No shit, Sherlock. Where are we going?"

"You look like you're going to faint," Wade said as he ushered her to the same patio restaurant where she'd been less than two hours ago.

"I don't faint," she shot back. "It's a thousand degrees out, and you shocked me, and I—I'm *reacting*."

"Gotcha. Well, you look like you're about to react, so let's sit down in the shade here, under this umbrella, and have a cold drink and talk about it, okay?"

His patronizing drawl infuriated her, but the suggestion had definite appeal. She needed something cold—and potent—to make sense of everything that had happened since she got off that boat.

"Two iced mineral waters," he said to the waitress.

"And a vodka tonic," Vanessa added. "But skip the tonic. And no lime."

One side of his mouth lifted in a half-smile. "You drink like you talk and walk. Tough."

"I hate limes. And tonic." *And you.* She crossed her arms. "You'd better have proof."

"There's no actual paperwork."

She slammed her hands on the tabletop and pushed back in the chair. "I knew this was totally bogus."

"But I have a picture." He placed a photograph on the table between them.

Wasn't that a fine twist? For the first time in three days, *she* was being shown a picture instead of the other way around. Though she wanted to be a complete brat and refuse to look at it, curiosity won out. She squinted at the photograph, half expecting—and half dreading—to see a reflection of herself.

"Oh." The word was a note of pure wonder, matching the sensation that rocked her. "She's beautiful." Then she shoved the picture back at him. "And she doesn't look a thing like me."

"You're beautiful." He slid it forward.

"Thanks, but I'm blond—natural, by the way—

and my face is longer, my mouth is wider, my eyes are shaped differently." Unable to resist, she took one more look. "She's really . . . delicate-looking." Willow-thin and fragile. No cleft in the chin. No glasses. No boobs.

No dice.

"We don't even look related." She gave the picture a good shove.

"Triplets aren't always identical," he said. "Some-times two are, and one is from a different egg. That might explain the difference in your looks and makes it possible that you're a match for the marrow, when she's not."

"She's not?" That hit her hard. If this alleged sister had been a match, would Eileen Stafford have dis-patched an investigator to find *her*? Or would she have let Vanessa go to her grave without ever initiating con-tact? Of course, she would have. God, she despised the woman right down to her last bad cell.

She turned toward the bar, lifting her hair with one hand to get a nonexistent breeze on her neck. "Where is that drink?" This was so ugly, so complicated, and so *not* what she wanted to be doing with her time in St. Kitts. Or anywhere, for that matter.

With impossible purpose, Wade inched the picture back across the table, like a gambler willing to risk a decent card for the remote possibility of a better one.

"Her name is Dr. Miranda Lang."

Something slipped inside Vanessa. *Miranda*.

She didn't care what her name was. She didn't *care*. Didn't he get that?

"What kind of doctor?" she asked, so casually it couldn't be interpreted as anything but small talk.

"An anthropologist. She has a book out that's been getting some media coverage, about the Mayan calendar and the myth that the world is going to end in 2012. Have you heard about it?"

She lifted an indifferent shoulder. "Unless it moves money, changes the Dow Jones Industrial Average, or otherwise generates cash with at least seven, preferably eight, figures involved, no." She fanned her sticky neck, wishing something wasn't pressing so hard on her chest.

Finally, a drink tray landed on their table.

"Thank God," Vanessa mumbled, her gaze sliding over the much-needed vodka only to land on the much-hated picture.

Wavy auburn hair. Wide smile. Pretty. An anthropologist.

She grabbed the ice-cold glass and plucked out the damned lime. "There's obviously been a mistake. I'm sorry she's going to be disappointed. But my father and I did exhaustive research, and there were no sisters."

She put the cold glass to her lips.

"I have another picture."

She didn't drink. She couldn't. She watched as he slowly reached back into his billfold, methodically drawing out another picture. Part of her wanted to kick him into faster action and get this hell over with. But it was easier just to watch his stunningly masculine hands as they moved to find something she just knew she didn't want to see. Nice hands. Sexy fingers. Bad, bad news.

"I think you'll be real interested in this one." He burned her with a look that might have been a warning or might have been something else. It was hard to read this man, hard to get past the eyes and the body and the face.

Was that a calculated move? *Send an irresistible hottie to sway her. I need bone marrow.* Her stomach tightened, and she pressed the icy cold glass on her cheek.

"This picture," he said, his voice as measured as his movements, "is actually of the back of Miranda's neck."

Her vodka splashed over the rim of her glass. Oh, no. *No.*

"Right here." He reached a hand around her head, making a tiny circle with his fingertip, right above the hairline, a million little hairs rising up at his touch and sending shivers down her back.

"She has a tattoo right here, and all three babies were marked with them. You have one, don't you?"

The drink slipped out of her grasp and clunked on the wooden table, drenching her shorts and legs with ice and vodka.

She pushed back from the table and swiped the spill much harder than necessary. "Screw you."

He instantly grabbed a napkin and started wiping her soaked thighs. His hand was hot on her thigh, and she jumped back, standing up.

He looked up at her. "I'm gonna take that as a yes on the tattoo."

"Then you'd be mistaken." She whipped the napkin from his hand, despising the crack in her voice. Crack? That was a bona fide sob. "I hate this. I hate that you're making me . . ." *Feel.* She flicked the napkin at the picture, a clinical-looking thing showing a close-up of a woman's head, her long hair pulled away to show a tiny dark mark. "Oh, my God." She leaned down closer, pushing her glasses up her nose. "Does that say 'hi'?"

"Miranda thinks it might be the numbers one and four. Which, upside down, look like 'hi.'" He straightened the picture. "Did you say you don't have a mark like this?"

"No, I don't." Not since her laser tattoo removal. "And I'm glad. I don't want any connection to a killer."

"I understand that. However . . ." He sat back in his chair. "Some people believe her trial might have been unfair and that she's serving time for a crime she didn't commit."

Not a chance. "I read enough about it to know she didn't take the witness stand, she had the gun in her possession, and she was jealous of the woman she shot. Pretty incriminating stuff."

He shrugged a shoulder. "Two sides to every story. Do you have the tattoo?"

"No." *Damn him. Damn that evil woman. Damn this whole situation.*

"Are you certain?" he asked. "It's kind of a hard place to see yourself."

"I'm certain." Certain she had a faint red scar that he

could see in this sunshine. Certain the scar didn't look anything like the design in the picture. And definitely certain that she just couldn't handle this right now.

She wanted to find Clive, get back to the familiarity of New York and the cool, controlled comfort of her office at Razor Partners. Maybe then, in the vault of protection she'd built around herself since her mother flew the coop and her father was killed, she could figure out what to do. But not here, beaten down by a blistering sun and an equally blistering man on his own mission, with his own agenda and his own pictures.

Vodka dribbled down her thigh like a tear.

"Could you excuse me?" she said, as calmly as she would to an enemy attorney in the middle of a merger negotiation when she needed to change the direction from give to take. "I'd like to go wash this off."

"Certainly. I'll order you another."

"Thanks," she said, grabbing the shoulder strap of her bag.

He stood, gesturing toward the back of the restaurant. "I'll wait for you."

He didn't sit as she walked away. A Southern gentleman. Great-looking, polite as hell, and carrying a wallet full of news she didn't want.

She rounded the bar and gave a questioning look to the bartender. "Ladies' room?"

He pointed his thumb to a hallway that led into the building behind the bar. It was much cooler in the dimly lit passageway. As she reached for the doorknob, a clammy hand seized her upper arm and made her spin with a gasp.

She half expected to see crystal-blue eyes, but the ones she met were dark, bloodshot, and sunken inside the face of a thin Hispanic young man.

"What do you want?" she asked, wrenching from his weak grip.

"For you." He stuffed a piece of paper, folded into squares, into her palm. "From a friend of Clive's."

He disappeared out into the sunlight, leaving the scent of pot in his wake.

Her heart stuttering, she turned over the note. A friend of Clive's?

She shouldered the door open into a dingy bathroom with a yellowed toilet and a cheap vanity, lit only by sunlight filtering through a window over the sink. As soon as she locked the door, she unfolded the note.

The man you want is in Nevis.

Nevis? Clive was in Nevis? That was what, just seven miles away? A bunch of the passengers onboard were taking a ferry from St. Kitts to that island today.

Who had sent her this message?

And more important, should she act on it? Did she have time to go to another island and get back before the ship set sail?

Who cared? She couldn't give a rat's ass about the cruise. She not only wanted to find Clive, now she *needed* to. He'd jump all over this; he was great at stuff like this. When he took his Zoloft, anyway.

Once she found Clive, she could get him out of whatever life crisis or love affair he was caught in, and then he'd help her. He'd know whether she should take this new, twisted road in her life.

Her brain raced, planning the steps.

She could run back to the ship, grab just one bag, and go to Nevis. After she found Clive, she could have her stuff sent back to New York, or if it was in a day or two, they could catch up to wherever the ship was docked.

Oh, yeah. This was totally doable. Nevis was a small island, and the gay community was tight-knit everywhere. She'd find him in no time.

Besides, it would get her away from Wade Cordell. The man with the pictures and the news and the connection to a woman—to *women*—Vanessa wanted no connection to.

She fingered the note. *The man you want is in Nevis.*

Two cryptic messages in one day. This and *watch ur back*.

Which should she believe? The one from Clive's cell phone or the one that came from out of nowhere? And then there was the complete stranger sitting fifty feet away with the worst message of all.

If she spent too much time with Wade Cordell, he'd wear her down with those insanely blue eyes and those masculine hands and all that Southern comfort. Slow and gentleman-like, he'd polish her down until she said yes.

Because, in her heart, isn't that what she wanted?

No. *No.* She owed far more to Clive than to Eileen Stafford. Sometimes water was thicker than blood—especially if the blood was tainted.

She eyed the dingy countertop around the sink. Kneeling on it, she pushed the window higher, checking out the alley through the sizable opening. One quick hop and she'd be gone. Wade would probably wait another ten minutes before looking for her, but by then she could have grabbed the tender and be well on her way to the ship before he figured it out.

He may be good, but she was better.

Flipping her bag over her shoulder, she climbed through the opening, dropped to the ground, and ran all the way to Port Zante without stopping.

"She bolted," Adrien Fletcher said, his Australian accent filled with disgust and disappointment.

"She *what*?" Jack Culver clunked down his coffee mug.

"He had her, told her, and lost her. Never even got to see the tattoo." Fletch snapped the cell phone closed. "Wade said she bugged off through a window in the loo."

"Well, that bites." Jack took a sip of the cold decaf he'd been nursing since they'd sat down in the infirmary cafeteria to wait for Miranda. "Doesn't she want to meet her mother and her sister? Why would she run away?"

Fletch gave him a look of total disbelief. "What the bloody hell do you think Miranda did when you asked me to go to California to do the same thing?"

"Fell flat in love with you?"

"Aside of that." He grinned, flashing his world-class dimples and looking every bit the rangy rugby player he was. "She ran like a wounded roo, and she didn't even know there were sisters involved. I know this is a big-ass deal to you, mate. I know you been on this one since you met poor Eileen Stafford and got this bug about finding her daughters for her. But put yourself in the girls' shoes. It's not easy to find out your mother's a murderess, dying, and needs your marrow." He shook back his long hair and twirled the cell phone on the table. "And trust me, it isn't easy to be the one who has to tell the sheila the truth."

"*Maybe* a murderess," Jack said, the only word of Fletch's speech he'd really heard. "When you dig into the past like I've been doing for a few months, the inconsistencies in that trial are jaw-dropping. It might have been thirty years ago, but the system of jurisprudence hasn't changed that much. Eileen Stafford didn't get a fair trial."

"Then why did she accept it?" Adrien leaned back in the plastic chair and crossed brawny arms. "Why didn't she take the stand? Her fingerprints weren't on the weapon, but someone's were—someone they never identified. She had no gunshot residue on her clothes, and her motive was downright piss-poor. So why didn't she mount a defense?"

Jack picked up the cup, then put it down again. He'd give his right ball for a beer, but Fletch, being the self-appointed sobriety police and the son of a gutter drunk, would put a stop to that.

"Ever since I interviewed her for another case and got caught up in this one, she's said the same thing over and over. 'He can do anything.' "

"And you take that to mean what?"

"That there is someone in the world who terrifies Eileen Stafford."

"The woman's in a coma, knocking hard on death's door. I doubt she's terrified of anyone right now."

That's where Fletch was wrong. In the last few months, he'd talked a helluva lot to Eileen, and two things were consistent. She was scared of someone, and she wouldn't say who had fathered the babies.

"That's what I want to know the most," he said, half thinking out loud. "Who is the father of those three?"

"Don't get your hopes up, mate," Fletch said. "That farmhouse on Sapphire Trail had a lousy filing system, and Lucy's investigation machine is mighty. There is absolutely no record of who their father is."

Jack had been a Bullet Catcher long enough to know Lucy Sharpe's *everything* was mighty. It was one of the things he missed most about the job. One of many.

"There might be a record," Jack said.

Fletch shook his head. "Trust me, while you've been off trying to find Miranda's sisters, she and I have been looking for any records. She wants to know who her father is, too."

Jack looked hard at his friend, considering just how much of his hand he could show. He trusted Fletch, but could he trust him not to tell Miranda? Or, worse, Lucy?

He had to. "I think," he said, leaning forward and lowering his voice, "I think the answer might be in the tattoos."

Fletch's amber eyes were full of doubt as he waited for Jack to elaborate.

"But I have to see the other tattoos before I can be certain or formulate some kind of theory," Jack said.

"We will. Wade will get Vanessa. Lucy says he's very good."

Jack snorted. "If you ask me, he just failed his Bullet Catchers test."

"I didn't ask you. Go on about the tats. Is this something Eileen said to you or just conjecture?"

"Nothing she's said outright and plenty of conjecture. After I saw Miranda's tattoo, I dug through every court record and newspaper clipping from Wanda Sloane's murder, looking for someone or something with a connection to the letters *HI*."

Fletch's eyebrows lifted with interest. "You think the tattoos are initials? That's brilliant, mate. Isn't there anyone from back then that you can talk to? What about the cop who arrested her? You talked to him, right? Did you tell him this theory?"

Willie Gilbert was the last person Jack would confide in. "I was a cop, and I was damn good at sniffing rat droppings. Willie Gilbert's no good."

"He's retired."

"Yeah, and he lives better than any retired cop I ever knew. He ain't golfing and living in a resort on his pension."

Fletch nodded, getting the implication.

"I have a better source," Jack continued. "Remember I found the nurse, Rebecca Aubry, who did the tattoos? She's the one who gave me the Whitakers' name in Virginia. I'm going to try to talk to her again. I just have to figure out some way to get her to talk."

"Guess your usual way won't work on a woman of seventy."

Jack smiled. "She's got a connection to one of the girls, I think. That's why she wanted the picture I found in the Charleston newspaper files of her holding a baby at Eileen's trial. Once I tell her I've found one, maybe two, I think I can get her to talk. But she's been out of town for weeks now."

"What's your theory? That she tattooed them with the father's initials?"

"Or birthday. Or something. When I first met her, Rebecca told me that tattooing a black-market baby isn't that unusual. It's a way for the mother to put her mark on a child she might never see again, since there are no legal records."

"Could be the mother's mark, not the father's," Fletch said.

"Maybe." Jack pushed his cold coffee aside and propped his elbows on the table. "Fletch, what if the father is the person who killed Wanda Sloane?"

Fletch's eyebrows shot up.

"Just hear me out," Jack continued. "Her battle cry before she slipped into the coma was 'He can do anything,' and I've always thought she took the blame for this murder to keep the babies safe. Well, who better to know Eileen's secret than their father?"

"It's not impossible," Fletch said, stroking the golden soul patch under his lip. "But the timing doesn't work. She had the babies in July 1977, and they were tattooed and sold almost immediately, right? So they were tattooed eight months before Wanda Sloane was killed. Why would she do that? Kind of a stretch to think there's a connection."

"Kind of stupid not to."

Fletch grinned. "I've always said you were a bonzer investigator."

"I'd ask her point-blank if she'd wake up." Jack glanced toward the door that led to the infirmary. "So far, she's refused to discusss the murder. But now that we've brought her Miranda and might bring her the other two sisters, she might. In the meantime, all I have is hi or HI or 14."

"Why don't I run it by Lucy and—"

"No." Jack's tone left no room for argument.

"Why not?" Fletch said, giving Jack a dark look. "Look how fast she was able to produce Vanessa Porter. She's got amazing resources, and I've finally cracked the door open, so she'll at least be civil to you. Take advantage of her—"

"No one takes advantage of Lucy Sharpe, Fletch. And yeah, you cracked the door by doing me the favor of finding Miranda. But anything happening on this case since then is not because Lucy's developed a soft spot for her least-favorite former employee. She's offering help because of Miranda, and because you and Miranda are getting married."

"Who cares why she's doing it? She's got the goods to help you investigate—"

"No fucking way am I letting Lucy Sharpe in on

this." He narrowed his gaze. "She's a control freak, and this case is mine."

Fletch shrugged, too good a friend or too loyal to his boss to push it any further. "Your call, mate, but you really don't know her that well."

Fletch was wrong again. Jack knew her better than any other Bullet Catcher, including her golden boy, Dan Gallagher.

"Just don't tell her this theory," Jack said. "Lucy's not the only one with 'amazing' resources. Now that I know Rebecca Aubry is coming back from Florida, I'll start there."

"How did you find that out?"

"Stellar computer hacking."

Fletch let out a dubious laugh. "Since when did you touch a keyboard?"

"I didn't. I have a . . . friend who used to be a travel agent and cracked the reservation system for me."

"I should have—" Fletch's smile evaporated as he rose from his seat so fast it hit the ground with a clatter. "What's the matter?"

Miranda ran into the cafeteria, her face flushed. "She's awake!" She grabbed Fletch's arm and pulled him toward the door. "She mumbled something, opened her eyes, and looked at me!"

"Let's go," Jack said, hustling around them toward the infirmary.

"The doctor's in there," Miranda said. "They made me leave."

"Don't worry, luv," Fletch assured her, draping his arm around her as the trio rushed down the hall. "If she wakes up, you're the one person in the world she'll want to see."

An armed security guard stood in front of the door, his expression and stance forbidding. "No entry," he said, in case they were not fluent in body language.

"I'm sorry, Jack." Risa, the most efficient and thorough nurse he'd ever met, came toward them, her dark eyes full of warning. "You cannot go in there."

"Risa, honey, come—"

"Don't 'Risa honey' me. This is the first sign of lucidity in almost two months. I can't bend these rules, and you know it."

He did know it, although it was easy to forget the infirmary was part of a women's prison.

"When?" he asked, undeterred.

"Let me check. Stay here." She disappeared into Eileen's room, and Jack turned to Miranda.

"What did she say when she woke up?"

"I don't know," Miranda said. "It happened so fast. I was just sitting with her, holding her hand, talking like I always do on the off chance she hears me."

"What were you talking about?" Fletch asked.

"You." She smiled. "I told her how we'd met and what happened. Then I told her we were getting married, and I swear she tightened her grip on my fingers just then." She rubbed her arms. "I got chills. It was like . . . she heard me."

"You said she mumbled something," Jack said. "What did she say?"

"I couldn't quite get it. She was just moaning at first. Then it was jibberish. I want to go back *in* there."

"Risa will get us in," Jack assured her. "If anybody can do anything around here, it's Risa."

The guard snorted softly. "Got that right."

The door opened, and Risa stood between them and Eileen, shaking her head. "I'm sorry."

Miranda gasped and put her hand on her mouth. "No."

"Oh, no, she's not gone," Risa said quickly. "She's just back to sleep. Deep. But the doctor wants to talk to you, ma'am. He'd like you to tell him if her eyes opened and how clear they looked."

"They opened. She looked right at me." Her voice cracked a little. "Are you sure she's back in the coma? She was definitely waking up."

"I know it's frustrating. You feel like you were so close," Risa said.

Jack gave Miranda a nudge. "Go on in. Maybe she'll wake up when she hears your voice."

He turned to Fletch, his only real friend in the Bullet Catchers now. "Keep my theory to yourself. I mean it."

"I will. But I still think you're making a mistake, not involving Lucy."

"No, I'm not." He'd made enough mistakes where Lucy was involved. He wasn't about to make another.

CHAPTER
FIVE

STELLA FELDSTEIN HUNG over the railing of the *Valhalla,* waving a bright orange sun hat and calling Vanessa's name. "I'll meet you down there!" Stella called above the forty-some sails slapping against masts that stretched into the blue sky.

Great. Just what she needed. Hurricane Stella.

From the moment they'd met the first day on-board, Stella had made it her mission to find a man on the ship for Vanessa. Fortunately, they were all traveling with wives and girlfriends. So Vanessa and Stella had dinner together, and by the time the entrée was served, Vanessa had shared the whole story about Clive.

It had been a relief to have someone to talk to, but Stella had adopted Vanessa's problem as her own and had threatened to accompany her on every island stop to search for Clive. So far, Vanessa had held her at bay.

But Stella was a force to be reckoned with, and right now Vanessa didn't want to reckon with anyone.

And she certainly didn't want to share what she'd learned in St. Kitts.

My mother, the murderer, is dying and finally decided to find me since she needs my bone marrow. Oh, and I have two sisters I didn't know about.

Vanessa's stomach rolled with the ship as she accepted help onto the boarding platform.

"Welcome back aboard, Ms. Porter. Hope you had a wonderful time in St. Kitts." The efficient crew members not only knew everyone by name, they had itineraries memorized.

She navigated the curved stairway to the Clipper Deck, followed a teak-lined passageway, and slipped into her cabin without seeing anyone. Inside, she pulled out a small carry-on bag from the closet and tossed it onto the bed, then started packing underwear, some T-shirts, jeans, shorts, and a cotton skirt. She wouldn't need much. She'd only be gone two or three days.

If she didn't find him by then, she'd get on an island hopper and fly back to wherever the ship was in port. She grabbed the itinerary on her dresser and looked a few days ahead. St. Maarten. She could resume her island-to-island search there. After that, St. Barts. Then what?

She'd figure it out. Just as she figured out the streets of New York City when she was fifteen and the games of Wall Street when she was twenty-five. She could figure anything out, and fast.

She stopped for a moment and pulled out the only tangible clue to Clive's whereabouts. *The man you want is in Nevis.*

Was this crazy? No. She'd been in that bar asking about Clive. She'd been all over and had probably talked to about forty people in the last few days. Someone had noticed or overheard and wrote this.

"Vanessa!" Stella knocked on the cabin door. "Did you find him?"

Vanessa crossed the room. "No, not yet." She invited her in with a wave. "But I've been told he's in Nevis, and I'm going there to find him."

Stella frowned at the half-packed tote bag. "Alone?"

"Yes. I'll only miss two days of the cruise."

"It might not be safe."

Vanessa gave her a surprised look before returning to packing. "This from the president of the Women Should Travel Alone club? It's Nevis, not Afghanistan. Don't worry."

Stella flung her tangerine hat across the bed as if it were a Frisbee. "I don't like it. It's one thing to be on a cruise, or in a hotel, or even on a day trip, but without reservations, you never know what you're going to find there."

"Hopefully, Clive."

"I think you ought to stay on the cruise and keep talking to people. That's a very good approach, and you get a little vacation from all that financial hoo-hah. Besides," Stella added, her voice dripping with implication, "you never know who you could meet."

"I'm not in the Caribbean for a vacation or to find a man. Although . . ."

"What?" Stella dropped onto the bed, her eyes bright. "You met someone?"

Did she ever. "Yes, but not like that."

"Why? Is he ugly? Fat? Poor? What's he look like on a scale of one to ten?"

"Eleven. But he's got . . . issues."

"Dolly, we all come with"—she lifted the handle of the partially packed tote—"a leetle bah-gahge."

"More than a little, I'm afraid." Killer mothers, secret sisters. Mongo bah-gahge.

"Did you take your glasses off so he can see how pretty your eyes are?"

"Nope, I kept my glasses *and* clothes on. I did spill a drink all over myself, though."

Stella sighed, devastated. "What's his name? Is he on vacation here?"

Vanessa flicked at the air. *Go away, subject.* "Business. Long story. Listen, can I give you my key so you can keep an eye on my cabin? I'll meet up with you in St. Maarten."

"You'd better tell the captain and someone on the crew. Or better yet, the owner. He's onboard. Did you see him?" She picked up the hat and fanned herself. "Ooh-la-la. Married, though, to a busty little Italian thing with a kid in tow and another one on the way. I talked to her. Did you know that one of these ships—"

Vanessa let her chatter, stepping into the bathroom for toiletries and cosmetics, checking her watch to calculate when she could get the launch back to Basseterre and grab the afternoon ferry to Nevis.

Suddenly, she realized Stella had gone silent and sensed she wasn't in the bathroom alone.

"*This* is what you call being told he's in Nevis?"

Vanessa didn't even have to look to know what Stella was holding. Damn, the woman was nosy. Sweet and well meaning but so freaking *meddlesome*.

"This crappy little piece of paper with chicken-scratch handwriting is what you call information?"

"Someone gave it to me in a bar where I know Clive has been in the last few weeks." She snapped it from Stella's hands. "And, honestly, this is not your business."

"Dolly, I'm a Jewish grandmother from Fort Lauderdale. Everything's my business. Why would someone hand you a weird note like this?"

"I've talked to a lot of people about him, and one of them wants to help, I'm sure."

"Why not just walk up to you and tell you?"

Vanessa had thought of that. "Because there are still people on this planet who are not cool with being gay or knowing gays. Whoever wrote this might want privacy or think Clive does."

Stella folded her arms and leaned against the doorjamb. "All right. You win. What time are we leaving?"

Vanessa choked a laugh. "No."

"You can't do this alone. I'll travel just as light as you. I know I'm in my sixties." At Vanessa's look, she shrugged. "All right, seventies. And I know you tear ass through these islands like a steamroller on amphetamines, but I'm a seasoned traveler. I can help you."

"I don't want your help." Hurt widened Stella's eyes. "I'm sorry, Stella. I'm so sorry." She reached for the other woman's hand. "I've had an unbelievably nasty day, and that was just mean-spirited, and I'm sorry."

"That's okay." Stella patted Vanessa's cheek and straightened her glasses, the gesture already so familiar and sweet that it just twisted the guilt knife even further. "I've got a daughter. She gets testy sometimes when she hasn't had sex for a while."

Vanessa didn't know whether to laugh or blink at the moisture in her eyes. "Your daughter is lucky to have you, Stell." The truth of it squeezed her chest. Her daughter was lucky to have a real mother, not a shrew who slinked away into the night, and not the psychopath who gave birth to her.

Stella slid Vanessa's glasses down her nose. "You really ought to get that LASIK surgery. You're hiding this *shaina punim*!" Her voice was light, barely covering hurt feelings. " 'Pretty face' in Yiddish, honey."

Vanessa's shoulders sank under the weight of all the kindness. "I don't even deserve friendship like yours, Stella."

"What a stupid thing to say. Everyone deserves friendship."

"And as much as I really appreciate the offer, I'm going to fly solo. I have your cell-phone number, and I know service is spotty, but I'll try to call you. And you call me anytime. Remember, I programmed my phone with your song. When I hear "Some Enchanted Evening," I'll know it's you and pounce on the phone." Vanessa smiled. "And I promise that when I find Clive, I'll get the word to you, no matter what it takes."

Stella nodded with a quiet sigh. "Okay." She stepped aside to let Vanessa finish filling her bag. "So what was his name?"

"Who?"

"The eleven."

She zipped up the case and flung it over her shoulder. "Oh, I don't remember, but he's definitely not my type." She took the card key off the dresser and held it out to Stella. "Here."

"Thanks. I might move in here for a few days," Stella said. "Your cabin's bigger than mine."

"Make yourself at home." Vanessa hesitated a second, then reached both arms out, fighting the demon that made the gesture feel so unnatural and stiff. Another one of Mary Louise Porter's legacies. "And thank you."

Stella took the hug and returned it with ten times the strength. "When will I see you again?"

"If I don't hook up with one of the day trips to Dominica or Guadaloupe, I'll be on the dock in Gustavia when this ship arrives. You have my word."

Stella sighed, cupping Vanessa's face. "I don't like it, dolly, but all right. I'm here if you need me. Though I know, I know: you don't need anybody."

"I need Clive." More than ever. "And that's why I'm doing this."

It had nothing to do with the man who'd shaken her world upside down. Nothing.

The minute Vanessa rumbled the rented Jeep into the over-the-top and under-the-radar elegance of the Four Seasons Resort in Nevis, she knew that if Clive had been to this island, he'd been here.

Clive Easterbrook didn't do quaint, precious, historical, or natural, which wiped out the Victorian gingerbread houses, the museums, forts, and excursions up the side of the mountain and into a rain forest she'd just spent a few hours searching. But this, she thought as she flipped the keys to the valet, drinking in the elegance and ambience, *this* place would appeal to Clive.

He loved nothing as much as the smell of big, fat, colossal sums of money, and the Four Seasons reeked of it. And if he'd been traveling with a new man, as he'd implied in one of his texts, it would be a man who would stay here.

Buoyed by that certainty, she headed toward the deck, where a sparkling infinity pool spilled into a waterfall, surrounded by clusters of palm trees and rows of white Haitian-cotton-covered chaise longues.

Strains of jazz floated on citrus-perfumed air. No steel drums for this set, no tiki bars or hot tubs. Just soft music and bubbling water and the occasional sound of laughter from the tanned, moneyed guests.

Oh, yeah. Clive would be at home here.

She took a seat at a softly lit bar under a classic thatched roof, and instantly a cocktail napkin was in front of her.

"Good evening, madame." The island native bartender's voice lilted with accented English as he touched his slim brass name badge. "I am Henry. What can I get you to drink on this beautiful tropical night? Something cold, with spicy island rum and sweet juice?"

"Just water, thank you."

While Henry poured mineral water over ice and added a garnish, she retrieved her picture of Clive. It had been examined by at least twenty more people in the last few hours. One said he thought he'd seen Clive but didn't remember when or where; one winked and said he *wished* he'd seen Clive. Two guys at a place called Papaya's thought he'd been there, but they'd been so drunk that night, they couldn't be sure. The rest gave her the blank stare she'd come to know all too well.

When the bartender served her water, she launched into her speech. "I'm looking for a friend of mine who's been on vacation in the islands."

Taking the picture, he tilted it toward a flickering candle. "A Four Seasons guest."

"I don't know," she said. "He might have stayed here."

"That wasn't a question." He looked up. "I've served him several times."

"You did?" She practically shot off the barstool. "When?"

"A week or so ago." He smiled at the picture and handed it back to her. "Very amusing man, from New York."

Hallefreakinglujah. "Yes, he's funny and from New York."

"A stockbroker," the bartender added with a gleam of pride at knowing his customers so well.

"A hedge-fund manager, but that's close enough."

"Drinks gimlets and loves Diana Krall," he continued, as though it were a game.

"Loves every song she ever sang. Oh, I am *so* happy!" She dumped her bags on the next stool and settled in. "I was beginning to think no one in the entire Caribbean had actually spoken to Clive."

"Clive?"

"Yes," she said. "He did the 'drop into the islands, drop out of life' thing, and I'm trying to coax him back home. He's been down here a month, and he's more of a workaholic than I am, so it's time for . . ." She hesitated at the look on his face. "What is it?"

"His name is not Clive. It's Jason Brooks."

Jason Brooks? Would Clive travel under a fake name? "Did he tell you that?"

"No, but it is our job to know the name of every guest, to be certain their drinks are charged to the proper room." He indicated the photo on the bar. "He is Jason Brooks, a guest in the Palm Grove villa, one of the private cottages on our property."

"Maybe he was staying with Jason Brooks. He's traveling with someone, and they could have put the room under either name."

"No." He shook his head. "That man is Jason Brooks. I am certain of that."

But he could be wrong; he didn't work the front desk. "Was he with anyone when he was here?"

He hesitated, then shook his head. "Not that I noticed. But he spent a lot of time . . ." He held up his thumb and pinky to his ear. "On the cell phone."

That would be Clive.

The bartender nodded to an older couple who'd just taken seats, then placed a drink menu in front of Vanessa. "Do you drink gimlets as well, Miss? I make the best."

"No, thank you. Can you just tell me when he checked out?"

"He did not check out. He has not been here for a while, but he is still registered in the villa."

"He *is*? Where's the villa?" she asked eagerly. "How do I get there?"

He shook his head. "I'm sorry. You may speak with the concierge, but I doubt they will take you there. Palm Grove guests are our most private, and it is not resort policy to disturb them for any reason."

"I understand, but he's my friend, and these are extenuating circumstances."

He inched toward the other customers. "I'm sorry. Our guests demand privacy, and we give it to them."

As he walked away, she said to herself, "If the guests demand privacy, then why did you just tell me his name and villa?"

"That is an excellent question, ma'am."

She spun around and blinked into electric-blue eyes, slack-jawed. He couldn't have. He *couldn't* have.

"The bathroom window." Wade pointed to her. "Not original, but you get points for sheer nerve."

"How did you find me?"

His smile was lazy, and a little bit victorious, as he used his pointed finger to close her mouth gently. "An eleven, huh?"

Stella. "I'm gonna kill that woman."

"Don't be too hard on her. You left a trail that a blind man could follow." Brushing her bare legs with those still-crisp khaki pants, he slipped onto the next barstool and gestured to the picture. "Sounds like you're making progress."

"You were listening?"

"I was just a few feet away."

Heat and chills clashed over her skin at the thought. "For how long?"

"Let's see. I picked you up somewhere around . . . Hurricane Hill? You took that hairpin turn a little too fast, don't you think? Considering you probably don't drive much in New York, and if you do, it's on the other side of the road."

He plucked the stirrer from her glass and bobbed the lime with it. "I thought you hated limes."

"What I hate is being stalked."

"I'm not stalking you." He removed the straw and slipped it between his lips. "What? No vodka?"

She turned away from the unwanted impact of seeing the straw slide into his mouth. "Listen, I can't help you. I have to concentrate on one problem before I jump into another. I need to find my friend. For the time being, I'm not going to meet Eileen Stafford or these other women—"

"Only one so far. We're still looking for the other."

"Whatever," she said, trying not to let that new information take hold of her heart. "Like I said, I'm busy with something else."

She sneaked a peek at him, just in time to catch him sucking the straw again, his mouth puckered, his cheeks not quite as clean-shaven as they were hours ago when she'd run away from him. The little bit of whisker made him even more rugged, and the look he gave her was downright sinful.

"Why are you staring at me like that?" she demanded.

"I'm just curious about how badly you want it."

"How badly I want . . ." She raked his face and chest with a long, slow look, lingering on his wide shoulders and the few golden hairs at the top button. "What?"

"To get into the Palm Grove villa."

She held his gaze, awareness and understanding sparking at the same time. He closed the space between them enough for her to smell the wind on him and the salt of the sea.

So he'd been in an open-air car, too. Right behind her on that hairpin turn that she *had* taken too fast. Warmth curled up inside her, tightening her belly and kicking up her pulse.

"You'd like to go there and see who answers the door, wouldn't you?"

Of course she would.

"And if no one is there, you'd like to go inside to look for his things or a clue to where he might be, am I right?"

So, so right.

He took his own slow trip from eyes to mouth to body and back, leaving every inch well scrutinized and warm. "How badly, Vanessa?"

"Not badly enough to make deals with the devil." She gave him her profile again in an act of sheer self-preservation. "Nice try, but forget it."

He leaned right in to her ear. "I can get you in there." He breathed just enough to move her hair and curl her toes. "I can do that."

She'd bet her next commission check he could. "How?"

"I found you, didn't I?"

She tightened her fingers on the glass. "In exchange for what? A big happy family reunion at the South Carolina jailhouse?"

"Dinner. With you. Tonight."

Her fingers slipped. "That's the price for getting me into that villa?"

"You make it sound like torture. It's just dinner."

Right. Dinner, where he would wear down her every last defense with that silky drawl and warm breath on her hair, with meaningful gazes and teasing touches. And, of course, his pocketful of pictures.

But the fact was, he probably could get her into that villa, and that could take her one giant step closer to finding Clive. Who might be in that very villa right now.

"Tempting, but your price is too high." She backed away from him and this dangerous negotiation. "I'm sure I can get the help I need from the concierge. Enough cash will persuade him to bend the rules."

"You think?" He cocked his head toward the lobby. "Why don't you try? I'll wait here."

"Don't bother. I'll have them take me to the villa. If no one is there, I'll convince them they should let me inside."

He pointed the straw at her. "Good luck with that."

Damn it all, he was right. She was *so* losing this one. The problem was, she was bargaining blindly. She needed to know more about her opponent.

She settled back into the chair and took a drink of water. "So, what's your background that you know all this hide-and-seek stuff?"

"I've spent most of my life looking for things that didn't want to be found." He got close again. "Like you."

She didn't back up but met his smoky gaze with a direct look. Did he really think she was some hopeless female who'd melt from his cocky flirting? "And how did you learn to do that?"

"First, I ask questions of the right people. Then I use all my senses to track." He drew in a slow, deep breath as if he was sniffing her. "I get all the necessary intelligence, move at an effective speed . . ." He brushed some hair from her forehead, curling the strand around his finger. "And then I zoom in . . . and . . ." He tugged the hair gently. "Getcha."

She corralled the three brain cells that hadn't turned to hormonal mush and gave him her best power stare. "Nicely done. But that doesn't answer *how*."

"How isn't important." He was so close that anyone watching would take them for lovers about to kiss. He looked at her mouth as if he was thinking about doing just that.

What would that feel like? He had a wide, sexy mouth and perfect teeth. Very . . . kissable.

"What matters," he continued, "is that I'm giving you a choice."

To kiss or not to kiss. "Which is . . ."

"You can sprint on over to that concierge and make some demands that they will ignore and put yourself on their radar as a problematic patron who should be closely watched while on property . . . or . . ." He ran a fingertip over her knuckles, a touch as hot as fire. ". . . you can sit here with me, drink a tonic-free vodka, and get more information out of the extremely observant bartender who knows more about your friend than he's telling you."

She surveyed his face, the thick eyelashes, angular bones, soft lips. All that easy-going Southern charm was a very deceptive mask over some serious brains. She liked that. Even more than his kissable mouth. "How do you know that he's not telling me everything?"

"The same way I knew to find the woman in orange to get a lead on where you went." He shrugged. "I know stuff. And I can help you."

He could, damn it. "So, what are you proposing? We suck Henry dry for info, then crack the villa?"

"I prefer to think of it as friendly interrogation, but yeah, let's gather some useful intelligence. After that, we'll thoughtfully plan our next move—a strategy you would do well to learn, by the way. That may or may not include circling the villa, observing the occupants, or having a few quiet conversations with someone in housekeeping. We have options. But first, why don't we get some food? You haven't eaten all day."

She *was* starved, and not just for food.

"Considering the way you're dressed," he said, putting a warm hand on her bare knee, "you might be more comfortable with room service."

She shivered. "I don't have a room here."

"I do." He reached into his pocket and set a card key on the bar. "And as luck would have it, it's on the second floor of the main building."

Just the thought sent her pulse spiking. "Why is that lucky?"

"It overlooks the eastern grounds of the resort— where the Palm Grove villa is." He lifted his eyebrows. "What do you say?"

"I know what my father would say."

"Run, little bunny, run?"

She smiled and shook her head. "He'd say, 'Nessie, bulls have balls. Use 'em.' "

That earned her a surprised look. "Was your dad a Marine, by any chance?"

"Worse. An investment banker." And a master negotiator. He'd say she hadn't won this round, but she hadn't exactly lost, either. As long as she had something to gain, she should stay at the table and barter.

She signaled the bartender with the slowest, most welcoming smile she could muster.

"I think I'll take that drink now," she said. "Vodka. Rocks."

"No lime," Wade added, winking at her. " 'Cause she's tart enough."

CHAPTER
SIX

"THE FIRST THING you need to do," Wade said after they'd clinked her crystal tumbler of Grey Goose to the long neck of his Kubuli, "is go to the bathroom. He's more likely to open up to a man."

She rolled her eyes. "Jesus. Oh, wait—that comment about my dad being a Marine? Tell me you're not."

He laughed. "You say that like it's a communicable disease."

"I'm a pacifist."

"Well, good for you. I'm a realist." He was actually way worse than that, but something told him that cozying up to her and telling her about his last two kills wasn't going to get him where he wanted to go.

"All that Semper Fi and ooh-yah shit gives me the willies."

"It's ooh-rah. And by the way, you swear like some

of the guys I fought with," he said. "Don't you know that ladies don't curse?"

She let out a hearty laugh. "Guess what? We can vote now, own property, *and* say bad words." She notched her head toward the bartender. "Want me to get him over here to talk?"

"I want you to go to the ladies' room and stay put for five whole minutes. Is that a remote possibility?"

"You would trust me to do that again?" She lowered her glasses and looked at him over the frames, finally giving him a chance to look directly into her eyes. The pupils were surrounded by a dark ring of navy, and her eyelashes were long and thick. Why would a woman hide artillery like that behind horn-rimmed glasses?

"Of course I trust you," he replied. "We just toasted. Where I come from, that and a handshake are as good as a written contract."

"Where I come from, that and a handshake mean you met in the bar and may or may not exchange accurate cell-phone numbers."

"Since this is technically south of the Mason-Dixon Line, let's call it a deal. Agreed?"

She hesitated, then got up.

He stood instantly, and she acknowledged the gesture with a wry smile. "That's right. South of the Mason-Dixon Line. I forgot."

He tilted his head to the lobby. "Five full minutes."

She took a quick sip of vodka, snagged her handbag, and trotted off while Henry worked his way over.

Wade lifted his bright green bottle. "Great recommendation. Local brew?"

"In Dominica. The secret is the island fresh water."

Wade shot the breeze about local beers for another minute, but since his idea of five minutes and hers were probably not the same, he nodded to the empty barstool to get a subtle interrogation going. "She tells me you've seen her friend."

"I have." Henry glanced toward the lobby, then back to Wade. "She is with you? She is your woman?"

"If I'm lucky." Wade leaned back, keeping his body language loose and unthreatening. "Maybe you can help."

Henry smiled at the conspiratorial tone, like any guy who'd want to help the male species in the quest to get laid.

"But she's real uptight about this guy she's looking for."

"Yes, she is." Henry touched the top of one of the bottles. "I'll make her a strong one, if you like."

Stronger than straight vodka? Wade laughed softly. "What I'd like is a tip on her friend, so she can find him and I can get down to business."

Henry nodded understandingly and rubbed his wiry goatee. "A bartender can be in a difficult position when someone asks about a guest."

"I bet that's tough." Wade nodded sympathetically. "But I'm a guest here, and she's not. Check the registration desk."

Henry leaned closer. "He's gay. Does she know?"

She'd never really said. But given Gideon Bones's establishment and the men he'd seen Vanessa talk to this afternoon, he'd already surmised that the missing man was gay. Vanessa was too smart not to know that as well.

"She knows," Wade assured him. "They're just friends."

"Whatever. Believe me, I see it all here."

The clock was ticking, but he took a slow sip of his beer. "So, what did you see with this guy?"

"Jason? Well, he was traveling with a man," Henry said as he wiped the bar in front of Wade. "A good-looking fellow, built even bigger than you. The man—I do not know his name, because he never once ordered a drink—was very attentive to Jason." He lowered his voice. "Until they had a very bad argument. Then—"

"Excuse me." At the end of the bar, a middle-aged woman wearing the cream-colored shirt of Four Seasons management glared at Henry. "Those people are waiting."

"Pardon me, sir," Henry said, averting his eyes at the reprimand. Then he gestured with the rag. "Here she comes."

Through the lobby glass, Wade could see a flash of platinum locks flying and shapely tanned legs devouring the marble. Vanessa at warp speed.

She sailed back to her stool and looked from him to the departed bartender. "Doesn't look like you did much male bonding while I was gone."

"As a matter of fact," he said, turning to face her, liking the direct contact of his pants legs against her knees and the way it made her try not to react, "in the scant time you gave me, I've learned that your friend was traveling with a muscle-bound man and that the last time they were seen together, they had an argument."

Her jaw unhinged. "Really? He told you that?"

"Then he got his knuckles rapped by his boss, so we have to be patient."

She was already gripping the edge of the bar, ready to climb over and shake Henry down for more information. "Who was this guy? And when did this happen? Which bar? Here? Were they registered together?"

He put his hand on hers. "Relax, and give him a minute." He inched the drink in front of her. "He'll come back."

"I don't want to relax," she said. "This is the first person who actually has some concrete information. Waiting is bullshit."

"Honestly, Vanessa. Where'd you learn to talk like that?"

Her look was lethal. "I was born with it."

"Must be your business. All that screaming on the stock-exchange floor."

"How do you know what I do for a living?" She drew back, on guard. "I never told you."

"I have a file on you. It's all public information," he assured her. "Remember, I work for a security and investigation firm. Obviously, we did some research to locate you."

"What's this firm called?" she asked, whipping out an iPhone. "I'll look it up on the Internet right now."

"You won't find it on the Internet."

"Then as far as I'm concerned, it doesn't exist." She touched the screen. "Naturally, no wireless." She put the phone down, disgusted. "What kind of company doesn't have a Web site?"

"A secret one."

"More bullshit," she said, locking her gaze on the bartender. "Tell me everything he said."

"I did already. He'll be back in a few minutes. Meantime, we can talk. Why are you so dead set against meeting your mother?"

"I thought we toasted and were pals now. Like this." She lifted the drink, touched the neck of his beer bottle, and took a deep drink. "Please don't make me talk about her. She's not my mother."

"She's your birth mother," he corrected.

"A mere technicality."

"What about your adoptive mother? Is she opposed to you meeting Eileen Stafford also?"

"I don't know what that woman is opposed to or not, and I don't care, and neither did she when she took a one-way flight to Arizona when I was fifteen." The pain in her eyes was raw.

"How about your father?"

Her expression softened. "Greatest human being ever to walk the face of the earth. His death was a travesty. And the reason I'm a pacifist."

He filed that but stayed on his target. "When did you find out about your birth mother's past?"

"After my father divorced Mary Louise Porter, he helped me launch a massive search, and we eventually found her."

"So, when you found out she was in jail, you decided you didn't want to meet her?"

Her laugh was quick and mirthless. "I admit it shattered my fantasy."

"Which was what?"

"That my dad and my birth mother would meet, fall in love, get married, and I would have a mother who really wanted me, instead of one who considered me just this side of Satan's daughter." She shot from the chair as the bartender passed. "Henry, can I talk to you for a second?"

"You need another, Miss?"

"I need to find my friend," she said, reaching out and closing her hand over his wrist. "You're the first person I've met who has actually seen Clive since he went on a cruise about a month ago. Tell me everything, please."

Wade knew better than to step in and stop her. If she wanted to do this her bullish way, let her.

Henry glanced around, but the management woman had disappeared, and the other bar patrons seemed fine. "I can only tell you this. He is registered here under Jason Brooks, and he introduced himself to me as Jason. I don't know anything about a Clive."

"What about this man he was with? Do you know his name?"

"I don't, but . . ." He hesitated, his dark eyes unsure of how far to go. Wade would have coaxed it out of him nice and easy, but Vanessa squeezed his hand and leaned so far over the bar she looked as if she'd bite the poor guy if he didn't cough up some facts.

"You have to tell me."

No, he didn't. But there was no proving that to her.

"You do this job long enough," Henry said, "you learn to pick out the people who are here for fun and those who might be running away from trouble, you know?"

"And you think he's running away from trouble?" Vanessa asked.

He sighed, glanced at Wade, then said, "There are some people who live on this island and over on St. Kitts who are very, very secretive. Do you know what I mean? Hiding from the tax collector, the police, the FBI, selling drugs, laundering money, doing stuff that might not be completely . . . good. The islands attract that type."

"He didn't do anything bad," she insisted. "He's totally legit. He's a hard worker and a good friend."

Henry looked unconvinced. "Most people on vacation in Nevis at a resort like this, they don't use the cell phone a lot. Most are happy to be off it for a week or two, you know? But this man, all the time on the phone—"

"Talking on the phone doesn't make him a criminal." She couldn't hide her indignation. "He lives on the phone. He's a hedge-fund manager."

Henry shrugged and started moving away. "Yes, of course. You are right."

They'd lost him.

Wade stood, surreptitiously sliding a fifty-dollar bill over the bar. Vanessa didn't see, but Henry did.

"You've been a great help," Wade said.

Henry didn't even look at the money as he curled it into his palm. "I'm sorry I did not hear what they were arguing about," he told Wade, ignoring Vanessa. "But Jason was very upset, very mad. The other man left, and Jason made a phone call, drank two gimlets, and disappeared. The next night, he was down here again. Alone. He answered his phone, talked, then took off."

"Is that all?" Wade asked.

"Well, a little while later, someone I'd never seen came into the bar. A large native man with beady eyes. He also asked me if I'd seen Mr. Brooks. I told him he'd been there a few minutes ago, the fat man left, and I haven't seen either one since. Really, that's all I can tell you. I just don't know where he's been or when he's coming back. Sorry."

Vanessa fell back onto her chair. "A really fat man? Smelling like cigar smoke?"

"Yes, and then—" Henry straightened as his boss sauntered toward the bar. "Excuse me, please."

"Bones," Vanessa said, a little pale as she looked at Wade. "That's the guy I met up in the hills on St. Kitts. The one who had some goon stick a gun in my back. Why would he be here looking for Clive?"

Wade had a few theories developing. Maybe Clive met someone at the house and left with him, owing money to the "madam," Gideon Bones. Or maybe Gideon and Clive had something going, or it was an old-fashioned love triangle. He reached for her bags. "I think we're done here. Time for Plan B."

She slipped off the stool and shouldered her handbag. "B as in B-and-E?"

He smiled. "Yes, we can break and enter if we have to. But it's an art and has to be done right, or we'll end up in a Caribbean jail. You won't like that."

"Wouldn't be the first in the family, now, would I?"

No wonder she was so tart. It was an act to cover a truckload of pain. Maybe if he could get her to admit all that, and find her friend, then he could get her to South Carolina.

And Lucy called this a gimme? Man, it was easier knocking off drug lords.

Remarkably, it was cool.

Clive opened his eyes and realized that for the first time in more than a month, his sweat glands were actually taking some time off. And his shower had removed almost all the sand that clung to every pore and made him feel like a human nail file.

But the hut was dark. And lonely. And, he hoped, safe.

He blinked at the horizon melting from silver blue to inky black on the Caribbean Sea, the only visible lights from some faraway island where tourists were drinking and locals were resting—and someone was searching high and low to find him so they could kill him.

On the stone mosaic cocktail table next to him, the drink he'd mixed hours earlier had turned to water. The last of his cigarettes was gone. His phone flashed with a message he'd missed because he kept the ring tone silent while he slept. He knew who it was but listened anyway.

"She's chasing wild geese. In Nevis."

Clive punched in a few buttons, and the phone was answered in one ring.

"Why Nevis?" he demanded.

"Because it's small, and I can have her watched and send her places where she will get nowhere. She's racing around like Christopher Columbus discovering the West Indies, flashing your picture, spilling your name, and leaking all kinds of personal information. Nevis is a good place for her."

Despite his misery, he smiled. The image of Vanessa on a rampage through the islands, waving his picture, tossing that hair, flapping that unstoppable mouth, was priceless. "You're worried she's drawing too much attention."

"Damn right I am. And so should you be."

"She'll never find me." The truth was, he'd never dreamed she'd come after him. He might not have taken a vacation day in five years, but she hadn't had one in six. Her last day off was her dad's funeral. "Anyway," Clive added, "I sent her a little warning."

"*What?* Why? How?"

"Don't worry, she can't trace it. I just wanted her to know I'm not dead."

"Everything can be traced. Now that she knows she is close, she will look even harder. It's not good. It's not safe. And tonight, she is not alone."

Clive frowned at the ominous tone. "What do you mean?" Who would she bring down here? Someone else from New York?

Someone who knew Charlie?

"She picked up a man, or he picked her up. My guess? He's looking for you and using her to find you. These people, they will stop at nothing. You know that."

Oh, yes, he did. He only had to think about Charlie French . . . and . . . no, he couldn't even think about Russell yet. The pain was unbearable.

"By the time she's exhausted herself over there, I'll send her somewhere else. Eventually, she'll give up and go home."

Clive choked and it turned into a coughing fit, his lungs burning from Marlboros. "Give up?" he finally said. "You do not know Vanessa Porter."

"Since you do, then perhaps you have a better idea, since it is your sweet ass on the line?"

"The only way to get her to go home is to offer something more appealing than the idea of finding me." He sifted through his cigarette butts to see if one was long enough to light for a few puffs. He braced a filter in his teeth and grabbed the lighter, then took it out and flung it back into the ashtray. "Money."

"She can be paid off?"

"No. But if she thought she was missing out on some huge deal on Wall Street, she'd put me on hold and go after it."

"What kind of deal?"

"An IPO, a leveraged buyout, a merger—something where her clients could make a killing. Give the girl a copy of the *Wall Street Journal*, and she'll eat out of your hand."

"I can try something."

Clive closed his eyes. "You can try, but she's very smart, so be clever. Who is this guy she's with?"

"I don't know. Very hot. Built like he has a big gun. A military type."

Just like Russell. His heart skidded at the thought. "Well, if some dude is using her to get to me, she'll figure it out. And on Nevis, she can actually talk to someone who's seen me."

"Some people will talk. And some people will lie. She'll lose a few days, and maybe just give up her whole quest and go home."

"Not Vanessa." Clive could just see her, striding toward the Razor Partners conference room, legions of the investment firm's lawyers in her wake, her game face on behind her glasses, her blond mane loose and long and all over the place. When she started kicking ass and taking names, she was a thing of freaking beauty. "When she wants something, honey, don't even get in her way."

"Precisely the reason I'm controlling and watching her every move. She'll lead them right to you, and, my friend, you don't want that. Or did you forget the number of stab wounds you counted?"

"Only when I'm drunk or asleep. Then I forget everything."

"Stay that way. For now, she's occupied. It'll take her two days to find out where you were—if she even does."

"It doesn't take her two days to put together a Fortune 500 merger," Clive told him, fingering through the ashtray again. "She's fast at everything."

"Yeah, well, I'm faster. And more motivated."

"She loves me."

The phone went silent for a moment, and Clive thought they'd lost the connection. But then he heard a soft chuckle. "So do I."

Guilt squeezed his heart. He knew what he should say, but it would be a lie. Instead, he let a few seconds tick by.

"Bet you could use some more cigarettes and gin."

"Actually, I'm sick of this diet. I need something healthy. Do you freaks have any macaroni and cheese on these islands?"

He laughed. "For you? I will find it."

"I prefer Kraft."

The snort on the phone was affectionate. "I will do my best, my friend."

"Thanks. And hey, listen . . ." Clive cleared his throat. "I really appreciate this, man. You're saving my life."

"Like I said, I'm motivated. I love you."

Clive didn't know how to respond. He didn't love back. But he needed to stay in hiding—and this man was proving to be indispensable in that regard.

"Thanks," he said again, knowing he sounded gruff and distant. And that it probably made him even more attractive.

After they clicked off, Clive thought about getting up and attempting to run, but it was too much. He'd rather just lie there and think how grateful he was for a friend like Vanessa. After all she'd been through, after how hard she worked to put a shell around herself and protect her heart, she chucked New York and got on a plane to find him.

Now, *that* was love. Not sexual, not romantic, and not celebrated enough, but so powerful.

Her selflessness put a lump in his throat, just as the phone lit with a silent notification of a text. He didn't read it, worried that someone, somewhere, would pick up his signal. He turned the phone off and let the screen go as black as the night around him.

Still, his fingers itched to send Vanessa another message. Could he tell her part of the truth and expect her to leave, in one piece and without him? Because if she knew the whole truth . . . she'd be the next to die.

And he couldn't risk that. He had enough guilt on his soul without adding her death to it.

CHAPTER
SEVEN

"HOLY SHIT," VANESSA whispered. "It'd be easier to get into Fort Knox."

In the moonlight bouncing off the white sand, Vanessa could see Wade's frown.

"It's not getting in that worries me," he said. "It's getting out."

"What do you mean?"

He pointed to the solid wood fence draped in foliage and painted the same yellow as the clapboard villa and pool house it enclosed. "That's tighter than I thought."

"You saw that barrier from your balcony and said it shouldn't be a problem."

They couldn't see much else from the balcony of his suite, which was not exactly the "full villa view" he'd used to lure her up there. Before she could get too worked up about that, he'd fed her an excellent room-service meal she'd desperately needed. Then he produced a laptop with some ultracool software that allowed him to download a satellite image of the property and produce a damn near 3-D snapshot of the villa. And true to his word, after she changed into jeans and sneakers and borrowed a navy hooded sweatshirt, they'd slipped out at midnight to follow shadowy, secluded paths that led to the Palm Grove villa.

If it hadn't felt so risky, Vanessa would have enjoyed the cool adventure with a hot guy. He moved like ink through the night, holding her hand in his much larger, slightly callused one, getting right up to her ear to whisper instructions and send vibrations down her skin. He was so totally confident on his mission, so thorough and alert, that every cell in her jumped with awareness and attraction.

If he hadn't been the messenger she wanted to shoot, she would have thanked him for his assistance with a night he'd never forget back in that suite. Just the thought kicked her hormones into gear.

She stole a sideways glance to catch his mouth set in a firm line. It was impossible to look at those lips and not think about kissing. Her stomach fluttered as she studied the breadth of his shoulders. He was tall, probably six-two, and broad, but not grossly muscular. Ripped and strong and—

"You want to climb up?" He tapped the shoulder she'd been admiring, his smile teasing enough to know she'd been busted.

"I can, if that's the best way to get over the fence."

"We just want to avoid the cameras." He pointed to a spot a few feet away. "There's one about every ten feet along the top. See?"

She squinted into darkness and greenery, seeing only tropical flowers and an overabundance of palm fronds covering much of the seven- or eight-foot-tall fence.

"I don't see a thing," she admitted. "How can you tell there are cameras?"

"Years of avoiding them. I assume a video feed from each one is being monitored this very minute. My guess is that this villa is a favorite of celebrities who want to hide from the paparazzi and too-friendly fans."

"It's not like Clive to seek privacy," she mused. "He loves attention."

"So maybe security."

Why would he worry about security? And, bigger question, was he in there or not? She'd called his cell phone to no avail, but Wade had talked her out of having the resort ring the villa directly. They tracked that sort of thing, and the move would only put security on alert that someone was trying to find a guest. Better not to get their attention at all.

Which made sense. Like everything else he said.

"I think we can get over the wall right there, between those two cameras. Once we're on the property, we'll stay back, to see if there's any activity or light in the house."

"If there is?"

"We'll figure that out after we watch their movements and determine if it's your friend or not."

"And if there isn't anything? What if the villa is deserted?"

He threw her a look in challenge. "It's your call. We go in, or we walk away. I say we storm the place."

A surge of adrenaline mixed with something much more sexual inside her. "Spoken like a true Marine." She smiled. "Let's roll, Sarge."

He took her hand, guiding her to the midsection of fencing. Just as they approached a spot in the deepest of shadows, a low motor rumbled, and headlights illuminated a narrow asphalt path that ran the perimeter of the resort and ended at the fenced-in property of the private villa.

"Down," he ordered in a whisper, pulling her flat to the ground. "It's hotel security."

Through the blades of grass, Vanessa could see a lone driver doing a cursory check of the area. He turned the little vehicle around at the back fence along the beach. When he glanced their way, Vanessa held her breath. After a split second, he hit the gas and rumbled back toward the main building.

"Your heart's pounding," Wade said, his mouth inches from her ear and his hand on her back.

"My heart's beating," she corrected. "Proof that I'm alive."

"You sure you want to do this?"

"Yes, I'm sure." She rolled to her side, putting her face to face with him, inches from that kissable mouth. "I want to find Clive. This is the closest I've come to . . ." *A man this sexy in a while.* ". . . finding him."

His eyes traveled over her face in assessment. "You're pretty brave for a girl, you know that?"

"For a *girl*? Well, you're pretty cute for a Neanderthal."

He blew out a laugh and slowly pulled her up. "There's nothing wrong with a little fear. It can keep you alive."

"I know all about survival. I work on Wall Street, and I've been roaming the streets of New York City since I was a kid. I'm not too worried about some hotel guard in a golf cart. Unless . . . he has a gun."

He pushed some bushes out of the way, clearing a section of the fence. "He probably does."

"But can he shoot it?"

"Can he, or will he?" He glanced over his shoulder. "My guess is that he would if he thinks we're breaking the law. Which we are." He cupped his hands, giving her a step. "After you, ma'am."

She put her sneaker in his palm. "You really are from another century. 'Ma'am'? I'm barely thirty."

He just looked at her.

Oh, yeah. The file. "All right, thirty-one. But can the ma'ams, please."

"I'll do my best. Grab my shoulder and push."

She did, closing her fingers around rock-hard muscles and positioning her sneaker in his hands. "When I get on the other side, what do I do?"

"Just roll into a ball, and keep your face and hands covered with the jacket. I'll be right behind you. Now, go, before the guard comes back and takes a shot."

She swiftly hoisted herself up, using the fence and

his sturdy shoulder to leverage herself. When she stood, she could see right into the back of a sizable villa, the pool, and an enclosed cabana. It was totally silent, dark, and empty. Not even a pool light on, just complete blackness.

"Doesn't look like anyone's here," she said.

"Can you get over?"

She leaned over to see if there was something she could use as a step to the other side. Nope. "I'll have to jump." A long freaking way.

She glanced at the house again. Was this worth it? Was Clive in there, hiding in the dark with a bottle of depression relief?

She shifted her weight, set one foot on the fence, and went over, landing with a jolt that cracked her teeth together before tumbling onto the grass. In a second, she heard a whoosh and a thud, and Wade landed next to her on the balls of his feet like a panther.

"You okay?" he asked, pulling her closer to the ground.

"Yeah."

"Good work. Now, stay low and close to the fence. We'll move along the ground; otherwise, a camera over there will pick us up."

She followed his lead as he slithered army-style toward the house, trying hard not to think about what she was doing but why, and for whom. When they reached the pool house, he cupped his hands and peered into one of the windows.

"Not much in there, and I don't want to risk the

cameras by going all the way around the front. Let's run along the side of the pool and head to the sliding doors near the bar. Got it?"

She followed the visual path he pointed out, got steady on the balls of her feet, and sprinted when he did. They rounded the unlit pool, passed a few chaise longues and a table, and slipped under the patio overhang.

When they stopped, Vanessa waited, half expecting a bullet to fly by or an alarm to screech into the night, but all was silent, except for the beat of her pulse in her ears.

"Should we just knock?" she asked.

He cupped his hands again to look inside before he tapped lightly on the glass. "My guess is, it's unoccupied." He pointed to a corner of the overhang, where a tiny camera was aimed at the sliding glass door. "Stay right here, out of range. I'm going to change the picture."

He lifted his black T-shirt to his mouth, bit the cloth, and yanked, the sound of tearing cotton loud in the silence. He tore halfway up the shirt, exposing his stomach, then two more tugs until he had a square of black fabric. He stepped around a table, pulled a chair out without making a noise, and climbed up to drape the camera lens.

He did it all so quietly and smoothly, with such ease and capability, that Vanessa gaped in amazement.

"You rob banks in another life?"

"Nope."

"Just a regular residential thief?"

"I told you, I consult for a security firm. When you put it all together, you usually know how to take it apart."

She really *couldn't* have done this without him. Did she owe him something now? A trip to South Carolina? She watched him climb down from the chair, the torn shirt making him look ridiculously tough, dangerous, and sexy.

Maybe they could renegotiate, and she could pay him off the more traditional way. Then they'd both win.

He tested the slider, walking his fingers around the aluminum rim, and jimmying it. "We just need to open this thing right here."

"How?"

"Piece of cake, ma'a—" He shot her a look. "Sorry." He turned, scanning the patio. "I just need a little something from the bar." He walked to the bar, stepped behind it, and looked around. "Perfect. This oughta do the trick." He held up an ice pick that glinted in the moonlight.

"What trick is that?"

"I believe this would be called the unauthorized removal of a sliding glass door from its mounted, operable position within a supporting frame structure." Back at the door, he ran his hand along the bottom track, his eyes closed and the tip of his tongue just peeking out of his lips. "That'd be the technical term for poppin' the slider."

"Did you learn that in the Marines?"

"Nope. My mama used to lock me out if I missed

curfew." He looked up and smiled wickedly, making her heart speed up more. "That happened a lot."

She'd bet it did. She could imagine all those Southern belles keeping him out *way* past midnight.

"Unless"—he reached farther along the glass—"this two-grand-a-night villa has upgraded every door with a . . ." He knelt down, bending over just enough to draw her attention to his jean-clad backside. ". . . Yamamoto apparatus that was patented not long ago to prevent just this kind of criminal behavior. If they have, it'll just mean I'll have to resort to more . . ." He wiped a hand on his thigh and tried again. "Aggressive measures."

There was a low rumble, then a crack, as he lifted the door right out of its frame.

He stood, holding the door steady. "After you."

She nodded in admiration as she opened the screen door. "Nice work." Nice *everything*.

The screen glided soundlessly on its track, and she stepped into a dark, air-conditioned room. In a moment, Wade had the slider back onto the rail.

"Whatever you do, don't turn on a light," he said, closing the door behind him and locking it again. "If someone comes by to do a security check while we're looking around, we don't want to tip them off that we're in here."

"No chance that you brought a flashlight, is there?" she asked.

"No, but gimme a sec." He rounded a counter into the kitchen. "The fridge'll give us enough light."

Soft light spilled over the room, revealing that

they were in a large, high-ceilinged gathering room decorated in Four Seasons elegance, with a gleaming marble floor and hardwood accents.

Hope and surprise lit in her chest as she took in the signs of life all over the room. A newspaper open on the coffee table, a pair of familiar-looking flip-flops by the sofa, a half-finished bottle of wine, one glass, and an ashtray overloaded with cigarette butts.

And the ultimate signature of Clive Easterbrook: a self-help book. This one was called *You, Understood.*

"He's here," she whispered. "At least, he was." She picked up the book and nudged the disgusting ashtray. "He's a marathoner who only smokes when he's hopelessly depressed, and he's addicted to therapy books." The wine was merlot, his depression companion of choice, with a bluesy babe crooning on the iPod, no doubt.

How low did he go this time? She glanced around again, taking in the coat of dust on the mahogany wood, the crumbs, and a few drops of some dried-up drink on the floor. "I wonder why no one's cleaned the place."

Wade was already headed back from the front door. "Because there's a privacy key in the main entrance," he said.

"Henry said he hasn't been by the pool in a week or so." Vanessa lifted the newspaper and angled it to the light to read the date. "Would they really leave his room empty for a week? Don't they worry that someone . . ."

"Vanessa. Come in here."

. . . might have died in here?

She tried to silence the thought. Holding the paper, she followed Wade's voice down a short hall, then forced herself to step into the doorway and face anything.

It was just a very messy room, lit softly by the closet light.

"What's the matter?" she asked. "What did you find?"

The drawers gaped open, some full of unfolded clothes, some empty. A four-poster antique bed was unmade, and loose change, a watch, and tourist guide-books were spread on the dresser. In the closet, a few shirts and a jacket were pushed to one side. Some dirty clothes were strewn on the floor. A phone charger hung from an electrical outlet.

"The whole place is a mess," Wade said, as if he suspected that was meaningful.

"Clive borders on being a slob. So this doesn't mean he left in a hurry or anything. The cigarettes and wine tell me he's miserable." Not to mention *You, Understood,* prime evidence that he was feeling anything but *understood.* "My guess is that his heart's been broken."

"There's only one head groove on the pillow."

She'd have never thought to make that observation. "True. But this is all his stuff. I recognize it."

"So maybe he had a lonely, drunken night, and he woke up and—"

"Went off to find the one that got away," she finished. "And he didn't think he'd be gone that long, so he didn't check out of the resort." Disappointment curled through her. "God, I really expected to find him. Or something that would lead me to him."

"Let's keep looking around."

With a sigh, she leaned against a bedpost and tossed the newspaper to the side. She skimmed the room slowly, taking in Clive's favorite nylon tank top balled up on the floor next to the gel-soled Asics that she'd spent a whole Saturday afternoon schlepping around Midtown to help him find.

Where would Clive go without his running shoes? It was like her leaving without her iPhone. Imflippingpossible.

She could hear Wade opening and closing cabinets in the bathroom.

"Does he have any Zoloft in there?" she called. 'Cause, boy, he needed it.

"Don't see any . . . but . . ." She heard something like porcelain grating on porcelain. *"Whoa."*

"Whoa what?" She pushed off the bedpost and headed toward the bathroom.

He stood with the tank lid in his hands, staring into the tank. "I know you said he's a slob, but would he stuff clothes into the toilet?"

She peered inside and instantly recognized the corporate lime-green and navy-blue T-shirt Vexell Industries had given out at a 10K they sponsored last year. "That's one of Clive's favorite running shirts. Why the hell would he put it in there?"

With two fingers, Wade gingerly plucked a corner of fabric, water rushing off as he lifted it.

"He came in second in that race, and he—" She froze and stared at the dark marks, chills rolling over her as she noticed the maroon color of the water. "Is that blood?"

He let the shirt fall back into the tank. "Yes, it is."

She took a few steps back, her hand over her mouth, stumbling over a balled-up towel on the floor. Was Clive hurt? Was that his blood? Her chest tight, she stepped out of the bathroom, vaguely aware of Wade passing her.

She heard the refrigerator door close with a soft pop. In the dim light from the closet, she looked around the bedroom, searching for a different kind of clue, something more nefarious than signs of a man who took off after he and his lover had a fight.

Dropping to the unmade bed, she squeezed her burning eyes closed. *Clive, what happened to you?*

"Do you want to call the police now or wait until morning?" Wade asked, standing in the doorway.

She looked up. "I don't know what to do."

He pointed to the newspaper. "Not that it's proof of when he was here, but what's the date on that?"

She lifted it and read the top again. "The sixth. Eight days ago." She looked farther down, the newsprint swimming before her. "I just wish I knew if . . ." The print stopped moving as her gaze fell on a picture of a man. *A man she knew.* "Oh, my God."

"What is it?"

She frowned at the words and the image, trying to process it. "Russell Winslow. He's Clive's ex-boyfriend. They broke up months ago . . ." Her voice trailed off as she read the words. "His car went off a cliff." She looked up at Wade, her head spinning. "Oh, God, Wade, do you think Clive was with him?"

He snagged the paper and read. "It doesn't say if he was in the car alone, just that they found the car and . . ." He skimmed the article, then looked up, his eyes narrowed. "They suspect foul play because of the way the accident happened."

She inched back, the weight of the words and his look of accusation pressing hard. "You think *Clive* killed him?"

"I think you have to assume Clive's involved somehow. Look around, Vanessa. Someone abandoned this place. He hasn't been seen for more than a week. What was their relationship like?"

"The breakup was nasty, but they seemed to be getting back to being friends. I know what you're thinking, but you're wrong," she said defiantly. "Clive isn't capable of murder. He's good, kind, funny, and . . ."

"Depressed, missing, and hiding bloody clothes in the toilet tank," he finished.

"And sending me messages to be careful."

"For you to watch your back. Maybe you're next on his list."

She shot up. "Stop it! You don't even know the man, and you're ready to send him to the electric chair. Haven't you ever heard of circumstantial evidence?"

"Down!" He dove at her, taking her to the floor in one lightning-fast move, stealing her breath and knocking her glasses off as she hit the floor. "Some-one's out there. I saw a flashlight."

With one solid push, he had her halfway under the bed. "Don't make a sound. Don't breathe. Don't move." He snagged her glasses from the floor and shoved them at her. "Just hide."

CHAPTER
EIGHT

WADE KEPT ONE arm around Vanessa, bending his right leg so that his other hand was only inches from his ankle holster. When the bedskirt fell back into place, he couldn't see, but he could hear everything. Footsteps on the patio. The slider door being tested.

And the erratic heartbeat of the woman next to him.

The footsteps grew distant, moving away from the patio.

"They're gone," she breathed.

He tightened his grip on her. "Wait."

In seconds, the front latch clicked, and the door opened. Wade closed his eyes to focus on sound, to determine if this was a standard security check, a late-night visit from housekeeping, the return of her buddy Clive . . . or someone else.

The footsteps were heavy—probably male—and

quick, moving through the villa and turning on lights as he went. Whoever it was, he wasn't worried about being seen or heard.

Could it be Clive?

Wade and Vanessa shared a silent look, neither one moving. Through the centimeter of space between the bedskirt and the floor, they could see a man's feet in slightly worn Docksiders and no socks. He slid clothes against the closet rod, then moved to the bathroom, the shoes quieter on the marble floor. The shower door clicked open and closed, and Wade listened for the sound of the porcelain tank being removed. Instead, he heard the soft tones of a cell-phone dial pad.

"No one's here," a low male voice said.

She looked at Wade and shook her head, as if to say it wasn't Clive.

"False alarm," he continued. "I didn't think she could get in here, anyway."

Vanessa tensed, and Wade squeezed her to keep her from reacting.

Inches away, feet shuffled.

He'd been in this situation a dozen times or more. In his former life, he'd have a weapon out, ready to rid the world of a terrorist, a drug cartel leader, or some other threat. His heart rate hadn't even climbed yet, but he could feel that every muscle in Vanessa's body was viciously tight.

"Oh, she's definitely at the resort. She was at the bar for a while, hit the bathroom, then flirted with some dude before they took off for his room." Another pause. "Well, apparently, she *does* have time to get laid."

Wade slid a glance to his left. Vanessa's eyes were wide, and he'd bet her cheeks were bloodless, since about twenty gallons a minute was coursing through her heart.

"I'll find her," the man said. "Might cost me, but someone at the front desk will give me the guy's name and room number." He paused. "Yeah, I know what to do. If that doesn't work, we'll send her off to . . ." A low chuckle. "Excellent. She'll never see that coming."

He sat on the bed, his weight smashing the box spring against their backs and crushing Wade's arm over Vanessa's back. She bit her lip and didn't make a sound.

"Oh, I'll stop her," the man said, the threatening note in his voice barely audible over the newspaper rustling. "You should see this picture. Jesus. Those fucking idiot cops still haven't searched this room. I swear, they're going to buy the suicide angle, which doesn't help us at all." He paused again, standing. "Not a bad idea, since I'm in here. I would have said it was too obvious, but since it's taking them fucking forever to find the bloody shirt, I'll just push things along so there's no question who killed Russell Winslow."

He stood in front of the dresser and dropped something into a drawer with a thud. Then he slammed them all shut.

"All set. When they finally check in here, it will be obvious even to a moron who did the deed. Now I'm gonna go find Blondie and do some damage. She's probably screwing her bar pickup by now."

The voice faded, the front door slammed, and Vanessa finally breathed.

"Not yet," Wade warned before she launched out of there. "There are lights on everywhere. Wait."

"They're setting Clive up," her words burst in a whisper. "Did you hear that?"

"Maybe. Whoever was in here is looking for you and knows you're in this hotel. What we need to do is find out who they are and why they're following you."

She nodded, visibly working for control. "Okay. Right. How?"

"For one thing, we move slow and smart—not fast and stupid. You stay *right here* for ten seconds. I can get to the window, get a look at him, and never be seen."

She didn't argue as he slithered forward. At the wall, he inched up until he had a visual over the windowsill. Nothing moved, no light shone. But he couldn't be sure someone wasn't watching the villa. Now that the lights were on, they were moving targets inside.

She peeked out from under the bed. "Clear yet?"

"Hang on." He crawled across the floor toward the drawers. "I want to see what he put in the drawer."

Carefully, without making any noise or creating a shadow in the window across the room, he opened the top drawer and peered over the edge. Boxers, a bathing suit, and an undershirt. He felt around. Nothing that would thud.

He opened the next drawer. More T-shirts, shorts. And there, under a pair of socks, was a wallet. A wallet could have landed with that noise.

"Got something here," he said, plucking out the leather billfold.

He crouched back down and motioned Vanessa out from the bed. Opening the billfold, he immediately recognized the picture from the paper. "Russell Winslow's wallet."

"That guy had Russell's wallet and put it there? And what about the shirt in the toilet? Did they do that? We have to find out who that was. Because that's who killed Russell, not Clive."

"Could be. We'll let the police—"

She smacked her hand over her mouth. "Oh, shit. I've been shoving that picture into the face of every person I met since I got here. I never dreamed he was in trouble, in hiding."

"He's in something, that's for sure."

"What else is in the wallet?"

He flipped it open. "A couple hundred bucks. Credit cards. An ID." Wade angled it toward the light and squinted at the holographic imprint. "Environmental Protection Agency?"

"That's where Russell works. Worked," she corrected grimly. "Is there a driver's license?"

"No, but maybe he had that on him when he died." Wade glanced at the EPA ID again, studying the thick neck, skin head, and serious expression. "Military?"

"He's a former Navy SEAL," she said. "Clive just loved saying that."

He snapped the billfold closed. "We'll turn all this over to the police immediately. I don't think we should wait until tomorrow."

"But what about Clive?"

"What about him?"

"You heard that guy. They're setting him up as a killer. And what if they fail? They'll . . . kill him, too. And what if they manage to plant enough evidence that no matter what I say I heard—from under the bed when I broke into his villa, by the way? Then Clive still looks guilty of something he didn't do."

"All that could happen regardless of what you do, and you have a legitimate motive for entering his room. Your crime isn't as bad as whatever happened to this Winslow guy."

"The system doesn't always work like it should," she shot back. "And even if the truth comes out, Clive's reputation will never be the same. No one will trust him to handle millions of dollars. His career could be over—not to mention his life. I have to find him, Wade. I have to help him. Now that I'm on to them, I won't go where they try to send me. I'll do exactly the opposite."

"Someone sent you to Nevis, and you went instantly."

"And I was right to. Clive has been on this island. Might still even be here." She shook her head, her expression set. "I'm not going to give up now."

Add stubbornness to her list of irritating attributes. "Listen, Vanessa. You need to go to the police. They'll take it from here." He held up his hand to stop the protest he could see coming. "And then you really ought to get on a plane and meet Eileen Stafford and Miranda Lang. Do the right thing."

"*Your* right thing, not mine. I can't leave my closest friend to take the rap for a murder I know in my heart and soul that . . . that . . . he . . ." She stumbled at the words. "That he didn't commit."

He didn't have to say a thing, just watch her expression evolve from hard and determined to . . . less hard and determined. He gave her a full thirty seconds to let logic and emotion hold hands and settle in her brain.

"No one should be blamed for a crime he didn't commit," she whispered, looking away as though she couldn't meet his eyes, defeat coloring her tone.

He took her hand, pulling her attention back to him. "It could take days to find your friend, or more. Go to the police, tell them everything, let them handle it. Then let's go help someone else who . . ." He searched for the most persuasive, powerful words he could find. "Someone else who needs you to help her stay alive long enough to prove she isn't guilty."

She trapped her lower lip under her teeth and looked hard at him. "All right," she finally said.

"Good girl." He squeezed her hand with the victory. "That's the right—"

"If you help me find Clive first."

He stilled.

"Come on, Wade," she insisted. "You're so good at this. Help me search this island and any others, keep me safe from whoever is trying to find me, and use all the software and ice picks and whatever else you've got up your sleeve that I don't have. But no police. Not yet."

"And in return?"

She closed her eyes in resignation. "I'll do it. I'll go to South Carolina."

"Will you test for a bone-marrow match?"

"Only if we clear Clive."

"We may not clear him if he's guilty."

"He's not. But I will do it if he's completely safe, and we know who's behind all this and why. Are those terms you can live with?"

"This isn't a negotiating table, Vanessa. We might not find all that out in time."

"*Life* is a negotiating table, pal. You've got something I need, and I've got something you need. So, do we have a deal or not?"

Tough and stubborn and fast and pushy. What a waste of a beautiful woman. "If we can do it in three days," he said. "Not one minute more."

"Fine. How do we get out of here and get started?"

"Stay low, and do exactly as I say. That guy is off to find you, so we'll go where he goes."

She hesitated. "He thinks I'm off screwing you."

Wade grinned. "Then we better hurry up and get into bed."

Behind her back, Vanessa uncrossed her fingers. It was childish, but hey, in her business, a deal wasn't a deal until it was signed in ink and blessed by lawyers. Until then, terms could change. *Anything* could change. Right now, she was desperate for Wade's skills. And he had plenty.

He'd wordlessly pulled the hood over her hair,

tucked her hands into the sleeves of the sweatshirt, and made himself equally invisible before leading her to a gated exit on the beach that opened from the inside. He'd gotten them out of the villa undetected in less than two minutes. Working from memory of a resort site map he'd called up on his computer, he avoided the lobby with a back entrance, took a service elevator to the second floor, and got them back into his suite without encountering a soul in record time. Proving that she'd picked the right man for the job *and* that he could move fast if he wanted to.

In the room, he yanked his torn T-shirt over his head and dropped it onto the floor. "Strip down, and get into bed."

Very fast when he wanted to.

Moonlight streamed into the room and highlighted the planes of his chest, the dusting of dark blond hair at the center, and washboard abs so defined there were shadows in between all six of the pack.

"Vanessa," he said, dipping his head into her line of vision. "Drop trou, sweetheart. Strip."

She lowered the zipper of her hoodie and shouldered out of it, toeing her sneakers at the same time. "Everything?"

"Everything. You don't want the guy to know you're one step ahead of him. You'll lose the advantage that way. He thinks you picked up a guy in a bar and went to his room. We're not playing tiddlywinks. Get down to nothing, and get into bed." He kicked off a shoe and started on his belt, giving her a pointed look. "You need help?"

"Of course not." Heat rammed through her as he unzipped his jeans with a flick of his wrist. She fingered the bottom of her tank top. "You know, if he's really watching my every move, he would have seen us go into the villa."

He pushed his jeans down narrow hips, revealing more golden skin and smooth, ripped muscles, and very tight-fitting boxer briefs.

"No, because he hadn't figured out what room I was in yet or made the assumption that we were in for the night. Our best bet is to make him think that assumption was correct."

He was right. She pulled her tank top over her head and dropped it onto the floor, shaking her hair out of her face in time to catch him looking. She flipped the bra strap. "This, too, I assume."

He notched a brow. "Unless you generally keep it on."

Was he testing her? To see how badly she wanted to find Clive? Well, he was in for a surprise. She reached behind her, unfastened the strap, and let it fall to the ground, the air-conditioning—and his heated gaze—instantly hardening her nipples.

"Jeans, c'mon, hurry," he said as he slid one foot out. His thighs were like carved granite, dusted with light hair over tanned skin. Forcing herself to look away as she unzipped, she turned to look over the half wall that separated the living room from the bedroom. The king-size bed was completely visible; anyone at the door could see who was in it.

"What do you think he's going to do? Just barrel in here, or knock on the door and threaten us?"

"I have no idea. We need to be ready for anything."

Her backside to him, she pushed her jeans down to her ankles, managing to keep her thong in place.

"So, we should act like we've been interrupted in the middle of . . ." His voice trailed off, and she looked over her shoulder. He sat on the sofa armrest, leaning over his ankle, but was staring at her ass. "The good thing."

"The good thing?" She faced him, naked but for a tiny piece of satin between her legs. "Is that a Southern euphemism for sex?"

His blue eyes darkened as he drank in every inch of her with raw appreciation. "That is a Wade Cordell euphemism"—he reached under the bottom of his jeans—"for what a man . . . does to a woman"—he pulled something out at his ankle—"with a body like that."

She started to smile until she realized what he was holding.

A gun.

She gave a shocked gasp. "What the fuck?"

He pointed the shiny barrel toward the floor. "You really need some soap in your mouth, young lady."

"I didn't know you were armed."

"I believe your words were 'Use whatever else you've got up your sleeve.' In this case, it's up my pants."

She backed up, pointing. "That changes everything. I hate guns."

"Not to worry, sweetheart. I'm real good with it."

"I don't care if you're the goddamn best shot in the country—"

"I am."

All the heat and sexual buzz evaporated, leaving her cold and wickedly disappointed. "You have to get rid of it. I can't be in the same room with it."

He snorted as he rid himself of his jeans and unclipped some kind of ankle holster. "Not an option. But don't worry." Naked except for his boxer briefs and the weapon, he opened his palm, revealing a wood-grip pistol with some gold trim. "I can handle any firearm made, in my sleep."

"Not if I'm sleeping next to you."

"Vanessa, guns don't kill—"

"I know, I know." She held up two hands to stop him. "I know all that NRA crap. I've debated with the bastards, fought them at city hall, held the hands of broken-hearted wives and mothers." *Stood at my father's grave and wept.* "Just keep that out of my sight, if you can."

The sound of footsteps coming down the hallway halted the argument. Wade held up a finger to his mouth, then pointed to the bed. "Go."

She hesitated but knew it wasn't the time to fight. As she turned toward the bed, he bounded past her to whip decorative pillows to the floor and throw back the spread.

"Get in," he ordered.

The footsteps stopped outside the door.

She dove for the sheets just as he did. He was on top of her instantly, covering her body, the gun in his right hand.

Without taking his eyes from the door, he slid off

her glasses and set them on the bedside table. "Don't worry, I can see enough for both of us."

The door handle rattled, and he held her still, then put his mouth over her ear. "We either let him know we're here and maybe scare him off, or stay real quiet and see if he comes in, then ambush him. Your call."

The door handle rattled again. "There's no security lock?"

He shook his head. "If he has a pass key, he can come right in." He lifted the gun. "I'm cool with that."

She nodded. "Then don't scare him off. Let him come in, and we'll surprise him."

This time, the handle turned, and the door inched open. From the bed, they could see only the back of the door, not who was on the other side. Vanessa instinctively inched up, but Wade held her steady and motionless, the gun visible in her peripheral vision, his body taut.

The door hit something and stopped moving. She lifted her head to see her sneakers probably at the same time the person entering did.

The door slammed shut, and footsteps pounded in the hall.

"Shit," she mumbled, trying to scoot up. "He chickened out."

"Shhh. Just wait." He lifted his head a little to listen, which pushed his chest harder into hers. His legs were spread over hers, and his cotton briefs warmed her stomach and hips. She arched a little to push him off her, but the move had the opposite effect, causing crotch-to-crotch contact.

"He may only have been verifying that we're in here. Just wait."

She did, staring at his face, his thick lashes just inches from hers, his jaw clenched and angular, tiny squint lines at the corners of his eyes. He was hard and hot and strong and covered every inch of her with corded muscles. All man.

Damn if her body didn't betray her with the first twist of desire.

She closed her eyes, which just made her other senses go on alert. He smelled like a man. And certainly felt like a man. And . . . oh, if she put her mouth on his, she'd bet he tasted like one helluva man.

A minute passed, and nothing happened.

Except every cell in her body got warm.

She shifted under him, her legs brushing the soft hair of his, her breasts rubbing his chest. He seemed so unfazed by this, while she felt so vulnerable. "Can I have my glasses back?"

He picked them up from the pillow and put them on her eyes. "You really need them?"

"Why else would I wear them?"

"They aren't very strong," he said, lifting them above her brows to look directly into her eyes. "Camouflage, maybe. Or to deflect enemies."

"Spoken like a true Marine. I happen to like the way they look. And the way I see," she added quickly.

He continued his scrutiny of her face, zeroing in on her eyes. "You're pretty." He said it as if he'd just figured that out, and it surprised him.

She patted his face with one hand and tapped the

glasses back into place with the other. "You've already got me naked in bed, so you can save the pickup lines."

"It wasn't a line. You are pretty. Pretty and tough is an unusual combination."

"Then you've been hanging out with the wrong girls." She shifted to her right, but that put her thigh against his crotch. "You should hang out on Wall Street instead of Peachtree Street. We're all pretty and tough up there."

"Maybe I should." His lips lifted in a smile as he settled his attention on her mouth. Against her leg, he hardened. The sensation shot fire right through her, making her want to give into the need to rock against him. Instead, she stayed perfectly still while he studied her mouth, her cheeks, her nose.

Then he lifted the frames of her glasses again, sliding them all the way up her forehead. "I'm probably close enough that you don't need these to see me," he said softly. "And I like to be able to look right into a woman's eyes . . . when I kiss her."

He lowered his head, keeping his gaze on hers, and opened his mouth as he closed in for the kiss. Her heart slammed up, and her stomach dropped down.

"I thought this was pretend," she said breathily.

"Yeah." His lips touched hers, but only enough to tease. "Pretend I'm not human." He let his teeth graze her bottom lip. "And pretend you don't want this as much as I do." He touched the tip of her tongue with his, his eyes still open. Then she closed hers, ready to—

The latch clicked with a snap, and the door opened. Instantly, he flipped off her, the gun out again.

"Housekeeping!" a woman's voice called as the door opened. "Turn-down."

"No thanks," he called back, already partially sitting. Instinctively, Vanessa pulled the blankets up, her attention torn between the gun and the door and the naked man poised to fire a bullet.

"Do you need towels, sir?" the woman called. "Toiletries or bottled water?"

He leaned over and put his mouth on her ear. "She could be the messenger."

"Then let her in," she replied softly. "But please don't shoot her."

"We'll take fresh towels," he called out, sliding the gun under the spread.

The door opened, and all they could see was a pile of white towels. Vanessa fisted her hands, bracing for someone menacing to pop out from behind them.

But only the friendly face of a young hotel maid appeared as she ambled in and muttered an apology as she looked at the bed.

"Mighty late at night for a turn-down, ma'am," Wade said.

"I'm sorry. I am running very behind tonight." She nodded toward the bathroom. "May I?"

"Go right ahead."

She went into the bathroom, and Wade stood, stashed the gun in the back of his boxer briefs waistband, and reached over to turn the light on.

Vanessa blinked at the brightness and watched him

move to the bottom of the bed, positioning himself so that when the maid came out, she couldn't see his back. She scooched deeper into the covers, listening to the woman hum quietly as she placed towels on the shelves.

Then she stepped out, looking from one to the other. "I am so sorry for the interruption."

Wade lifted a shoulder. "No problem."

She glanced at the wake of clothes between the door and the bed and gave Vanessa a knowing smile. "Honeymoon?"

Did Wade really think this petite and tired-looking woman was dangerous? Maybe a bit presumptuous, but not involved in some conspiracy to pin a murder on Clive Easterbrook. She was probably a single mom who lived in a run-down part of the island and worked her ass off sixty hours a week for tips from the rich folks.

"Just a vacation," Wade said, remarkably casual for a man who was one slice of cotton away from naked, with a gun slung at his backside.

The woman didn't move, still looking expectantly at Wade. No doubt, she was waiting for a tip. "Have you been to Pinney's Beach yet?" she asked.

Definitely stalling for a tip. Should Vanessa get up and get it? If Wade turned, she'd see the gun.

She looked at Wade for a clue, but he was completely focused on the young woman.

"Not yet, Shayla," he said.

She looked surprised at the use of her name, then glanced at the badge on her uniform.

"You should go," she said. "And on the way, you should visit the batik makers in the mountain, right off the main road. Nevis is famous for our batik."

"Is that so?" he asked.

"Yes. In fact, my sister lives in Jessup's Village, just a little ways up the road, and she makes the most beautiful shawls, like no others on the island. You should go see her. She'll be there tomorrow morning. I will call her and tell her an American couple is coming. She will give you an excellent price on a batik shawl."

Vanessa's veins turned to ice.

She was *sending* them there.

"Maybe we will," Wade said to her, then looked at Vanessa. "You up for that, sweetheart?"

"Sure, I'd love to go," she agreed, then asked Shayla, "Anywhere else you suggest we see while we're here?"

"You should go to St. Kitts, too."

"We've been there already," Wade said.

Did she know that? Vanessa studied the woman's face, looking for a clue but seeing nothing. But Wade didn't look as if he trusted her at all.

What did he see that she didn't?

"Well, then you know that it is all beautiful in the West Indies," the housekeeper said. "Enjoy your stay, and thank you."

Wade nodded, ushering her to the door without revealing his gun.

Vanessa waited until the door closed, ready to launch into a debate on whether or not they'd been intentionally sent to a local village. But he returned with the same dark and intent look on his face.

"Don't say a word," he mouthed as he marched into the bathroom.

In a few seconds, she heard a clicking noise, as if he was . . . snapping his fingers?

"She was a nice lady, don't you think?" Something about his voice, not to mention the weirdness of the question, caught her.

"Uh, yeah."

"We should go look at those batik shawls. I'll buy you one."

Was he serious? Didn't he suspect that woman had been the very person they were waiting for, and her suggestion was more than a friendly tip on where to buy a nice souvenir?

"Wade, don't you—"

He snapped again. Louder.

What the hell? Vanessa rolled out of bed, far too curious to care about her near nakedness. In the bathroom, Wade was crouched in front of a stainless-steel shelving unit where the towels had been placed, pointing to something stuck on the bottom shelf.

She got down on her knees and followed his finger.

"Let's go in the morning, after breakfast," he said, pointing at a black square about the size of her baby fingernail, so well hidden she'd never have seen it. "What was the name of the place again? Jessup's Village?"

He tapped his ear as if to say someone could hear them.

A listening device?

"Don't you think? Tomorrow morning?" He continued the faux conversation without missing a beat as he stood and pulled her into his chest. "Or would you rather stay in all day?"

His voice was low and sexy, a little muffled as he kissed her neck, taking a direct path right to her ear. "Work with me, Vanessa," he whispered.

"Uh, gee . . . tomorrow. I don't know." She closed her eyes, pressed against him, and tried to think of what she would say if they were really alone. But her mind went blank, and all she could do was respond to his mouth on her skin, hard and firm and hot. "I can't think straight when you do that."

"All right," he said with a low, knowing laugh. "Let's go think about it in there." He walked her backward toward the bedroom, and as they passed the sink, he flipped a faucet on full blast. "Just let me wash up, babe."

He pointed her toward the bedroom and followed her, closing the bathroom door behind him so carefully the latch didn't make a sound. Then he instantly covered her mouth with a kiss before she could speak.

"Be careful what you say," he murmured into her mouth. "We have an audience." Sure that he'd gotten his message across, he broke the kiss, his blue eyes full of warning. "You're being tracked by someone who knows what they're doing," he whispered.

"Why?"

"My guess is that either someone thinks you can find Clive and they don't want you to, or someone wants to find him and hopes you can lead them to him."

She frowned, considering the options and hating them. Either Clive was in danger, or he'd done something seriously wrong.

"What should we do?" she asked. "Try to fake them out about where we're going? Or should we really go to the batik place tomorrow and try to find out who it is and what they want from me?"

"We keep the game going. You don't want them to know you're on to them."

She could feel her heart pounding against his chest. Or was that his? They were so close it was hard to tell.

"Can't you disassemble that device?" she asked.

"That'll tip them off." He took the gun out from his waistband, silently setting it high on the chest of drawers. "Right now, they think you are completely occupied with a man, and we're going to make sure they think they're right. Then we'll—"

"I know. Make a plan."

He grinned. "You're catchin' on, darlin'."

"What do you have in mind?"

Against her stomach, she felt him—all of him—stir.

A tease was buried in his smoldering stare. "All you have to do," he said, tightening his grip on her waist and sidestepping them both to the bathroom door, "is be loud and convincing. Can you do that?"

She nodded, and in an instant, he pulled her into the bathroom, turned her around, and hoisted her onto the vanity.

"For real this time?" she whispered.

He spread her legs with his hips. One hand slid her glasses off, the other turned off the faucet. "If it has to be."

His mouth covered hers before she could say a word, and he kissed her so hard he stole her breath.

CHAPTER
NINE

SHE WAS SOFT, sweet, sexy, and way too smart to question the kiss.

But was she good enough to pull this off, or would he have to elicit genuine moans of ecstasy from her? The device looked professional, and even a cheapo from a spy-gear shop could pick up a whimper, a whisper, or a gasp of pure delight from three hundred feet away.

Which was exactly what he wanted their audience to hear.

He opened his mouth and added the tip of his tongue to the kiss. She responded with plenty of enthusiasm but still no sound.

How far would he have to take her to get some noise?

He cupped the backside he'd been admiring a few minutes ago, the curves as firm and smooth as he'd imagined. That earned him the first little moan. He delved his tongue deeper, appreciating the taste of her, the fullness of her lips, and the slick line of her teeth as he took a swipe over them.

He pulled away for some silent eye-to-eye communication, but hers were closed. And her lips parted with a shudder. He leaned back to steal a glimpse at the slope of her breasts, her skin pink with heat and the nipples peaking wickedly. Her hips rocked in an instinctive sway, and inches away from her crotch, the pressure of a hard-on strained his briefs with that same instinct.

Nobody here was acting.

He kissed her again, sliding his palms up her bare back, aware that she'd unclasped her hands from his neck and was running them over his shoulders and biceps.

Finally, he got the kind of moan he needed: low, long, rich, with a nonverbal approval of his physique, and, best of all, loud enough to reach the mike.

She stopped the mouth-to-mouth this time, but only to nibble and kiss the shoulder she kneaded, tilting her head to give him access to her neck again. He suckled and smelled the skin, kissed her collarbone and the translucent flesh below it. She tasted like paradise. Like salt and sun and palm trees, mixed with the scent of excitement and *woman*.

"That's nice," he murmured, turning his face toward the mike a few feet away.

She responded with a breathy "Yes," but without enough volume. He pointed in the direction of the mike and mouthed, "Louder."

She nodded, her eyes glinting with the shared secret, her body quivering under his hands.

"Yes," she repeated, leaning toward the shelves, her voice still little more than air but not the least bit fake-sounding. "That's nice."

"How 'bout this?" He stroked her back as if it were as alluring and sexy as her front, urging her into the moment for the benefit of their act. He kept the touch innocent enough, his thumbs at the sides of her breasts, definitely not crossing the line. "You like that, baby?"

Her skin was buttery smooth, warm and tight over defined but feminine muscles, shooting a sexual shockwave through him.

"I do," she said, giving it a note of believable desperation with an audible catch in her voice. She leaned into his touch, inviting more. "I really like that."

They shared a quick look, his brow angled with a question that was answered by a nod, another groan, and a little hand motion that said, *Keep it going.*

He stepped closer into the space between her legs, making contact. She quivered at the pressure, rocked forward, and let out a whimper of surprise and pleasure.

A very genuine whimper.

"And that?" he asked.

"Oooh, yes. That." She added a sexy laugh and lifted her hips to ride the length of him with the flimsy little of patch of nothing she wore as underwear. "Definitely that."

The line between real and fake was disappearing

as fast as his control, blood draining from his brain, where he needed it, and down to his cock, making him achy and stiff. She arched toward him, her hair falling over her shoulders and down to her breasts, the ends grazing her nipples the way he wanted to.

His mouth watered. His chest tightened. His entire lower half constricted into a full-blown erection.

He put his lips against her ear. "More?" If that question got picked up by a supersensitive device, it wouldn't sound out of place, but he had to know how far he could take this cover.

She drew back, gave him a blistering gaze, and touched his lower lip with her fingertips.

"Oh, yeah. More," she said, her voice just forced enough for him to know it had to be for effect. "I want this." She dipped her fingertip into his mouth and curled around his tongue. "And this." She trailed the wet tip over his chin, down his throat, and over his chest, traveling over one ab muscle after another, a sneaky smile pulling at her lips as her finger took its private joy ride over his six-pack.

She stopped less than an inch from the tip of the hard-on bursting through the waistband of his boxer briefs.

She wet her lips. "And, oh, honey, I *really* want this."

He clenched his jaw and braced for the mind-blowing impact of one slender female finger, but she didn't touch him. Instinctively, he tightened his hold on her ribs, squeezing enough to plaster the soft flesh of her breasts against his wrists.

It hurt so bad not to touch her he gave a loud groan of frustration.

"Good one," she mouthed.

Did she really think he was faking? She closed her eyes and released a long, sensuous sigh, drawing him closer until her breasts were fully pressed against his chest.

She sucked in a deep, noisy breath.

Heat and arousal hammered through him, kicking his pulse into double time, stealing another bona fide rumble of desire from his chest.

She released another sex-kitten moan, totally and maddeningly in control. He'd been worried she couldn't fake it? She was giving an Oscar-worthy performance, while he was fighting for command over his hormones.

He channeled the burn into a long, wet kiss, slamming his hands on the counter to add credence to the sound track and give him something safe to grab.

She opened her mouth and vacuumed up his lower lip, sucking with enough force to punch a sound needle to the red, along with every yearning cell in his body. Sweat stung his skin, and heat rolled over him as his balls tightened and throbbed.

"Vanessa." He yanked her to him, shocking them both with a roll of his hips. "You're killin' me, honey."

She tensed her legs around his thighs. "That's the idea, isn't it?"

With a sultry laugh, she flattened her hands on his stomach, stroking his skin and caressing his muscles. Her fingers dipped low again, the tips of her thumbs so close to his engorged head he could swear he felt her nails graze the moist droplet there.

He leaned back, hoping she could read his warning look.

"Don't stop now," she replied, far too loud for it to be anything but an act as she pulled him right back for a searing, brutal kiss.

"You go one more inch . . ." He growled into her mouth, only half caring if he chose the perfect words to get his point across *and* fool anybody listening. "And I'm not responsible for what happens next."

"Oh, yeah?" Under his lips, he could feel her smile just as her fingers stroked his slickened head, punching the breath out of him. "So what happens next?"

"We move to . . ." He lifted her from the vanity, forcing her to wrap her legs and arms around him to hang on. "Bed."

She mixed a moan and a laugh while he carried her out the bathroom door, kicked it closed with far more force than necessary, and threw her onto the bed.

"You are really playing with fire." His voice was strained and gruff.

"I'm doing what you—"

He put a hand over her mouth and dropped on top of her. "They can still hear," he whispered into her ear.

She clasped her hands around his neck, forcing his face to her mouth. "Then stop talking," she whispered back. "Or we're going to get busted."

Her kiss was wet and long and uncharacteristically *slow*.

Screw the mike. They didn't need to *try* to make noise; it was already deafening.

Insane bursts of pleasure beat deep in his belly. His chest vibrated against the moans in hers, both of them taking unsteady breaths. Her skin brushed the covers with every up-and-down movement as they rocked against each other in mock sex.

And somewhere in the distance, he heard another sound.

"God Save the Queen?"

He shot his head up to listen, recognizing it as a phone. "I hear music."

"Mmm. A choir of angels." She pulled his head back down to her mouth.

He stopped moving. "It's your phone."

"My phone never works here."

"It's working now."

She froze for a second, then practically pushed him off her at the third time through the melody. "Oh, my God! That's—"

He whipped his hand over her mouth again. "Don't say his name," he breathed.

"—the London office of my company," she finished.

He gave her a look of admiration at the save, but she shook her head. "That's Razor Europe calling." Rolling off the bed, she seized her bag and pulled out her iPhone.

"It's a text," she said, touching the screen.

He looked at her magnificent breasts, all sweet and creamy and round, and so freaking perfect it made him hurt not to devour them. With only a sex-dampened triangle of pink silk between her legs, her long thighs quivering from foreplay, and her hair a wild mess from his hands and the bed, she was enough to make a grown man cry.

"Are you okay?" she asked, glancing up from her screen.

Choking a laugh instead of howling the way he wanted to, he reached to the floor and tossed her his T-shirt. "Define okay."

She caught the shirt, slid it over her head, and popped through the neck. Then she took a handful of the torn fabric, brought it to her nose, and sniffed, revealing some smooth skin under her breast and letting out a soft sigh of appreciation.

If that wasn't the damn sexiest move he ever saw, he didn't know what was.

"I think I'll sleep in this tonight."

As if there would be sleep.

He put a finger to his mouth, and she nodded, instantly transferring attention to the screen and reading it intently, screwing up her face into a look of total disgust.

"What's the matter?" He kept his voice to a faint whisper.

"They're idiots," she muttered, dropping onto the bed and reading the message again.

"Who are?"

"The lawyers." She thumbed the device and nibbled on the lip he'd just kissed. "God, I hate them all. Do you mind if I handle this? Before we get back to . . . that."

That. As if *that* was something she could start and stop at will.

Well, apparently, it was for her. He lifted a casual shoulder, fascinated by the concentration on her face—just as fierce as it had been five minutes ago, for a very different reason.

She didn't look up from the screen, where she was already typing and *tsk*ing.

"Throw obstacles, that's what lawyers do." She bit her lower lip again, thinking, then thumbed the keypad. "Structure . . . the . . . exchange . . ." she muttered. "As . . . an . . . unregistered . . . private . . . placement." She stabbed hard. "Send. There, you assholes. Take that."

He dropped back onto the bed. If her words were being picked up from that bug in the bathroom, whoever was listening was either confused as hell or laughing their asses off at his dismal failure to keep a woman in his bedroom out of the virtual boardroom.

"All right. Done." She set the phone down and returned her gaze to him. "Where were we?"

"I don't know where you were," he said with a disgusted sigh, "but I was—"

The same digital ring silenced him, and she grabbed the cell phone, muttering a few more obscenities.

"I have to call Marcus," she said, clearly irritated. "They are going to totally screw this deal. What time is it in New York?"

"Same as it is here." He glanced at the alarm on the nightstand. "Two-thirty. Time for *bed*."

She heard the implication and nodded, leaning

toward the bathroom and raising her voice. "I'll be right there, baby, I promise." She had the phone to her ear. "I just have to leave this message. It's early morning in London now, and they could have this deal derailed in hours. He gets up at four-thirty, anyway—oh, Marcus, hi. It's Vanessa. I didn't expect you to be up at this hour." She waited a beat. "Then you know what those gargoyles are doing in London."

She slid off the bed and headed toward the glass doors of the balcony, the T-shirt too short to cover the heart-shaped shadow of her bottom.

Stifling a groan, he rolled off the bed, snagged his 1911 from the dresser, and headed into the bathroom. Without making a sound, he picked up her glasses and followed her out to the balcony.

She leaned against the railing, listening. After a minute, she switched the phone from one ear to the other and launched into a speech about tender offers and bond exchange rates.

He stood right in front of her, close enough to feel the current that still electrified the air around her. She looked up, held up a finger to say she'd be another minute, and droned on.

Amazingly, his hard-on didn't lose its intensity. He waited for her business talk to send a few hormone-drenched cells back to his brain, but they stayed south, torturing him.

He scoped the grounds behind her, zeroing in on the darkness of the Palm Grove villa property, barely able to see past the edge of the fencing. He looked anyway, certain she was following his gaze while she talked.

He took a few steps farther, peering into the night.

Still nattering on about amendments to the indentures, Vanessa looked where he did and paused midsentence. "No, I'm still here, Marcus, but I have to tell you, the cell service sucks, and I could lose you at any minute."

Another few beats passed as they both stared at the same spot. He pointed . . . at nothing.

"A couple of days, no more," she continued, obviously distracted as she stood on her toes to examine the spot he indicated, then frowned at him. "Actually, I'm in Nevis."

She winced as if she wasn't expecting a good response to that.

"I was really . . . honestly, I'm here for a couple of reasons." She shifted from one foot to the other. "But I did really need a vacation."

She sounded totally unconvincing, and he could only assume the guy on the other end wasn't buying it.

"Oh," she said, straightening a little, glancing over at the property. "Really? That would be awesome, Marcus, because I ditched the cruise for something . . . um . . ." She searched for a word. "Less commercial. So I could definitely do that for a few days. It would be amazing, actually."

She tapped Wade and added a thumbs-up, nodding as she listenend.

"Wait, I lost you for a second. Did you say Nevis Properties?" She closed her eyes, pressed her finger to her other ear. "What was that? Do I just go there and give them your name or . . . Marcus? Are you there?" She held the phone out and pressed a button. "Shit. I lost him."

He notched his chin toward the Palm Grove villa. "Did it look like there was a shadow moving to you?"

"No," she said. "But listen, that was my boss in New York. One of our clients has a house on Nevis and he said we can stay there. I think all we have to do is go to Nevis Properties, but we got cut off. I'm sure it's a tiny office. If we go there tomorrow, we can get a key to a place to stay."

He gave her a wary look. "Why didn't you tell him why you're down here?"

"I don't want him to know. He's furious with Clive for leaving the company and would be even more furious to know I'm blowing off work to help him. But this is a perfect offer, Wade. We can't stay here; the place is bugged. For all we know, it might have been bugged when we walked in and they heard us. This would be perfect. A secret hiding place where we can work out a plan to find Clive."

As if she ever made a plan in her life. "Why are you lying to your boss?"

"I didn't really lie," she said. "I just didn't tell him the whole story."

"And why are you lying to me?"

Her look was sharp and defensive. "I'm not lying to you."

"Oh, no? You saw what I saw out there."

"There was nothing out there but trees and some lawn chairs."

"How many?"

She frowned and glanced over again. "Four."

He lifted his hand, holding the glasses he'd taken from the bathroom, then slid them over her face. "Pretty good vision for a person who's nearsighted."

She opened her mouth, and he shut it with one finger before a sound came out.

"An addendum to our deal, Vanessa Porter. Don't ever lie to me. Ever."

"I didn't lie. I never said I needed them." She swallowed hard. "I like the way they look, so I wear them."

"Don't lie to me on a technicality, either."

"Fine." She adjusted the glasses and indicated the room on the other side of the glass. "You want to go back inside and act some more?"

He brushed by her. "I wasn't acting."

She snagged his arm to turn him around, then took her glasses off and looked directly at him. "Neither was I."

The last time Jack Culver visited the brick ranch house owned by Rebecca Aubry, he'd given the seventy-year-old former midwife's nurse a picture culled from the photo files in the library of the Charleston *Post and Courier*. In exchange, she'd given him an envelope with proof that a Virginia family named Whitaker had adopted one of Eileen's triplets.

For five brief minutes, he'd felt a surge of hope. Hope that his cop's instinct might be working again, hope that he was close to finding the missing daughter, saving Eileen, and helping to solve a murder that he believed in his gut she didn't commit.

Then a thug relieved him of all that hope, along with seventy-five bucks and the fucking envelope.

He'd memorized the information on the paper before he relinquished it and decided it wasn't worth the trouble to kick the shit out of the kid, squeeze his skinny neck, and get him to confess who'd sent him there. The last time he took a risk like that, he'd paid too high a price. There were less bone-breaking ways to get what he wanted.

He knocked hard on the door, loudly enough for an old deaf woman who might be napping to hear him and take a good three minutes to shuffle to the door.

Nothing.

He knocked again, gave it one more minute, then pivoted, eyeing the side of the house to consider the most efficient way to get in and look around if she wasn't home.

Behind him, the chain lock slid, and the front door opened.

"Are you looking for the old lady?"

He turned at the female voice, barely seeing the form in the darkened entryway inside the screen door. "As a matter of fact, I am."

"She's gone."

He slid off his sunglasses but still couldn't quite make out the face or age. He knew from the tone and pitch of a younger voice that it wasn't the companion who'd played gatekeeper the last time he'd visited.

"She's back from Florida, right?" He took a step farther. "Did her flight get in okay last night?"

The woman's form moved close enough to the screen so that he could see she was in her mid-twenties, dark-haired, and attractive—or at least made up to look that way. "She wasn't on it." She looked him up and down. "Who are you?"

He gave her a smile and matched the up-and-down. "Who are *you*?"

"I asked first."

"My name's Jack. I'm a friend of Rebecca's."

"Gina. I'm a friend of Rebecca's nephew."

Jack swiftly reviewed every fact he knew about Rebecca Aubry. She'd never been married and had no brothers and sisters. Therefore . . . no nephews.

"Hi, Gina." He put a hand on the doorjamb and hooked the other in the back of his jeans. "Is Rebecca's nephew here?"

She shook her head. "He had to do something, but he'll be back. If you don't want to wait, I can have him call you or just give him a message."

"I really wanted to talk to Rebecca," he said. "Any idea when she's coming back?"

"Never." She glanced over her shoulder, indicating two open cartons. "That's why we're here. He's set her up in an assisted-living place in Florida, and we've been here all day packing this crap to send to her. Scratch that. *I've* been packing. Willie's just been sifting through papers."

Willie? As in Willie Gilbert, the ex-cop who'd

arrested Eileen the night Wanda Sloane was murdered?

What the hell was *he* doing at Rebecca Aubry's house?

He glanced behind her into the dining room, where the table was covered with paper and files.

Maybe Rebecca *didn't* turn everything over to the police when the Sapphire Trail operation was busted. And Willie Gilbert was here trying to find, and destroy, evidence of who fathered those girls.

Because he was the father . . . or the father was paying him? He had to work fast and smart and come up with some way to get in and look around.

"What about Butterscotch?" he asked.

"What about it?" She crinkled her nose.

"The cat. Are you shipping him to Rebecca, too?"

"I don't know what he wants to do with that thing. All I know is I'm not touching it, because I'm allergic."

"Why don't I take him off your hands? I'll let Rebecca know I have him."

"I don't know . . ."

"Unless her nephew wants to keep him."

Curling her lip, she looked over her shoulder again. "I hope not. He sheds like hell." She gave him another checking out. "I'll sneeze for an hour if I go near him."

"I'll get him." He held his hands up and winked. "You can trust me, sweetheart. I'm not dangerous."

Opening the door, she stood up straight, showing

off some impressive goods. "How dangerous can a cat lover be?" she asked with a flirty laugh. She wasn't bad-looking, a little shopworn but shapely in a skimpy cropped T-shirt, painted-on blue jeans, and high heels.

He smiled and stepped toward the dining room. "Not dangerous at all. I think I saw him scoot in here."

"He's been on the sofa in the den since we got here." She indicated the back of the house. "Let me go see if he's there. You wait here, okay?"

She stepped down the hall, and Jack went immediately to the table, scanning what hadn't yet been packed or picked over. A box of cookbooks and recipes, a pile of crossword-puzzle books, magazines, and photo albums.

"He's not in here," Gina called.

Jack stole a look under the table. "Not here, either. Why don't you look in the laundry-room cabinet for some catnip? That usually gets him."

Hoping he'd bought a minute, he flipped open the cover of a photo album and saw an old black-and-white baby picture. He closed the book and opened a yellowed shirt box next to it, instantly seeing the gold-embossed edges of certificates.

Birth certificates.

"You won't find him in there."

Jack turned to see her standing at the dining-room entrance, a sharp, accusing look on her face.

"I know," he conceded. "I just thought I could snag a picture of Rebecca before you sent all this stuff down to her."

Her look was all doubt. "How do you know her, anyway?"

"I used to live down the street."

She lifted an eyebrow. "With that accent? You expect me to believe you ever lived anywhere outside of New York, let alone Charleston?"

"Why would I lie?"

She shrugged. "Be straight with me, dude. What are you looking for?"

He sighed. "A picture." He closed the photo album and turned to her. "I let Rebecca borrow a picture I'd taken from the library at the Charleston *Post and Courier* a while ago, and she never returned it. They want it back."

"I've been through a lot of her pictures today," she said. "What was it?"

"It was Rebecca, about thirty years ago, with a baby."

She snorted. "There are, like, fifty pictures of her with babies. She used to be–a midwife, didn't you know?"

"Could I see them? I bet I could find the one I need."

She shook her head. "Willie left with them when we opened that box. He said he wanted to make copies before he sent them to her."

"Well, she just got this one a few months ago, so maybe it's still here. Mind if I check?" He leaned a little closer with a smile. "I'll still take the cat for you."

She eyed him warily. "I don't know. We better wait until Willie gets back."

When Willie got back, Jack would be long gone. They'd met already, when Jack tried to get information about Eileen's arrest from the former cop. If Willie had anything to do with Wanda's death . . . if Willie was the father of those triplets . . . the last thing Jack wanted the man to know was that he was about to figure that out.

"I don't have time to wait," Jack said. "I'll just take the cat. Want me to go get him?"

She considered that and shook her head. "I can pick him up for a minute if I wash my hands. You wait right here in the hall."

The instant she disappeared, he grabbed the shirt box and turned to the open window, punching the screen just hard enough to pop it off its track. He stuck the box out, looked over the windowsill to see where it would land, and let it drop to the ground.

He was back in place before she rounded the corner.

"Here you go." She shoved the orange tabby into his hands with a sniff. "You better go. He probably won't like that I let you in here."

He grinned mischievously. "Then let it be our secret."

Her eyes twinkled in response. "Deal. I'll tell him the cat ran away when I opened the back door."

"If I go out that way, then you won't be lying."

"All right." She laughed lightly. "Follow me."

He did, watching her perfectly toned ass slide side to side for his benefit. She moved gracefully, totally at ease in her sexy clothes and the skin under them.

"You a dancer, Gina?"

She shot a sexy look over her shoulder. "Sort of."

"Let me guess. Exotic?"

She laughed and pointed a finger at him. "Some call it that."

"Where do you work?" Just in case he had to interrogate her again on the comings and goings of Willie Gilbert.

"Diamonds," she said as she opened the laundry-room door that led to the side yard. "Tuesdays and Saturdays."

"What night is Willie there?"

She grinned and looked right up at him as he paused next to her in the doorway. "Every Saturday, like clockwork."

He looked up and down her face, slowing on her mouth, then back to her eyes, watching her color rise. "I'll make it a Tuesday."

She gave him the same look, only she spent more time studying his torso. "You do that, Jack."

When the door closed, the cat wiggled and mewed, but Jack held tight as he slipped along the side of the house to the dining-room window. Just as he got there, a gray BMW whipped into the driveway, and out stepped Willie Gilbert.

Jack crouched down and grabbed the shirt box with his free hand, ready to run to where he'd parked a block away, curious to hear if Gina outed him. He stayed low, under the window, stroking the cat under the chin to keep him quiet.

The front door slammed, and Gina's greeting floated through the window. Willie answered, too softly for Jack to make out the words. Then "Aren't you done yet?" The question held just the tiniest hint of a threat.

"I got sidetracked," she said.

"Doing what? You had one thing to do, Gina, and you didn't finish it."

"Screw you," she mumbled.

Good girl. He'd definitely stop by Diamonds and give her a nice tip. He balanced on his feet, checking out the best route to the street without being seen.

"Where's the box, Gina?" The words boomed through the window. "Where's the fucking box that was right here?" A thud on the table punctuated the question.

"I . . . I don't know." But she didn't sound so sure. Would she rat on him now?

Jack straightened enough to start his run but froze at the sound of a slap and Gina's pained cry.

"Find it, you stupid bitch. It's the whole fucking reason I'm here."

"I swear to God, Will." Her voice faltered. "I don't know—" Another slap and a grunt of pain.

Aw, fuck. The sound sent disgust coiling right down to his toes.

"Maybe I accidentally threw it out," she mumbled with a sniff. "I'll check the back, by the trash."

"You better find it."

Jack eyed the box. There were answers in there, answers that might be able to solve a thirty-year-old mystery. And if Willie didn't find them, Gina the pretty stripper would pay for Jack's deed.

Damn it all.

He silently retraced his steps to the back, reaching the patio before the back door opened. He set the box there and the cat right next to it.

As he darted through the next-door neighbor's yard to where he'd parked his car, his cell phone beeped with a text message.

Lucy? Well, would you look at that. The lioness had invited him to her lair.

He texted right back. *Will be there at noon tomorrow.*

They had a lot in common, Lucy and him. She'd never admit it, but they were both suckers for justice. And each other.

CHAPTER TEN

"Wow. That was easy." Vanessa dangled the key to Mango Plantation as they left Nevis Properties and walked to Wade's rented Wrangler. She used the roll bar to hoist herself into the passenger seat, scooping her hair off her neck and fanning, the homemade breeze not nearly enough to counter the oppressive tropical sun. Even at nine in the morning, the vinyl seats burned her bare thighs like a waffle iron.

Wade appeared unfazed by the heat as he moseyed around the front of the vehicle and climbed into the driver's seat.

"No kidding it was easy," he said, lifting aviator sunglasses from the breast pocket of his navy cotton T-shirt while surveying the empty streets of Charlestown. "They gave you entrance to a house and never even checked your ID."

"Less complicated than the mandatory return of my rental car this morning."

"You're still bothered by that?" he asked. "It makes no sense to have a second car if we're doing this together."

"I like having my own wheels."

"If you need to go somewhere, I'll drive you." At her disgusted look, he added, "Or give you the keys."

"I just want to be sure I get concession credit on the imaginary bargaining table."

Though after last night, there was a lot more than an imaginary table between them. There was a little distrustful silence and a lot of . . . space.

"Yeah, Vanessa. That was a huge concession. You're from a city where no one but cab drivers can handle the traffic. It's no hardship for you to give up left-side driving on winding mountain roads."

He was right, but she wouldn't give him the satisfaction of knowing that. "I can do it. I did it all day yesterday. I don't like being dependent."

"I can tell." He rubbed a hand on a clean-shaven, perspiration-free face, checking out the scenery again. When had he shaved? When had he *slept*? She'd crashed in the bed, and he'd never so much as lain on top of the covers to sleep. She assumed he spent the night on the sofa in the living room, but he was awake, showered, shaved, and ready to roll when she opened her eyes.

All she knew is that she fell asleep inhaling the scent of his T-shirt, trying to forget their "audible" pretend lovemaking, and wishing he'd insist on faking some more.

She hadn't intended to swear off men for the past few years, but there was always an excuse not to get too close. Sex, unless it was raw and meaningless, usually came with some affection. And she just wasn't demonstrative that way.

She stole a glance to her left. Wade could probably do raw and meaningless very nicely and wouldn't require hugs and handholding afterward.

Wild monkey sex instead of a trip to South Carolina? She still had a few days to work on renegotiating their verbal contract.

"It was strange that they just gave you the key to a privately owned villa," he said as he adjusted his shades.

"Not strange at all when you drop Marcus Razor's name." She snapped an elastic around her hair into a ponytail. "There's a reason we call him the Rainmaker around the office. The man gets things done. They said he called and told them to expect me."

She frowned as he tipped the sunglasses down to train his eyes on a spot over her shoulder. "What are you staring at?"

"Will you look at that?"

She turned to see empty wrought-iron chairs in a deserted café's stone courtyard, all tucked under a huge poinciana tree. On the street, two locals, wearing bandanas and carrying water jugs, lingered in the shade to talk.

"What is it?" she asked.

"Look. Don't you see that?"

A dented, rusted yellow truck with the remnants of black stenciled letters on the driver's door pulled onto the road about two hundred yards from where they sat.

"What?" she asked again. "The truck? The people? The tree?" Impatience pulled. What was he looking at?

"Way over there to your right."

She twisted even farther, toward a stone wall around an ancient church and a white balustrade balcony over a tiny grocery store. Frustrated, she pivoted around to face him. "I don't see . . . *hey!*"

His sunglasses were way down his nose, and he was squinting at her neck.

"You bastard." She touched her hairline, exposed by her ponytail. "Even if I hadn't had it lasered off, you couldn't see it."

"Then why take it off?"

He'd never understand. No one would, which is precisely why she'd never tried to explain it. She waved her hand toward the road. "Move it, will you? You're the one who said anybody could be following us when we slinked out of the Four Seasons at the crack of dawn. Why are we sitting here?"

When he finally pulled out of the parking lot, she reached into the back and grabbed the Yankees cap from the side of her tote, jerking her ponytail through the back. The adjustable plastic band covered the curlicues of the faint lasered scar, a constant reminder of who she really was. A reminder of how her most powerful childhood fantasy had blown up in her face and how Eileen Stafford was responsible for her father's death.

"Tell me about our host who owns this place," he said, giving a "go ahead" wave to the yellow truck, which took its sweet time getting by.

"Nicholas Vex, a dickhead CEO of a big chemical company."

"Vexell Industries? Big is an understatement."

"So's dickhead. Vex is one of Marcus's cronies, and probably our biggest and most influential client. I've handled a few acquisitions with him. We make a lot of money off him, and since his company holds the patent on the plastic coating that's on every keyboard manufactured in the world, his stock has done exceedingly well for many of our clients. But the house is free, so who cares if he's a jerk?"

Vanessa studied the run-down clapboard houses with tin roofs that stood beside Victorian gingerbread masterpieces painted lavender, fuchsia, and cream, a total mishmash of poverty and cash, of new money and old culture. Ahead of them, the yellow truck turned off, but Wade didn't pick up any speed, just jostled them on the potholed road that might have been asphalt once but wasn't much more than gravel now.

Their destination, the town of Cotton Ground, was about six miles to the north—but they were winding, steep, and occasionally breathtaking miles, so it wouldn't go fast. The island smell of citrus and salt permeated everywhere, and since Wade was driving at a leisurely pace, Vanessa inhaled and leaned back, closing her eyes and letting some stress seep out of her pores.

"Let me ask you a question," Wade said, the intensity buried in that drawl tensing her right back up again. "Why don't you tell your boss the truth? Surely he wants to find Clive, regardless of the fact that the guy resigned."

"Don't you ever hide the truth from management because it could have a negative impact on your job?"

"No."

"Then you must have some impressive job security."

"Isn't your job secure?"

"On Wall Steet, nothing is secure. Clive is a traitor in Marcus's eyes, regardless of what he says he's going to do with his life."

"And you're not allowed to remain friends with someone who left the company? What kind of operation is that?"

"A successful one. When someone quits, he takes millions of dollars' worth of insider information. It's not just that Marcus hates to lose good people, although he does. I'm sure he thinks Clive's secretly planning to go to another firm, and that the whole 'I'm moving to the islands' thing was a fake-out."

"Maybe it was."

"I don't think so," she said honestly. "Clive would never make a move like that without telling me. We have no secrets."

"He obviously does, or we wouldn't be here."

She shifted her gaze to the mind-numbingly

beautiful horizon, where a line of turquoise water met robin's-egg-blue sky. *Did* she really know Clive that well? They were buddies, confidants, coworkers. But . . .

"I guess anything's possible," she conceded. "Clive is so damn good at what he does that the headhunters call him daily, just like they call me. And if Fidelity or Legg Mason waved obscene amounts of money, hell yeah, he might go. But he'd tell me. He wouldn't just disappear—he's got too much at stake. Money's important to him, but so is his reputation."

Wade put a hand on her arm. "I'm not trying to paint your friend in a bad light, Vanessa. I'm just trying to look at all the possibilities, because one of them might lead us to him. Is it possible he wanted to lie low while he orchestrated a move to another firm? Or, I don't know, maybe he's involved in some kind of insider trading?"

"Of course, anything's possible, but it just isn't likely," she said. "Clive's very ethical and aboveboard. He doesn't even cheat on his taxes—and, believe me, everyone at Razor does that."

"What does everyone at Razor actually do, when they're not cheating on their taxes?"

She smiled. "Well, not everyone cheats. And we're asset managers. We handle and invest about eighty billion dollars a year of funds and portfolios, with ten offices around the world. If you have an IRA or retirement account, chances are, whoever holds it uses a company like ours to grow it."

He let out a low whistle. "Eighty billion?"

She shrugged. "We're not actually huge in the investment world. Razor is considered a boutique."

"And you're pretty young for a VP, right?"

"Not really. My dad used to say if you weren't a VP headed for partner by thirty, you're not enough of a shark."

Wade threw the Jeep into a lower gear to start up a winding climb. "Are you a shark, Vanessa?"

She'd been called worse. "I prefer barracuda. Shark is so masculine."

"And you're *so* feminine."

"You thought I was pretty damn feminine when you attacked me in the bathroom last night," she retorted.

"Womanly," he responded. "You are that."

No argument on the "attack," she noticed. "So, womanly and feminine are two different things to you, huh?" She crossed her bare legs, stretching them into his line of view.

He dropped his hand from the gearshift to her leg. "This is feminine." He grazed his knuckles along the skin, leaving goose bumps in their wake. "What you do with it is womanly."

They went down a dip and took a sharp curve, taking her stomach on a roller-coaster drop. "I bet you prefer feminine to womanly."

"I prefer ladylike." He threw her a look, but she couldn't read his expression behind the sunglasses. "But they all have their place in the world."

"Which means what—that you'd fuck a woman but date a lady?"

He lowered the glasses, his eyes smoky blue and serious as hell. "I don't *fuck* women, but I'll make love to a lady."

"Well, good for you." She looked away, right up at Mount Nevis ringed with clouds. "And the lucky lady."

He took another tight turn and glanced in the rearview mirror, frowning. "We have company."

Vanessa checked the side mirror and instantly recognized the bright yellow pickup. "That's the truck we saw in town."

He didn't respond but kept his speed steady as they veered gently around a curve.

Vanessa watched in her mirror as the truck approached, noticing that even though the owner couldn't afford to restencil the name of his business on the side, he'd had enough money to tint the windows heavily.

He was easily going five or more miles an hour faster than they were; if Wade hit the brakes hard, they'd be sporting yellow paint all over the back of the Jeep.

"Asshole," she muttered.

The truck came closer.

"Where I come from, we call that brand of idiot a hammerknocker," Wade said.

The truck rumbled to within a car's length of them.

"That hammerknocker's getting too close, Wade."

She leaned back, bracing herself, but Wade calmly swerved to the left just as the truck revved its engine and tore by, so close she could have touched the side.

"Jesus!" she exhaled. "What the goddamn hell is his hurry?"

"Whatever it is, he's on his way." He eased them back to their lane, smiling at her. "Miss Potty Mouth."

"Oh, that's right. *Ladies* don't say *Jesus* or *asshole* or *hell* or *fu*—"

He held his hand up. "No. They don't."

Ahead, they saw the yellow truck turn onto a dirt road.

"Where do you come from, anyway? Alabama?"

"South of Alabama."

"Really? I didn't know there was anything south of Alabama."

"Then you ought to look at a map." He glanced into the rearview mirror and slid off his glasses, throwing them onto the dashboard, his expression darkening. "But you're right about one thing." He tilted the mirror a little. "This guy is an asshole."

"What the hell—" Vanessa swung around to stare down at the truck driver, who had apparently turned around on the dirt road and decided he wasn't finished with them. "Hey!"

The pickup's engine roared, and he tapped their bumper. Wade moved to the side again to let him pass, but this time he didn't. He bumped again, making the Jeep swerve.

Vanessa raised her fist and stuck her middle finger in the air. "Back off, Jack!"

Wade pushed her hand down. "Don't antagonize him. Just wait for him to pass."

"I'm a New Yorker. I live to antagonize." Space grew between the two vehicles. "See? He's backing off." She settled down a little but kept her gaze on the heavily tinted windshield behind them.

Wade took another smooth turn, then hit the accelerator and shot ahead. But the truck took off like a rocket, careening toward them at about eighty miles an hour.

Vanessa sucked in a scream, then covered her face with her hands. As they curled around another tight turn, she squinted through her fingers to see water and the cliff twenty feet in front of them.

"We're going to die!" she squeaked.

"Not even close." Wade threw the wheel to the left, spinning them, in total control as he worked the gas and brake and wheel in brilliant choreography. "Just hang on."

The truck flew right by, squealing on the asphalt as he slammed on his brakes. Wade whipped the Jeep in the same direction, punched the gas, and ate up the thirty feet between them in a spray of gravel.

"Get down!" he ordered, almost standing as he smashed the accelerator with a dark, determined look on his face.

When she didn't move, he yelled again. "Get down, Vanessa!"

His right hand moved so fast she almost didn't see him pull out his gun.

With a gasp, she flattened herself into the seat as they zoomed by the truck. She could see the hair on Wade's knuckles, the index finger locked on the trigger, the barrel of a gun aimed directly at the driver to their right. His hand didn't even quiver.

"Don't shoot him!" she yelled.

He kept the gun pointed until they passed the truck. Then he stood, his right foot still on the accelerator, his left knee on the seat to lift him higher. Driving with one hand, he fired.

"What are you doing?" she screamed, turning to see the front tire of the truck explode and the pickup swerve and roll into a thicket of palms in the hillside.

Calmly, Wade eased back into his seat and stuffed the gun into his waistband.

"Where I come from, this finger"—he wiggled his index finger—"is more effective than that one."

She breathed hard, trying to slow her heart rate.

"Look at that," he said, nodding toward a wooden road sign. "Jessup's Village is one mile down that road."

Her mouth dropped open as she put the pieces together. "The maid. The batik. The sister. Were we set up to be driven off a cliff?"

"I think that's a distinct possibility." He reached over and put his hand comfortingly on her thigh. "You okay?"

"Yeah." She actually shuddered as the adrenaline seeped from her veins. "Just remind me not to get on your bad side."

"That won't be too tough." He patted her leg. "I don't have a bad side."

CHAPTER
ELEVEN

"YOU'RE LATE." LUCY Sharpe didn't look up as the footsteps slowed and Jack stopped in the doorway of her library. "It throws my entire day off when someone is late, and I don't appreciate it." She tapped a few buttons on her PDA, sent a message, and set the device to the side, finally lifting her gaze to meet his.

And hid even a flicker of response at the way he looked. Unshaven, uncombed, untucked, unspeakably . . . dark.

He strolled in, long legs eating up the space between them, his insolent smile pulling at the corners of his mouth. "If control were an Olympic sport, you'd hold the world record."

"And if irritating me were in the same games, you'd get gold."

He laughed. "Good. I love to win." He dropped onto the settee in the middle of the room and stretched his legs, maddeningly at home in the very room where she'd confronted him, argued with him, and ultimately fired him.

She stood and got little satisfaction from the way he drank her in from head to toe.

"You always look amazing, Luce, but you've out-done yourself today. For me?"

"Don't flatter yourself." She came around the desk, picking up a file folder on the way. "Let's get to business; my schedule's tight."

He glanced at the folder, no doubt reading the words typed on the label. *Eileen Stafford.* She watched for a reaction and got nothing but a direct look from bottomless brown eyes.

"My schedule's tight, too," he said. "So shoot. You called me."

Lucy perched on the armrest of the chair across from him to maintain the advantage of height. "First, tell me about your investigation."

"*My* investigation," he said pointedly, "is going fine. Why did you need to see me?"

"I thought you'd like to know that Wade Cordell just checked in, and he's making progress with Vanessa Porter."

"Really." He locked his hands behind his head, a move that accentuated his well-formed biceps and made him look even more at ease in a room designed to make no one feel comfortable. "Last I'd heard, she slipped right through his fingers—and a bathroom window."

"He found her, as I knew he would. They've hit a

minor glitch and have to spend a few more days in the islands."

"Time's running out for Eileen," he said. "Not the best time for Mr. Cordell to have a little fun in the sun."

"No one's having fun, Jack. Evidently, Vanessa is down there to find a friend who is on an extended vacation, and won't leave until she does. They are staying briefly at a private home, and with some help from my team, they should be able to locate her friend. When they do . . ." She held out her hands as if she was about to announce a major coup. "She's agreed to come back and meet Eileen Stafford."

"Great." He didn't seem very happy about that, considering how invested he was in the case. He just ran a hand through long, wavy hair that hadn't seen a professional hairstylist in months, maybe more. Still, his eyes were clear, his skin looked tanned, and from the looks of the muscles under his black T-shirt, he'd been hitting the gym far more than the bottle.

He watched her, silent, waiting for her to show her hand.

"I've been doing some interesting reading, and I want to discuss it with you." She set the file on the coffee table. "Eileen Stafford's trial transcripts."

He didn't touch the folder. "What brought that on?"

"I like to know what my team is up to."

He gave her a sharp look. "I'm not on your team anymore, Luce."

"Wade Cordell and Adrien Fletcher are on my

team, and they've both been sidelined from fee-paying clients for this case."

"Not for *that* case," he corrected, pointing to the file. "They are helping to find Eileen's daughters—a standard adoption search for you. That's the only piece of this investigation that has anything to do with the Bullet Catchers."

She slid into the chair, curiosity winning over the advantage of height. "Jack, why are you so secretive about what you're doing to help Eileen Stafford?"

His eyes narrowed. "When you kicked my ass out of this company, you lost the right to ask me questions about anything I do."

"And when you purged your NYPD record, lied about an injury, and accidentally shot one of my men, you lost the right to borrow my resources and staff."

That impudent smile pulled again. "We both know that isn't the reason you fired me, Luce. So don't pull the self-righteous 'Jack Culver lied and can't be trusted' bit with me."

"You did lie to me. And you can't be trusted. And that *is* why I let you go."

He leaned forward and put a bold hand on her knee, instantly warming the skin underneath her thin silk trousers. She didn't give him the satisfaction of jerking away from his touch.

"You fired me because I did what none of your other hot-shot Bullet Catchers could do. I found your weakness."

"I see you still suffer from delusions of grandeur." She stood to look down at him. "I can help you on this case, Jack. I can help you save time, money, and effort. But you have to tell me everything."

"Forget it."

"You don't want help?"

"You don't help, Lucy. You control. Big difference."

She walked to the window and stood at her favorite spot to look at the rolling hills and river valley. "It must be big."

He didn't respond.

"My instincts," she said softly, "and many of the facts in that file scream that someone with some serious power pulled the strings that tied Eileen Stafford to the murder of Wanda Sloane. I want to know why."

"Yeah? Well, I don't care about why. I want to know who, and I want to see them pay for the years they stole from her."

She eyed him warily. "Very noble."

"It has nothing to do with noble. It's just what's right."

"Unless she's really guilty. Then it's wrong."

"My problem, not yours." He stood. "Is that it, Luce? We can wrap this up now, and you can probably get back on schedule."

"You know, I haven't assigned anyone to search for the third daughter yet, but I'm about to. I was waiting for Roman Scott to finish an assignment."

"I'm this close to finding her, Luce. You don't have to spend any more unbillable hours on my pet project." He headed for the door.

"Then you can be the unofficial Bullet Catcher on

that job. I'll give you anything you need to find the third sister."

He hesitated but didn't turn. "In exchange for what?"

"No exchange. You want to help a dying woman, and I want to help Miranda find her sister, since she's fallen in love with one of my men. I don't always have an ulterior motive."

His shoulders moved with a soft laugh, and he turned to her, his eyes twinkling. "Lucinda, your middle name is Ulterior Motive."

She tilted her head to the closed door on the other side of her office. Every Bullet Catcher knew what was behind that door: a war room and computer center so heavily equipped with state-of-the-art technology that it made the Pentagon look archaic. "You could cut the search time in half. It's a good deal for both of us, since neither of us is getting paid."

He didn't say anything.

"Jack, why are you being stubborn? I don't want the glory or the credit if we crack this case. I just want justice to be served."

Again, the slow smile, the teasing glint, the look that made women melt. "You know what always amazes me, Lucy?"

The fact was, she never had figured out what amazed him. "What's that?"

"That you and I are so much alike. Deep down, we both want what's right. Truth, justice, and the American way."

"That's not amazing."

"No, what's amazing is that you actually think you can control that. You think you can find out who really killed Wanda Sloane and drag him or her into Eileen's jail cell and replace the wrong person with the right one."

"Yes, I do. What do you think *you* can do?"

"There are other ways to mete out justice." He turned and headed out the door. "I'll take your help," he called as he disappeared down the hall. "Call me later."

She just stared at the empty doorway and took the deep breath she always needed after a round with Jack.

Wade stood on a plain wooden deck, propped his foot on the handmade bench that ran along the perimeter, and studied the rough-hewn wooden house with the grand and misleading name of Mango Plantation. "For a vacation home of a gazillionaire CEO, this place is pretty modest."

Vanessa flung open one of the shuttered doors that led from the main room to the unfurnished deck. "It has a private beach and a postcard view, and it rents for seven grand a week. I'd call it a gift from the vacation gods."

"If we were on vacation."

She went back into the shadows of the house, leaving Wade to continue his inspection alone.

The view *was* spectacular: a hundred and eighty degrees of crystalline water every imaginable shade of jade and navy, broken only by the tip of St. Kitts and a few majestic yachts that bobbed in the far distance.

He zeroed in on the access and security, which were less than spectacular.

The house sat perched on a hillside, surrounded by an acre or two of fruit trees and some crabgrass cut into the rain forest. While the lush foliage blocked them from general view, they were only about five hundred feet from the road, with no fencing, wall, or security gate. Worse, there was no driveway, so Wade had to park the Jeep on the road—a virtual advertisement that they were there.

The next set of shutter doors popped open, and Vanessa stood victorious in the archway. "This place is fantastic. They have cable TV and Internet, the fridge is ice cold, and the shower is huge."

"Great. We can watch movies, surf the Net, drink beer, and shower together." He shook his head. "We're not on holiday, Vanessa. I just want to find your friend and get the hell out of here before whoever bugged the room or followed us out of Charlestown shows up."

"I do, too," she said defensively. "But you could at least thank me for jonesing a great place to stay while we look for Clive."

"Thank you." His voice was dry. "But you realize we're out here like sitting ducks."

"It's completely private." She waved a hand. "We're surrounded by rain forest."

"Providing perfect cover for someone who wants to ambush us."

"Whoever built this place thought of that." She lightly jumped up and down on the wooden deck that encircled the house; the same planks formed a boardwalk from the road and a rickety set of stairs down to the beach. "It creaks if someone's coming. No one can sneak up on you. It's like an alarm system."

Not a foolproof one, though. "The whole place is accessible by someone intrepid on foot or quiet in a boat."

She put her hands on her hips. "So we'll have to be careful. Or if someone you don't like shows up, you can shoot them."

He clenched his jaw and turned toward the sea.

"You could have killed that guy in the truck," she said softly, sounding as if she'd been brewing over the incident.

"But I didn't."

"But you're capable of it."

"I have the skill, yes," he agreed. "That doesn't mean I go around murdering people." He brushed by her into the house. "I'll check out that—"

"Have you?"

He asked the obvious, but unnecessary, question. "Have I what?"

"Killed someone. With that gun."

"With this gun? No."

She closed her eyes. "With any gun?"

"With many guns," he said quietly.

She barely nodded. "Well, you are an ex-Marine."

There was no such thing as an ex-Marine, but he wasn't about to correct her when she was rationalizing his past. "Look, the faster we get out of here before our friend in the yellow truck comes back, the better we are. I'll find out if there's any progress on pinpointing that call made to your cell phone."

She stayed out on the deck while he made the call in the small bedroom nearly filled by a king-size bed. How many more nights would he spend sleeping in a chair, now that he had told her she wasn't his type and that he didn't *fuck* for fun?

Sage Valentine answered her phone on the first ring. "I wish I had better news, Wade. Your caller wasn't using a satellite phone, and in the Caribbean, cells are spotty because some of the cell towers are on ships. The tower used to send this signal was moved out because of a storm."

This was a complication they didn't need. "How long until you can get that reading, then?"

"A day, maybe two."

"Make it one, please."

"I'll do my best."

He disconnected the call and strode into the other room, where Vanessa stood at the kitchen island, jotting something down. He told her Sage's news, and she nodded, tapping her paper.

"Then we have to do our own digging. I have a list of places where people have seen Clive. Let's start with Papaya's in Brick Kiln. After that, we'll head down to a very remote place called White Bay Beach. I can't remember the name of this little hole in the wall there, but I can find it again. I had an interesting conversation with the owner, who definitely lied to me. Let's see how you do with them."

He glanced at the map. "Why do you think the responses would be any different this time?"

"Because you're going to ask, not me. And the

clientele in these places will react better to a man."

He looked up at her. "Now who's the chauvinist?"

"These are gay hangouts, Wade. You'll be like catnip to these guys."

"They're gay, not stupid. They can smell a fake a mile away."

"Then be a good actor. This time, you'll ask about Russell Winslow, and I'll stay in the background. Come on." She tugged at his sleeve. "You said we're sitting ducks here, and this is a plan. You love plans."

"Not this one."

"We have to do something," she said, "so let's go bar hopping."

Less than an hour later, they arrived at Papaya's, separating before they stepped onto the sprawling cliffside patio populated by scruffy-looking locals and tourists who wanted to look like them. Wade joined the bar crowd, mixing with the drinkers knocking back Carib lagers and dancers clomping on the wood boards to the calypso beat of a steel-drum band.

Vanessa tucked herself into the shadowy recess at a table close to the kitchen. With her baseball cap pulled low over her glasses, she peered over the top of a plastic menu to watch Wade, who sat at the bar sipping a beer, looking all sun-kissed and as edible as the fried conch he popped into his mouth. She glanced around to count five, six, no, *eight* women checking him out. And three men. And her.

No surprise there. Even under a loose-fitting T-shirt—sized to cover his gun, no doubt—you could tell his arms were cut, his chest was ripped. His hair looked highlighted from the sun, his face rugged but breathtaking, his blue eyes easy and inviting.

Picking up the ice water, she downed a gulp, glanced at the menu, then returned to the view at the bar, her gaze rolling over every incredible inch of him.

She sipped again, a strong and undeniable sexual tug moving at warp speed to raw lust.

What was wrong with her? He was a gun-carrying ex-Marine from south of Alabama, with an agenda to make a mess of her life and force her to face people that she loathed. All that slow, lazy, sexy drawling Southernness was the polar opposite of everything she'd ever found attractive in a man.

How could she lust after him?

He didn't even *like* her. She swore too much. Moved too fast. Wasn't freaking *ladylike* enough for him. Even if he didn't come right out and say it, she picked up the vibe of distaste, the rolled eyes every time she muttered *shit*. She wasn't his type.

And he wasn't hers. But that sure didn't stop her from enjoying every kiss and touch they'd shared while they were faking it the night before. That didn't stop her from looking at his hands and remembering how thoroughly they explored her, or studying his mouth and wanting it on her skin again. Lust didn't care that they weren't each other's type.

Had it been so long since she got laid that she was ready to give it up for a guy she basically didn't like and whose hard-on when they messed around the night before was equally blind?

Uh. Yes.

Vanessa lowered the menu enough to get a good look at the woman approaching Wade from behind. He turned before she even spoke to him and drank her in with a look and a smile that said he liked what he saw.

The girl *was* stunning. Maybe twenty-five, in a body-hugging pink halter, shorts that barely covered her ass, and auburn hair cascading over toned shoulders.

Wade smiled and stepped off his barstool, offering it to her. When the woman sat down, her back was angled to Vanessa, but she could see Wade's smiling face as he said something to the girl, who laughed, gave her hair a quick shoulder toss, and nodded enthusiastically.

Wade laughed right back, and Vanessa imagined she could hear that rare low and sexy chuckle. He leaned a little close to say something in her ear, getting more giggles. He sipped. She flipped. He waved for the bartender's attention to buy the babe a drink.

What was the deal? He was supposed to be looking for gay guys who might have talked to Clive, not doing the mating dance with a Mariah Carey lookalike.

Should she wander by, shoot him a dirty look? Call him? Wave her menu in the air? Did he really think—

A bowl of conch chowder thunked down in front of her.

She looked up, expecting to see the waiter, but this was an older man. Pale-skinned and drawn, he looked out of place—not a native, not a tourist, and, something told her, not a waiter.

"I'm sorry," she said, pulling her gaze away from Wade and his new friend. "I didn't order that."

"But you want it."

She gave him a tight smile. "It's kind of hot for soup, so no, thank you."

"Can I join you?" He sat down, taking the seat across from her and blocking her view.

"I'm waiting for someone," she said quickly, moving to the side to let him know she was more interested in watching the deck than chatting with a stranger. She was just in time to catch the woman putting her hands on Wade's shoulders to whisper in his ear.

The man inched to the right, blocking her chance of seeing how Wade handled that.

"I know who you're waiting for," the man said.

That yanked Vanessa's attention back. He parked his chin on his knuckles and stared at her. The lined face, the tailor-made dress shirt, and the buffed and professionally manicured fingernails seemed out of place at Papaya's. He'd fit right in at the conference table at Razor Partners, but here, he seemed like the odd man out.

"And I know where he is."

Her heartbeat quickened. "You do?"

"And you have . . ." He glanced at an expensive watch. "An hour before the first heat."

Heat? "What are you talking about?"

"Clive Easterbrook has more than one hundred thousand dollars on Calloway's Girl, a beautiful thoroughbred who has a chance of winning today. She's running in the fourth heat at the Jockey Club."

Clive had a hundred grand on a horse race? She stared at him, using all her skill to read a man who was . . . unreadable.

"You want to find Clive?" he asked. "He'll be there. It's the only racetrack on the island, just past Red Cliff, on the southeastern side."

"I know where it is." She'd seen the signs in her travels around the island.

"And you'd better pray hard that his horse has a good day, because if he doesn't . . ." He leaned forward and made a slice across his neck. "Not good for your buddy."

Her stomach clenched. "Who are you?"

"That's not important. Clive's a gambler; did you know that?"

"He's a hedge-fund manager. Subtle difference." As Wade had pointed out, there was plenty she didn't know about Clive's life. Who was she to question another vice? "Are you sure he'll be there?"

"He may not be running around the barbecue stands or shaking hands with the jockeys, but he'll be there. Quietly, hidden. Always hidden, our Clive."

Who *was* this guy? A lover? A bookie? She shifted on her wooden chair, forcing back a barrage of questions. She'd learned a little by observing Wade Cordell: no attacking and insisting. She'd *work* the guy.

She picked up the spoon as if she were going to eat some chowder and tried to change her body language from "desperate" to "conversational."

"So, when did you last see him?" she asked.

"A few days ago. Here."

She spooned the chowder, meeting his silvery gray eyes. "Was he with anyone?"

"Not anymore."

What did that mean? "Before that, had you seen him with anyone?"

He cocked his head to the side. "I'm sorry, dear. I just can't say."

Frustration trumped subtlety.

"Why not?" she demanded. "Who are you? How do you know Clive? How can I trust you?"

He flattened his palms on the table and pushed himself up. "How can you trust anyone?" As he walked away, he put an uncomfortably warm and friendly hand on her shoulder. "Enjoy the soup, dear." His voice was heavy with implication.

She stared at the bowl. *How can you trust anyone?* She pushed the bowl away and whipped around just as the kitchen door swung back into place. She bolted up and strode over to it.

In the tiny, bustling kitchen, the cooks and busboys stared at her. Pots clanged, and cloying waves of sweet fried plantains wafted over her.

Her waiter looked surprised but pointed to the right. "Ladies' room is over there."

"Where did that man go? The tall guy in the white shirt?"

"No man," someone said. The waiter shrugged and looked genuinely stumped by the question.

A back door was closed. There was no office, no

walk-in refrigerator, nowhere he could have gone. Sighing, she spun around and went back to her table, dropping into her chair and looking toward the bar.

Wade was gone, as was the girl. The barstool was empty, the drinks were cleared, and they'd both disappeared.

He sure was fast enough when he wanted to be.

CHAPTER
TWELVE

WADE GLANCED OVER his shoulder, but the young lady had taken him to meet her friend, and his view of Vanessa was blocked at this table. How long would she wait? Vanessa? Not long. Especially after the daggerish looks she'd shot his way when the lovely informant fell into his lap.

He turned back to Sarah and her friend, Maddie. He wasn't sure yet if they were the real deal, a setup, or just a couple of cuties from Chicago who were playing him. And he'd like to determine that before he and Vanessa went to the remote Newcastle resort where the two girls insisted Clive was a registered guest.

Because, worst case, it could be a trap.

"I'm telling you," Maddie said, her voice just a little loose from the juice, "that guy is staying at the Nisbet. Want me to take you there?" She raised a cucumber-colored glass to her bee-stung lips. "I know he'd remember me. We had so much fun together when we partied that night."

"Maybe I'll go there later," Wade said, leaning back in the chair far enough so Vanessa could spot him.

He'd only mentioned Clive's name to three or four people when Sarah had sauntered over and announced she'd heard he was looking for someone she'd met there a while ago. "A while" being relative. First it was a week ago, then two; then her friend Maddie said "a few weeks." The discrepancies had him doubtful—as did their fast approach. Still, he worked the informants. And they worked him.

"I really liked him," Sarah said for the fifteenth time since she'd dragged him from the bar to meet Maddie. "I mean, what a nice, nice guy. And not bad-looking, if you like tall and wiry. Which"—she laughed and pointed at him—"you must if you liked this guy."

Maddie clunked her elbows on the table, her eyes dreamy. "Why are the best guys always gay?"

She and Sarah shared a world-weary look while Wade lined up his next question, keeping it vague enough to fit his cover but trying to get some concrete answers.

"And you're sure he was alone that night?" Wade asked.

"Absolutely," Sarah assured him. "But he . . ." She glanced at her friend again. "He was really bummin' over some guy. That's how come we all got so drunk. We were doing shots, playing 'the one that got away.' "

Maddie leaned forward and put her hand on his. "Maybe *you* were the one that got away."

Wade took a long pull from his beer, then set the bottle down. "Maybe."

The girls exchanged another secret look.

He gave them a knowing smile. "Or maybe not."

One more look, and Sarah cracked. "He was flat-out *pining* over a dude named Charlie."

"Charlie?" Wade asked. *Not Russell?*

"Oh, yeah, he was big-time pining over Charlie," Maddie said. "Over and over, he said he really messed things up with Charlie. How he missed Charlie. What happened with Charlie was all his fault. He even started crying. Remember, Sar?"

"Don't even think about that, hon," Sarah told Wade. "I bet he's over that by now. And he wasn't *crying*-crying, 'cause he was *soooo* toasted. We all were."

"Are you sure it wasn't Russell he was crying over?"

"He mentioned Russell, too," Maddie said quickly. "Maybe this guy's too much of a player for a man like you, Wade."

"That's what I thought." He smiled and took another swig. "So you two are here, what, every day?" If so, they could be a real help. If not, they might be plants.

"Oh, yeah." Maddie nodded. "We come here after work almost every day since moving from Chicago. Did Sarah tell you we moved here for the summer?"

"Three times," he said with a wink.

"We work at Cliffdwellers," Sarah told Wade, for the second time. Once more, and their information was officially tainted with alcohol and useless. "It's a really nice resort. Have you been there?"

"Nope."

"But you should go to Newcastle and find Clive before he checks out of the Nisbet or something," Maddie said.

Should he? Or would the guy in a yellow truck follow him there and try to run him off the road again? These girls were good but not that good. If he had enough time, he could find out if they were working for someone.

"You know," Maddie said, her fingers trying to thread his, "you don't seem gay at all."

Sarah punched her in the leg. "*So* politically incorrect, girlfriend."

"I don't mean it as like an insult or anything." Maddie shifted uncomfortably.

Wade gave her an easy smile. "Don't worry, ma'am. No insult taken."

"Ma'am. That's sooo cute!" they both squealed.

He rocked back on the legs of his chair again, casually stealing a glance over his shoulder. No Vanessa.

But Sarah caught him looking, and her face melted in pity. "Oh, you poor thing, you really have it bad. I'm telling you, he said he was staying for a few more weeks. You should go check out that place up in Newcastle." Four times.

She was completely wasted, stupid, or determined. Or all three.

"Maybe."

Maddie winked at him. "You say that a lot, did you know that?"

He laughed and lifted his beer. "I have trouble with commitment."

"Don't they all!" Sarah joked, and offered a sloppy toast. "Here's to the commitment-phobes, both gay and straight!"

Maddie still hadn't let go of his hand, and Sarah patted him sympathetically. "There are lots of fish in the pond for a guy who looks like you." Then she curled her fingers around his wrist. "All kinds of little fishie-wishies you might try."

The girls shared a look again, then Sarah grazed his hand with her fingertip. "You ever been with a girl, sweetheart?"

"Maybe," he said, laughing with them.

They tightened their grip and asked in unison, "How about two?" They let out a squeal that could probably be heard all the way back to where Vanessa was sitting.

"We said that at exactly the same time!" Sarah giggled, still clinging to Wade's hand. "Just think about what that means."

Maddie pulled in closer, a lock of frosted blond hair falling into her eye. "There's a first time for everything, baby."

"As long as we use a condom," Sarah said. Then she looked over his shoulder, frowning as two hands gripped Wade's shoulders from behind.

"Don't worry," a familiar voice said. "Wade has cartons of them."

He knew she couldn't stay put and let him do his

job. He turned slowly, the glint in her eyes telling him exactly how she read—or misread—the situation.

"Hey, Vanessa," he said, keeping his voice steady and low. "What's up?"

She thrust her hand toward Sarah. "I'm Vanessa Porter."

"Sarah Clegg." Sarah took her hand. "This is my friend Madeline."

Vanessa nodded at the other girl, then surprised Wade by crouching down next to his seat. "Listen, it looks like you're going to be tied up for a while, so I need the car keys."

"For what?"

"I have to run an errand." She threw a look at the girls. "You can hang with your new friends while I'm gone."

Was she nuts? "An errand?"

Behind her glasses, her eyes bored through him. "A very important errand. I'll be back to get you later, but I have to go. *Now*." She lifted one brow. "If you want to stay and play, that's totally cool. You told me I could have the Jeep anytime I wanted it." She held out her hand. "Now I want it."

He searched her face, trying to read what she wasn't telling him, then pushed back his chair. "I can take you wherever you want to go." He spoke through a clenched jaw, narrowing his eyes at her. "I was just talking to Sarah and Maddie about a friend of mine."

Her gaze dropped to his crotch. "I heard."

"Vanessa."

She put a hand on his arm and leaned very close.

"It's fine, Wade. Do what you need to do here. I have to go *right now*. I know where he is."

He stood and reached a hand out to Sarah, then Maddie. "Ladies, it was a pleasure."

They looked at each other, then settled their attention on Vanessa, checking her out mightily as she stood, their smiles turning as fake as their hair color.

"It could have been a pleasure," Sarah said dryly.

"And thanks for all your advice," he added.

"Seriously," Maddie said. "Go to the Nisbet Plantation. You'll find what you want, honey."

He gave them a quick wave and followed the blond ponytail swinging from the back of a Yankees cap. When he reached her side, she picked up her speed.

"They met Clive," he said.

She didn't miss a step. "Yes, I heard you discussing that."

"You only heard part of the conversation." They reached the edge of the deck, and he grabbed her arm. "And where do you think you're going like a bat out of hell?"

She tugged away. "The racetrack. It's south of here, near Red Cliff. I just spoke to someone who really does know Clive and was not drunk or trying to get into my pants. He told me Clive is in trouble for gambling, and he has a lot of money on a horse running today, and he'd be at this racetrack in the next hour, when the horse runs. So I'm going there." She pointed her thumb over her shoulder, back at the bar. "But feel free to stay and flirt with the *ladies,* Wade."

She reached the Wrangler and flung herself into the

passenger seat. Pulling the keys from his pocket, he climbed in. "Who is this guy you talked to? Did you get his name? How do you know he's reliable?"

"I don't know; no; and I don't. I'm going on gut. He sought me out and just spilled. It's the first tangible lead I've had in a while, and I want to follow it."

He looked at her. "What you are doing, Vanessa, is going straight to where he told you to go, exactly in the time frame he told you to, and you are willing to do this unarmed and unprotected."

"I was unarmed and unprotected before I met you."

"Yeah, back when you thought your friend had dropped out to be a bartender or something. Now we know it's a little more dangerous than that." He slid the key into the ignition but didn't turn it. "You know what a trip to a racetrack might be?"

"A way to find Clive?"

"A *trap*." His fury at her stubbornness built. "Someone is sending you to a specific place at a specific time, and you are running there just like they want you to. Those two girls might have been doing the same thing, and if you hadn't barged in, I might have been able to find out who paid them to do that. I needed more time."

She rolled her eyes. "Those two girls were drunk sluts who wanted a threesome, for chrissake."

He grabbed her arm and forced her to look at him. "We have a deal, and I'm going to hold up my end of the bargain. They might have been girls looking for a good time, or they might have been on someone's payroll whose job it is to detour you. The same with the guy who wants you racing to the track."

She leaned back and closed her eyes with a sigh. "All right. That's true. I just thought . . ."

"I know what you thought. I'm better than that."

"Oh, yeah. You carry a semiautomatic, shoot it like some kind of gunslinger, but the possibility of casual sex with a stranger offends you." She shook her head. "Whatever, Wade. I don't want to argue. But this guy said Clive's got a gambling debt, and doesn't that make some sense to you? Maybe that's why he's hiding."

"Maybe. Or someone wants you to go there for some reason. Maybe because he's *not* there."

She turned to him, some of the spark gone from her eyes. "Should we just ignore a lead like that?"

"No, we should think about a lead like that. Consider the source, check out the various routes, find out if it's safe."

"There's not enough time!" she insisted. "Start the fucking car, Wade, and let's go and think it through on the way."

He twisted the key and rolled out of the lot, his blood pumping hard. He stopped at the road and stared straight ahead. "You're like a . . . a force of nature, you know that?"

"Thank you. Now, go right. Red Cliff is south of here."

He just stared ahead.

"I have an idea," he finally said. "Do you want to take thirty seconds to consider it?"

"Twenty-nine."

"My informants told me they'd met him a few weeks ago and partied with him. He said he was staying at a place called the Nisbet Plantation in Newcastle. You want to go south to Red Cliff; I want to go north to Newcastle."

She nodded, listening.

"And someone," he said, drawing the word out for emphasis, "could very well be sitting in that restaurant wondering which of the plants we're going to believe. They may even be prepared for us to go to either place."

"Okay. Then what should we do?"

He pointed toward the left. "Head toward Newcastle, pull off as soon as we find a place to hide, wait until someone who might follow us zips by, then take a circuitous route to the racetrack."

She took a slow breath, considering that. "Could we make the track in an hour?"

"I think so. There's a southbound road that's off the main road, but we should be able to get there in an hour."

"All right."

He turned the Jeep north and drove in silence for less than two miles, to a side road with thick bougainvillea bushes that blocked the view from the road.

He parked where they couldn't be seen and turned the ignition off.

"Just listen," he said, with a finger to his lips. "Listen for cars passing, headed north."

They sat quietly; the sun moved behind a cloud, and a car passed. Then another, and one more. She crossed her legs and stretched them. Her skin was smooth, toned, and flawless but for a little mole on her knee and another higher on her leg.

"Did you really think I was going to sleep with those girls?" he asked.

He saw her thigh tighten. "I don't know."

"I just met them."

"You've never had sex with someone you picked up in a bar?"

"Other than last night?" He glanced over and caught her smile. "No. Have you?"

"No. But I'm not a hot guy with a big gun."

He winked at her. "You're a hot girl with a big mouth."

"Very funny. But I thought you were supposed to be acting like you were gay."

"I was. They wanted to convert me. But you totally misread the situation."

She laughed humorlessly. "Yeah, there's a lot of room for interpretation in 'You have to wear a condom.'" She pointed to the road. "Can we go now?"

"I think so." He pulled out and turned right. "The road that cuts through the rain forest is just before Newcastle. It's probably pretty rough in spots, but we can take it down past the mountain, then cut over to Red Cliff. I studied the map last night while you were sleeping."

"All right, but hurry. We're down to about forty-five minutes now."

In ten minutes, they found the southern crossroad, and he knew it would be a challenge to make it in less than an hour. The asphalt was completely missing in places, and some of the foliage was so thick it nearly blocked the narrow road.

"What else did your girlfriends say about Clive?" Vanessa asked.

"They said he got drunk and cried over a guy."

"Not a surprise. He loved Russell. Always did."

He squinted through the palm fronds to gauge how far the next crossroad was, because he heard another vehicle but couldn't see it in front of them.

"Actually, they mentioned a different guy. Charlie. He kept saying it was his fault, which just shows you . . ."

"Who?"

At the sharp note in her voice, he turned to see she'd drawn back, her hand over her mouth. "What's the matter?"

"Charlie?"

"Yeah. Charlie. You know him?"

"What exactly did they say?" Her fingers closed over his arm, clammy. "Exactly, Wade. *What* did he say?"

He frowned at her, his attention divided among the road, the intersection, and the sixth sense that another car was coming. "They said he cried because whatever happened with Charlie was his fault."

They neared the intersection, barely visible from the thick fronds that hung far into the road.

"Are you *positive* that was the name? Not Charles?"

"Yes, Charlie."

"Charlie French?"

"I don't—" The sound of a revving engine pulled

his attention, and suddenly he saw a white van through the trees, careening full speed down the road to their right, straight toward them.

He had to get through the intersection before the van did, or slam the brakes so hard they'd probably skid into the ditch.

"Hang on!" he ordered, stomping the gas and weaving with the sudden acceleration. Gravel and asphalt spewed behind them, almost drowning out Vanessa's shriek of surprise.

The van shot onto the road right in front of them, forcing Wade to stomp the brakes and fishtail wildly. The second they got through the intersection, another engine screamed, and the yellow truck came roaring out from a hiding place like the one they'd used ten miles back.

"Oh, my God," Vanessa gasped. "It's him."

The truck sped up behind them just as the van slowed down in front, sandwiching them.

"Get down!" he ordered. "All the way! Before you get shot!"

She snapped off her seat belt and rolled to the floorboards. The van slowed to less than ten miles an hour but swerved every time Wade tried to pass.

Behind him, the yellow truck got closer and closer, then hit their back bumper hard.

Wade whipped the Jeep to the left just as the van came to a stop, so he hit its back corner and slid wildly. The truck rushed by on the right. Long dark hair whipped around a bearded face, and a hand reached out, middle finger poised in the air.

"Watch who you fuck with, dickhead!" He swerved viciously into the Jeep, forcing them into a four-foot gulley, where they crunched to a complete stop.

The truck roared away with the van, leaving only the echo of their engines and the clicking of the useless Jeep.

Wade reached down to help Vanessa up. "They're gone."

She climbed back into her seat with a grunt of pain, her face white, her eyes wild.

"They're gone," he repeated.

All she could manage was a nod, swiping the hair out of her eyes and righting her glasses.

"Don't worry," he assured her, a comforting hand on her shoulder. "I might be able to push us out of here. If not, I'll call the rental company. It's gonna be all right. We might not make the racetrack, but it's okay."

She shuddered, still looking at him with horror in her eyes. "It's not okay."

"I've been through worse, believe me. Even if they come back, I'll . . ." His voice trailed off as he watched her crumple before his eyes. "What is it, Vanessa?"

"Charlie French, she . . . she is . . . was *not* a man. Charlie was a woman we worked with at Razor." She closed her eyes and shuddered. "She was murdered. Brutally stabbed to death right in her own apartment."

"When?"

She swallowed, visibly struggling with the act. "The day before Clive suddenly disappeared on his first vacation in five years."

Chapter
THIRTEEN

THE FASTER HE ran, the more blood he left in his wake.

And wasn't *that* an appropriate metaphor for the mess that was his life?

Clive turned, jogging backward for a few steps to look at the bloody footprints he'd left in the sand, admiring the perfectly straight line, the even spacing of each step, and marveling at his time.

Even with a dozen cuts on his feet from broken shells and rocks, he could run fast. Even without his custom-fit Asics, even without comfort food, even without a finish line in sight, he could run really fast.

Damn good thing, considering how many people were after him.

Bending over to catch his breath, he pulled up his sweat-soaked T-shirt and dried his face, wincing at the sting in his eyes. Just as he blinked to clear them, a

frothy wave rushed the sand and wiped out his footprints. For some reason, that pissed him off.

And being pissed off was the best feeling in the
world.

Anger was always the first indication that the
inner pendulum that whipped from happy to sad had
peaked on the misery side and was sliding back to
normal.

God, as if. Normal? How about content? His lips
lifted in a bitter smile. How about *alive?*

Even that was a little shaky these days.

He looked left at the endless ocean and then right
at the thickest jungle he'd ever seen. Was someone
hidden in there, aiming a rifle at his head? He started
running again, imagining what it would feel like when
the bullet hit his back and bored a hole right through
his heart.

It was a bizarre feeling, knowing someone wanted
him dead. Even more bizarre not knowing who.

He concentrated on his feet, his legs, his oxygen,
slowing when he passed the four graceful coconut
palms bowed from years of tropical breezes and the
weight of their fruit. The trees marked the last stretch
before his little piece of "paradise."

He stopped again, propping his hands on his hips
and bending left, then right, to stretch his spine and
muscles, squinting into the copse of trees and rocks
where his house was hidden.

Something moved. Someone was in his house.

Swallowing hard, he took a few steps closer. His heart
rate ratcheted up. It could be anyone, friend or foe.

He trusted his friends. They'd gotten him here, fed him, aided him, and loved him. But his foes . . . Christ almighty—look what they did to Russell. Look what they did to Charlie.

He liked blaming their deaths on someone else. It eased the burn in his chest and the ache in his stomach. Guilt . . . *hurt.*

From the moment he saw her lying in her blood, Clive was sick with guilt for what he'd done. He should have stayed for her memorial service; that just made him look guiltier. But he couldn't stand in some church as people talked about the life of Charlotte French. What kind of hypocrite would that make him?

Through the trees, he could see the stone walls of the little hut, the thatched roof, the patio where he liked to sleep. Who'd violated his hiding place? He hadn't heard a helicopter and couldn't see a boat. There was no other way, unless someone was on foot and intrepid as hell.

He squared his shoulders and headed in. What was the worst that could happen?

Charlie's body. That was the worst that could happen.

"Hey, beautiful."

He gasped and spun at the words, whispered so low they could have been part of the breeze.

"I'm right over here." A low melody of male laughter followed. "You should be more attentive, my friend."

Relief washed over him as a familiar figure lumbered out from some bushes.

"You fucking scared me," he growled.

"Special delivery, Mr. Easterbrook." He held up his right hand. "And it's Kraft, too. Your personal favorite."

"Thanks." As Clive walked up the path, he saw a motorboat moored next to the little sailboat tucked into a cove, far enough away that he hadn't heard the engine. He let himself be hugged, tightly and for a long time, trying to return the embrace without showing too much affection. He walked such a dangerous tight rope with this man; falling meant death.

"I have news."

Clive stepped back and frowned. "That sounds ominous."

"It is. They've found Vanessa. They've got her."

"Jesus Christ! Is she okay? Did they—"

"They don't actually have her, but they're all over her every move. And if she is remotely successful in finding you, so will they. You must be hypervigilant. No more solo runs on the beach. No more lights on at night. And no more phone calls to her, do you understand?"

Clive leaned against the rickety column that held up the thatching. "I have to talk to her. I have to tell her to go home. She shouldn't be in the middle of this. It's crazy."

"She's crazy," he shot back. "Talking to the whole world, giving too much information away, drawing attention to herself. She is a huge liability to you, my friend."

"She is not a liability." Clive worked to keep from

sounding defensive. This protector could snap at any moment, and then where would he be? "Where is she now?"

The gaze that met his was sharp, midnight-black. "There's nothing you can do. Save your ass. That's all that matters." He grinned salaciously. "Especially to me."

"Where is she now?" Clive repeated. "Still on Nevis? I just need to know."

"She's back on that cruise. Surrounded by people and perfectly safe. Let it go."

He frowned in disbelief. "You mean, she gave up already?"

"Like you said, she moves fast. Maybe she's just back to Plan A to follow your footsteps on the cruise." He gave Clive a hard look. "And don't even think about it." The stern warning was accompanied by a pointed finger. "You *cannot* leave this house. You cannot contact that ship. You cannot use that phone." A large, warm hand landed on his shoulder. "Come on. I cooked for you. We'll eat this garbage you call food, then we'll smoke. And maybe we'll . . . talk."

The euphemism hung in the air as thick as the tropical humidity. They would not *talk*.

"I quit smoking," Clive said, dipping out of the touch to enter the single room. "Just this morning, as a matter of fact."

That earned him a solid pat on the back. "I am proud of you. It's a nasty habit. But you will start again." Low laughter rumbled.

Clive stopped at the sink, washed his hands, and threw water on his face.

No, he wouldn't start smoking again. Maybe this time, he could keep his pendulum on the right side. Maybe.

"Why do you eat this crap, anyway?"

"My mother made it for me," Clive said, inhaling the smell of cheap melted cheese. "It smells like my happy childhood."

His cell phone was on the sideboard. Clive glanced at it, considering the possibilities and risks. As he pulled out his chair, he blocked the phone from view and casually lifted it. When he sat down, he slid it under his thigh.

"I don't feel like talking tonight," he said, looking at his plate so he didn't need to see the hurt in his friend's eyes. He put his napkin on his lap, leaning forward to inch the phone between his calves. "You understand, don't you?"

"Of course. Maybe we'll just play hangman, or I'll leave after we eat."

Clive reached across the table. "You're good to me, and I appreciate it."

"Yeah, yeah. You don't appreciate it enough." He gave Clive a hollow smile. "But you will. You will eventually love me, Clive Easterbrook. By then, all the darkness in New York will be behind you and forgotten. And you will love me so much that you will never go back."

Was he really doomed to spend his life here? Was that the punishment for what he did to Charlie? "I have to go back. That's my life, not this. No matter . . . how I feel."

"I'll take my chances. Now, *bon appétit.* Eat your lousy meal that I have made you, and tell me about your happy childhood."

"No." Clive stabbed a forkful of yellow comfort and worked the phone down his legs without letting it clunk to the floor. "It'll make me homesick and depressed."

"You're funny when you're depressed."

The comment felt like a smack across the cheek. "I am?"

"And needy."

He just looked, the fork frozen in front of his mouth. "Really?"

"Yes, but don't worry. I like you when you're depressed. Everyone does."

Not Vanessa. Was she the only real friend he had? The only one who didn't encourage his weaknesses because they enjoyed the wry, bitter, sardonic Clive?

Yes, he thought as he took a bite. She'd proved it over and over again. Vanessa loved him as a true friend and proved it constantly. Not like the friend across the table, who was using him in his own way.

Vanessa's love was real—and he owed her that real love back. He had to get to her somehow. He'd tell her enough to get her to leave and stop looking for him. He'd convince her this was the life he wanted. He'd never tell her the truth about Charlie, and she'd probably never find out about Russell. But if anyone saw him . . . if he got caught, it was over.

This man would not protect him any longer.

Very, very carefully, he worked the phone to his

ankles, then used his bare foot to slide it deep under the table. Yes. He'd take the risk for friendship. And then he'd have a little less guilt on his conscience.

"What are you thinking about, my friend?"

Clive swallowed and smiled. "How truly good this crap is."

Wade smelled.

Even a few feet away, with the tropical breezes blowing the fragrance of saltwater and exotic fruits through the air, Vanessa could pick up his scent—a mix of sweat and earth and the last remnants of soap.

He smelled like a man who'd pushed a Jeep out of a ditch, fought and failed to start it, walked a mile in blistering heat to get a cab, rented another vehicle, drove like hell to the racetrack where three hundred crazed locals drank beer and ate chicken and bet wads of cash on second-rate horses, scouring the crowd and stands for a man who wasn't there, then drove all the way back up the island to crash a resort looking for a guest who had never been there under either of the names they had.

No wonder he smelled. She probably did, too.

Perched on the lowest of the wobbly wooden stairs that led from the deck to the beach, she nestled her chin on her knees, hugged her legs, and let the sights and sounds and smells and sensations of sunset in the Caribbean islands surround her. Along with guilt, worry, bewilderment, and, just to confuse matters more, an attraction that she didn't want or need.

Wade paced through the surf in front of her, on the phone to a woman he called Luce. His voice was low and steady as it drifted over the twenty feet of sand, allowing Vanessa to glean nuggets of the conversation.

He talked about Clive. About Russell Winslow. About Charlie French. He even mentioned Nicholas Vex. After a day of abusing his incredible body and applying his sharp brain to attack her problem, he was now seeking help from someone who, according to Wade, had a security company chock full of super-technology and legions of capable men and women to use it.

He'd made a deal, and he was obviously a man of his word. And he'd expect her to keep her end of the bargain. She curled her bare toes into the warm sand and stared at the cobalt horizon, where the sun melted like a massive ball of orange sherbet dropped on a hot plate, letting her thoughts go back to the strange connection of Charlotte French and Clive's disappearance.

Charlie's vicious murder a month ago had been called random violence, a stunning and unsolved act of brutality. Vanessa had suspected Charlie's death was a catalyst for Clive's sudden vacation, figuring it was his way of dealing with the shock. She even figured it had incited his latest bout of the blues.

He'd known their coworker much better than Vanessa had; Clive had done several deals with Charlie and had mentored her when she first joined the hedge-fund division.

Vanessa refused to believe he'd murdered her. Clive wasn't capable of murder.

But then why was he in hiding? Why did he have a bloody T-shirt in his hastily abandoned villa, along with the news story about the death of a man he'd once loved? And why, oh why, was he drunk in a bar crying that Charlie's death was his fault?

And who bugged her room and drove her off the road and sent her on wild-goose chases around Nevis? Clive? Could *he* be pulling the strings hard enough to get her to go home?

Wade snapped the phone shut and sauntered toward her, dragging his T-shirt over his head, wearing only dirty khaki shorts. His chest was sculpted as if Michelangelo himself had done the work. More of an assault on her battered senses, including whatever sense made her a woman.

He dropped his shirt on the sand and stood over her, blocking the last vestiges of sun. "I got Lucy's operation up to speed. They'll start supplementary investigations and research. She's certain we'll have a location for that call by tomorrow morning."

"Great."

"And just in case you were wondering . . ." He sat next to her, the soft hair of his legs tickling her. "Eileen Stafford is still in a coma."

She wasn't wondering. She inched away and rubbed her temples. "My head is throbbing."

"You're hungry. Let's go up and find something to eat."

"Good luck with that. I checked the pantry." She

let him pull her up when he stood. "If you don't like Campbell's tomato soup, extra-wide egg noodles, or buttered microwave popcorn, you're in trouble."

He shrugged. "I've survived on worse. And it had eight legs and bit back."

"Ewww."

"Spoken like a true girl." He gave her a smile so endearing she forgot to be insulted. "But you're discounting nature's bounty." He placed a hand on each of her shoulders to nudge her up the stairs. "There's enough fruit here to keep us alive for days. Let's go picking."

She let him push her up just because she was so tired, and fruit sounded good, and his hands were strong and solid and secure. At the top of the steps, he pulled her over to a thick tree, laden with golden red fruit.

"You allergic to mangoes?"

"I don't think I've ever had one—at least, not right off the tree."

"They're a treat. But lots of people are allergic to the skin. We'll do a test." He plucked a fat, football-shaped fruit from a low-hanging branch. "Give me your wrist."

She held out her arm.

"The reaction is instant," he said, gently rubbing the sun-warm fruit on her skin.

"What will happen if I am allergic?"

"The reaction varies. Some people get a light rash. Some people go crazy."

She blinked at him. "Crazy?"

"Only in severe cases." His eye twinkled just enough for her to be pretty sure he was teasing.

"How crazy?" She twisted her wrist, which looked normal. And delicate in his large hand.

"Crazy enough to do things you've never done before."

Something low and sensual in his voice tightened her tummy. "Like?"

"Like going into the house, finding a basket or a bowl, and helping me pick fruit for a picnic on the beach."

She laughed softly. "That's not crazy. You think I've never had a picnic on the beach before?"

"Not with me." He rubbed her chin with his thumb, a tender gesture that practically made her sink an inch deeper into the soft earth. Then he took her hand and raised her wrist to the fading sunlight, examining the skin. For a second, she thought he might kiss it, and she held her breath . . . and hoped.

"No rash. Looks like you can eat mangoes with abandon."

She slipped out of his grasp before she did something else with abandon, like press her wrist to his lips and force him to kiss the spot he scrutinized. "I'll get a bowl."

She headed up the boardwalk to the house, the wood squeaking under her bare feet. The spot on her arm still felt hot, tingly, and alive. She had a reaction, all right. To him.

There was a long night, a hot guy, and just one bed in her very near future. Anticipation and lust curled through her. He was no saint; he was human. He'd admitted that much.

And God, she wanted to see him be human again.

She went into the bathroom and looked in the mirror. Her hair was stringy and knotted. Her face was flushed from the sun and speckled with dirt. Her top was mud-splattered from the racetrack, and her eyes looked tired and shadowed.

She slid off her glasses and touched her cheekbone, feeling grit as she tried to see herself as he did.

Loud. Fast. A finger-flipping, cussing Wall Street barracuda, covered in dirt.

Well, she could do something about the dirt, anyway.

She threw some water on her face, then lathered up a bar of soap. Makeup was out of the question, but at least she could get the grime off.

And she probably smelled as bad as he did. She smeared a little soapy water under one arm, then the other. Turning for a towel and finding none, she saw a tiny cabinet built into the wall. Opening it, she found a few towels, along with a cluster of prescription medicine bottles, a hair dryer, shampoo, and some lotions.

When she grabbed the towel, it knocked over the shampoo, which hit the meds and sent them to the floor with a clatter.

"Son of a bitch," she muttered, dabbing her eyes and scooping up the plastic bottles. "Nothing like raiding the host's drug cabinet."

She set the bottles back in their approximate spots, then spotted one more by the wastebasket. She bent to pick it up, noticing the Duane Reade logo known to any New Yorker. Curious about where the über-rich Nicholas Vex bought his meds, she looked at the label to read the drugstore address. Huh—that was her Duane Reade right near Broadway and . . .

Sertraline 50 mg. Substituted for Zoloft.

Jesus. Was everyone on this shit nowadays? She lifted her thumb to read the name on the bottle. And froze. And blinked. And tried to make sense of what she read. But couldn't.

Clive Easterbrook.

Holding the bottle tightly, she ran to find Wade.

CHAPTER
FOURTEEN

WRAPPED AROUND A papaya tree five feet above the ground, Wade heard the urgency in Vanessa's voice as she called his name. He dropped the fruit to the sand and shimmied down the trunk. "I'm over here. What's the matter?"

She spun toward him, her eyes bright, her arm outstretched. "Look at this!"

"You got a rash?"

"Clive's prescription Zoloft. I found it in the bathroom!"

He brushed his hands before he took the little medicine bottle. "Seriously?" He read the label, noting the scrip was issued two months ago, then opened it and peered in, doing a quick count. "This is for sixty, and there are fewer than thirty in here."

"How is this possible?" she asked, stabbing her

hands in her hair as if she could pull the answers out of her brain. "He's *been* here."

"Well, maybe it's the same deal as you got. Maybe your boss offered him the house after his cruise was done, for a place to work things out."

"But wouldn't Marcus have mentioned that to me on the phone? Wouldn't Clive have told me?"

Wade examined the bottle again. "You said you've had only text messages from him, and you got cut off last night when you were talking to your boss. Plus, why would he mention Clive? I thought he was a non-person at your firm."

"Yes, that's true." She took the bottle back and reread the label. "And that wasn't until he resigned, about a month later. So, I guess it's possible he had the same deal and stayed here."

Still, she didn't sound convinced.

"Was he steady on Zoloft?" Wade asked. "Or only when he got depressed?"

"He hates taking it. He only takes it when he feels like he's headed into dark days."

"How was he on May 15?" The date on the bottle. "Headed there?"

"Two months ago, he was fine."

"Until a coworker was murdered a month later, and he bolted."

She shot him a look. "He took a vacation. Which I realize he hadn't done in a long time, but . . ." She sighed, staring at the bottle for answers it couldn't give her. "I still think Marcus would have mentioned it to me."

"Could Clive have gotten permission to stay here directly from the owner? Do they know each other?"

She brightened at the thought. "Yes, they do. Clive managed a lot of accounts heavy on Vexell stock, so he spent a lot of time at the company. He knows Nicholas Vex, though I wouldn't say well enough to borrow his vacation home."

"Did Charlie work with them?" he asked.

"Sometimes. She specialized in mezzanine funds, so it would depend on the situation, but overall, the group was tight." She shook the bottle again. "One thing we do know for sure: he's been here."

"And gone."

"I'm going to call Marcus and see if I can get him to tell me if he arranged for Clive to stay here."

"I thought you didn't want him to know you're looking for Clive."

"I don't, but I could do it very casually. Tell him I found something of Clive's and ask if he'd rented the place. I'll be very subtle. I can be, when I want to."

"I'm sure you can. While you do that, I'll pick dinner from the trees."

Wade finished getting fruit, found a blanket, and set it halfway between the bottom of the stairs and the surf. He started peeling a mango with his penknife, considering all that he knew about Clive Easterbrook and just how long Vanessa was going to remain in denial.

The guy was obviously in trouble. Either he was guilty of murder, possibly on two counts, or he knew who was. He was hiding from the authorities or a killer, and Vanessa probably wasn't doing him any favors by searching high and low for him. How could he convince her of that?

And could he persuade her to abandon finding her friend and still agree to go to South Carolina? He'd seen the shadow cross her face every time the subject came up. She was looking for any way out of the deal, and if they didn't find Clive, that'd be all she needed.

He couldn't force her to go, and he couldn't leave her in this situation, either. Whoever wanted Clive— or didn't want her to find him—was tough enough to play hardball with the yellow truck.

Now he was jumpstarting Jeeps and cruising race-tracks and getting flipped off by angry locals and eating fruit on a beach with an opinionated, pushy, high-speed *tart*.

She'd been looking lustily at him, and while that wasn't the worst way to pass a night on a tropical island, if she thought that was going to meet her end of the bargain, then she was wrong. Although he wouldn't mind . . .

At the sound of her footsteps, he looked up the stairs and practically dropped his knife. The three triangles of her bathing suit barely covered the essentials. Oh, man. No wonder she kicked butt on Wall Street. The woman did not play fair.

"He's not around anywhere. I finally managed to get a signal, but Marcus's voice-mail box is full on every number I have for him in my phone. Of course, the office is closed. I'll try again in a little while. He's never out of contact for more than a few minutes." She trotted down the steps and dropped a towel on the sand next to him. "I thought I'd take a swim, since I'm pretty dirty from the day." She toed his thigh. "So are you."

The last streaks of sunlight bathed her in a golden glow. Dirty? She looked beautiful, with her hair tumbling over her shoulders, her hands on narrow but nicely curved hips.

"That's a polite way of telling you that you smell."

He laughed. "I thought you had a headache and were starved." He held up a mango. "Eat first. Then I'll join you."

She eyed the fruit hungrily. Or was she eyeing him? "I thought you weren't supposed to swim after you eat."

"That's an old wives' tale." He reached up and took her hand. "C'mon. Have a taste."

She slipped out of his grasp but lowered herself to the blanket.

He carved a thick slice and held it to her mouth. "You don't like to touch people, do you?"

Her eyes widened, and he slid the mango in before she could answer, forcing her to close her mouth and chew.

"That's one way to shut you up."

She narrowed her eyes at him, ready to argue, but then closed them, letting out a tiny moan. "God, that's amazing."

He raised another piece to her mouth. "Yep. They're kind of like you, don't you think?" She opened her mouth to suck in the bite, a trickle of juice drawing his attention to her lips and holding it there.

"Why? Because they're tart and juicy and give some people a rash?"

He laughed. "No, because they're surprisingly sweet once you get past the tough exterior."

Her expression softened.

"And they make people crazy," he added.

She wiped her chin, then sucked the juice off her finger, staring at him, surely knowing his cock was getting stiffer every second. "Do I make you crazy, Wade?"

"That move just did, yeah."

She smiled, deliberately licked another finger, then grew serious. "I don't mean to be a pain, really. And you were really great today. Thank you for all you did to help me."

"We didn't find Clive," he said, lifting a bite of mango to his mouth. "So hold your gratitude."

"We found a big clue, though." She looked back up at the house. "And you know, I was thinking. Maybe he comes here at night."

Wade lifted his brows. "That's a thought. And it would be so easy. He shows up, we've officially found him, then you can keep your end of our deal."

That shadow crossed her face again—the almost imperceptible expression of a lie.

"You do remember our deal, Vanessa? As I recall, you initiated it."

She turned to the sea, nibbling on her lower lip. "Yep. I remember."

He started digging the center out of a papaya, flicking the shiny black seeds onto the sand. "Tell me something," he said as he slid the blade under the skin. "I can understand your feelings about your birth mother, considering she's in jail for murder, but now that you know you have two sisters, aren't you even curious about them?"

She kept her eyes on the water. "No." Wordlessly, she pushed herself up. "I want to swim."

But he had a hand on her wrist and tugged her back down. "I want to know."

"It's not your business to know," she shot back. "I haven't asked you about your family, and you don't need to ask me about mine. This isn't a date. This is . . . an arrangement."

"Well, as part of this arrangement, I'd be happy to tell you all about my family," he drawled. "I was raised by my mama and my grandmama, and I have two younger sisters, Bonnie Sue and Becky Lee." He added a killer grin. "At home, I'm known as Billy Wade."

Her own smile threatened to bloom. "Billy Wade?"

"William Wade Cordell, Junior."

"And where's William Wade Cordell, Senior?"

"He was killed when I was little. When my mama was pregnant with Becky."

She hesitated, obviously torn between escape and interest. "How?"

He dug a chunk of papaya and held it out to her. She took it by hand, denying him the pleasure of feeding her again. He waited until she'd taken a bite and swallowed.

"He was shot."

"Really? So was my dad. What happened?"

"Hunting accident. My moron uncle mistook him for a deer." He shook his head, wishing he could muster up some hatred for Uncle Gil, but he never could. "It was an accident, plain and simple, and poor old Gil has suffered for it every day."

"You're kidding me. And after that, you . . ." She pointed to the gun that lay a foot away, still in the leather holster he'd worn all day on his belt. "You carry a gun?"

"A gun is part of my job, Vanessa. It always has been, no matter what job I had. Anyway, my dad's death was an accident and a result of being in the wrong place at the wrong time."

"My dad was in the wrong place at the wrong time, too. But it was no accident. He was shot in cold blood by a carjacker at a rest stop in Baltimore." Her eyes narrowed at him, sparking with accusation. "And guess what he was doing there?"

He shook his head.

"He was on his way home from Columbia, South Carolina, after a visit with Eileen Stafford." At his stunned look, she nodded. "*She's* the reason my father is dead."

"No, the reason your father's dead is that some hammerknocker with an agenda and a drug habit picked your dad out of the blue. You can't blame the gun, and you can't blame Eileen Stafford."

She rocked backward. "I can blame whoever the hell I want. He wouldn't have been there if not for her. We'd learned her identity ten years earlier, and we'd already agreed she was dead to both of us. But he had to go."

"Why?"

"He never told me. But I think . . ." She reached down and scooped up some powdery sand, studying the grains as they poured through her fingers. "I had to piece it together after he died, going through his office and his phone calls. But I think he might have wanted to talk to her about her trial. Based on what I found."

"What did you find?"

She flipped her hand and threw the rest of the sand down. "Enough to know that she's a murderer, plain and simple."

"Is that what your father found out when he met her?"

"I have no idea what he found out, because he was too dead to tell me." She pushed herself up.

He was up in a flash, putting his arms around her. "I'm sorry, Vanessa. I'm sorry your dad was shot, and I'm sorry that it involved Eileen Stafford."

"Yeah, yeah, yeah." She tried to pull away, but this time, he wouldn't let her. "But you're not sorry you want to drag my ass there and meet her, are you? Because you'd back off that plan if you were."

"I have a job to do." Plus, he believed that deep inside, she wanted to meet her sisters; she was just stubborn to the bone. "Why don't you think of it as finishing the last project your father was working on when he died?"

She narrowed her eyes again. "My father was working on an M&A for a meatpacking company when he died. I did finish it, and made half a million in commission. Thanks for the suggestion, though."

She started to walk, but he got hold of her elbow. "Maybe it's time you let go of some of that bitterness. Maybe you can forgive her."

"She doesn't want forgiveness. She wants my bone marrow—and, you know, I've sacrificed enough blood for her."

He took her hand and put his mouth on her palm, softly kissing it. She closed her eyes and took a quick ragged breath.

"I'm sorry for you," he whispered, keeping her hand at his mouth.

"And now that you know how much I *really* don't want to hold up my end of the deal, why don't we . . ." Taking a step closer, she slid her other hand up his arm, stopping at his neck and pulling his face to hers. "Swim."

He froze just as her lips reached his. "You don't want to swim, Vanessa."

"You're right." She kissed him, softly at first, then opened her mouth, but he didn't take that invitation, so she broke the kiss. "I'm just going to go out there and feel sorry for myself for a while."

"You'd better hurry. It's getting dark."

"You'll find me—if you want to."

Then she turned and ran over the sand, diving face-first into a crashing wave.

Of course, he could see in the dark. Of course, he could swim like a goddamn Navy SEAL. Of course, he would find her like a heat-seeking missile, wrap those impossible arms around her, drag her to the surface, and smother her with tenderness, affection, kisses, sympathy, and sex.

So why didn't he?

Vanessa waited until her lungs nearly exploded before she popped to the surface, just in time for the next swell to break over her head. Salt burned her eyes, and the ninety-degree summer Caribbean water chilled her overheated skin.

She fought the next wave to get to a sandbar, where she could stand while the swells passed chest-high before they broke at the beach. She let her head fall backward, the water dragging her hair off her face. Then she scanned the sea around her, certain he would emerge at any minute.

Naked. Hard. Needing to drown her with sexual sympathy.

Nothing but the waves moved.

Where was he? Hadn't he followed her in? Had he left her and gone back to the house?

She peered into the darkness. The house was completely black, the beach barely lit by moon shadows. Treading water, she finally spotted him when a cloud drifted away from the moon and silver light poured over the sand.

He was on the blanket. Watching her and letting her soothe herself, find her own sympathy, drown her sorrows all alone.

She fell back into a dead man's float, stared at the first few stars, studied another cloud wisp over the moon, found the tiny red dot of a plane. Then she looked at Wade.

He didn't move.

What if a shark attacked? Or the undertow pulled her down? Didn't he care if she was alone in dark water?

Didn't he *want* to swim with her? Didn't he want her as much as she wanted him?

The realization rocked her. It had been a long, long time since she'd wanted a man with an ache so deep and impossible to ignore. She wanted Wade Cordell's hands on her body, his mouth on her body, his *body* on her body.

And he was peeling fruit.

There was a time to be a gentleman, and there was a time to be a lady.

And this wasn't that time.

She rode the next swell in, dragging her feet over the frothy surf, taking slow, sure steps on the glistening path of moonlight that led right to him.

He sat very still, watching her approach, silent, expressionless, expectant.

She reached behind her, pulled the tie of her top, and released it, lifting it over her head and dropping it onto the sand without missing a step.

He sat a little straighter.

Three feet from him, she put her fingers on the hip ties, held his impenetrable gaze, and pulled. The bikini bottom fell to the sand.

"Billy Wade." She knelt in front of him. "I don't care what you call it or why. I don't care if it's part of a deal or just for fun. I want you."

His smile was slow, easy, as sexy as sin. He snapped his knife closed and set it to the side, never taking his eyes from her. "Even though I smell?"

Inhaling slow and deep, she nodded. "I'm starting to like it." She brushed her fingertips over his mouth. "I'm starting to like you."

"That's funny," he whispered, kneeling to meet her mouth to mouth. "I was just thinking the same thing."

His kiss was gentle at first, and slow, of course. Even though she was inches away and completely naked, he didn't throw her down and stuff himself all over her and inside her. Not this man. He was . . .

Deliberate.

He glided his tongue into her mouth.

Purposeful.

He grazed his hands over her breasts and teased her nipples into hard points under his palms.

Calculated.

He leaned back so she could unsnap and push down his shorts, then he guided her to the blanket so she could watch him finish undressing. When he had, he lay next to her, his erection touching her hip, then his hand on her breast, his breath warm on her cheek.

Too slow.

She crushed his mouth with a kiss, closing one hand over his shaft, hungry and desperate to stroke him. Under her lips, she could feel him smile, then laugh.

"We're gonna have to take turns, sweetheart," he said softly. "Once we'll do it my way. Then we'll do it yours. But not both at the same time. That won't be pretty."

"I don't care about pretty." She stroked his buttocks, hard and curved and cut, trying to pull him on top of her so she could ride that hard-on.

"Well, I do." He rose above her and kissed one of her nipples, then circled it with his tongue, holding himself high enough to deny her contact with his erection. "And so should you, because you are so damn *pretty*." He moved to her other breast, sending sparks through her body, making her let go of his backside to travel up his back and dig her fingers into his scalp, pressing his hot, wet mouth against her.

He chuckled again. "Easy, baby; it'll be over too fast."

"I like fast." She ran her hands over his chest and down his abs, then closed her fingers over him, rubbing the moist head and sucking in a breath as she squeezed her way down the shaft, glorying in how it grew harder in her fingers. "I like this." She nestled her fingers under him, cupping his balls to squeeze gently. "I like these."

His smile was a little lopsided from the distraction. "You know what you are?"

"Ready?"

He released a breath of laughter. "You are one beautiful . . ." He nibbled her chin. "Brilliant . . ." He licked her throat. "Sexy . . ." Another swipe over her nipple. "Funny, relentless, sexy, speedy . . ." Then the other one. "Crazy, wild—did I say sexy?" He kissed her mouth. "Woman."

"But not a lady," she whispered.

He held himself above her, braced on his hands, looking into her eyes. "A woman," he repeated. "Whom I very much want to make love to."

She closed her eyes, and he kissed her, sucking in her tongue so she could taste the sweet tang of mango and papaya in his mouth.

"You know what else you are?" he murmured into her ear.

"About to scream if you don't get inside me?" She tried to maneuver toward him again, but he lifted his body to glide his hand between her legs.

"You're always, always, always in a hurry." He slipped one hand around her bottom and lifted her from the blanket, his other hand lightly stroking the wet and swollen center, gently rolling her clitoris between his fingertips. Slow, sweet, and leisurely as hell.

Blood hammered in her ears, and a soft, desperate moan trembled through her whole body. Was that her? Him? "Then I can have three orgasms in the time you have one," she whispered to him.

"And you will." He inserted one finger, kissed his way up her neck, fluttering his tongue into her ear and nibbling her earlobe. Then he delved a second finger into her. He curled the tips and stroked inside her, shocking her with a sexual jolt from head to toe, gliding over her nub as he suckled on her earlobe and grazed his nipples against hers, coarse hair against tender, sensitive skin.

She didn't know where to feel. What to feel. Just . . . bliss. His mouth, his hands, his hips, his chest, his legs—pure pleasure and delight coiled deep inside her.

He controlled her with his hand, his thumb on her clitoris, his fingers deep inside, and she rocked with a swift and furious climax that twisted and coiled and then released with brutal urgency. She slammed her teeth against his shoulder, stifling a scream, letting the sensations career over her, all wicked and warm and not nearly done with him.

"There's one," he murmured as he rolled off her, then scooped her up in his arms and walked straight into the surf as if she were some kind of holy offering to Poseidon. Spent, lost, and completely under his spell, she let her feet and hair and fingers trail through the water as he carried her deeper into the blue-black sea.

A wave crested under her, and she rose with the water. He strode further, her body rising with each swell, high enough so that she floated right into his mouth. He suckled her breast, cupping her bottom in one sure hand.

Finally, he reached the sandbar, stepping up the underwater hill to where the water was only waist-high. They were utterly alone, surrounded by miles of moonlit Caribbean Sea.

He turned her so she could wrap her legs around his hips. "Here's two." He kissed her, wedging his rock-hard thigh between her legs. The wet hairs of his leg tickled like a million delicious fingers, torturing her until one more shuddering climax took her like the relentless ocean waves.

"Wade . . ."

"Shhh. I believe," he said, his large hands clamped over her hips, "that my woman ordered three."

His woman almost drowned at the sound of sex in his voice. "One *with* you."

His eyes were like blue steel in the moonlight, his focus as insanely sexy as anything she'd ever seen. He braced his legs wide and lifted her, positioning her right above his erection. "Open your mouth and kiss me," he ordered softly. "Then open your legs and let me inside you."

"Oh." She barely sighed the word, covering his mouth with hers as he plunged into her in one steady, unrelenting stroke. He went all the way in, taking her, shocking her, invading her so completely that she threw her head back and let out a helpless, strangled cry.

The warm ocean splashed around them as he filled her body. Another kiss, another thrust, timed perfectly for full body assault. Then faster—and faster, until he pumped so hard that he broke the kiss, his eyes half closed, his mouth half open, every muscle tight and throbbing as he groaned with the pleasure of his release.

She came slower, with less fury this time, like dessert—sweet and unnecessary but perfect. She rocked with a little whimper of defeat and delight as the tropical breeze carried scents of salt and sex.

She was completely peaceful. Spent. Safe. Satisfied.

All she could do was close her eyes and rest her head on his shoulder, buoyant and blissful. Finally, she lifted her head, blinking into the darkness to get her bearings.

"Did the tide take us away from the house?" she asked, frowning at the golden light that wasn't the moon, wasn't the stars, and . . . wasn't on before. "Oh, my God!"

He turned to face the beach. "Well, look at that. We've got company."

"Maybe it's Clive!" She wrenched herself away, but he snagged her with a solid grip.

"Maybe it's not." Lights poured from their patio and living room. "Whoever they are, they're not trying to hide."

He set her down and started wading toward the beach, clasping her hand, instantly on full alert.

"It could be anyone," he warned. "Including our friend in the yellow truck."

On shore, he circled them far to the left, avoiding the light that spilled over the beach.

Suddenly, it all went dark, and Wade immediately pushed them down into the soft sand.

"Do you think he's leaving?" Vanessa whispered.

"He saw us." He gave her a solid squeeze. "Stay here. *Don't move.* I'm going to get my gun."

A shadow appeared at the top of the steps, then footsteps pounded down toward the beach.

Wade sprinted, sand kicking from his feet as he leaped toward the blanket, rolled, and came up with his gun pointed at the stairs.

"Drop it," a voice said, accompanied by a distinct click. "Or I'll shoot her."

CHAPTER
FIFTEEN

A FLASHLIGHT INSTANTLY bathed Wade in white as he cautiously lowered his gun. Vanessa cringed, bracing for a shot as the blinding light in her eyes made her blink.

"Get the hell out of here," a gruff—and vaguely familiar—voice demanded.

Vanessa put her hand over her mouth. *Fuck! This isn't happening. It can't be.*

"Don't shoot him, Wade," she said softly, completely mortified. "Uh, hello, Mr. Vex."

He took a few more steps down, and out of the corner of her eye, she could see Wade sliding into his shorts. "Vanessa? Vanessa Porter from Razor?"

His shocked tone told her he had no idea they'd been invited to use his house.

"Yes," she said, shielding her nudity with crossed arms. "Marcus arranged for me to stay here for a few days. Didn't he tell you?"

"Marcus gave you the key?"

"Actually, he just made the call, and we got the key from Nevis Properties," Wade said, walking toward Vanessa to hand her the blanket.

She shot him a grateful look and wrapped it around her. "There seems to be a misunderstanding, and I'm so sor—"

"You have to leave." Vex whipped around, pointing the light up the stairs and leaving them in the dark to watch him take the steps back up to the house two at a time, thudding on the wood, his shoulders stiff in palpable displeasure.

Vanessa let out a little sigh. "Nothing like royally pissing off the company's biggest client by invading his vacation home."

"And embarrassing yourself." He lifted the blanket higher on her shoulder.

"No," she said, anger starting to burn. "I'm single, free, and allowed to have sex on a private beach on my vacation. I'm not embarrassed. But I'm furious with Marcus. *How* could he not tell the client he was going to let one of his employees use the house?"

The house lights came on again, and they could see Vex's silhouette lumbering around the patio and the main room.

"Shit!" She punched the air. "My stuff is all over the bedroom. I dumped my tote on the bed to find a bathing suit and threw my cosmetics bag in the bathroom."

"Let's go get it, then. We're obviously not staying here tonight." He put his arm around her and led her up, pausing to pick up his pen knife, the bowl, and her bathing suit.

Above them, something hit the boardwalk with a thump.

Sharing a quick look, they hustled up the stairs to find her tote and his duffle dumped outside, clothing spilling out.

"Jeez," she said. "He doesn't have to be a total prick about it. It's just a little communication misunderstanding."

"Nothing that involves Marcus Razor is a little communication misunderstanding, Ms. Porter." The voice boomed from inside the house, rich with disgust. "If you don't believe him, just ask him." Vex stepped into one of the open archways, his bulky six-foot frame filling it. "If you have a job when you return."

Vanessa lifted her chin. "Mr. Vex, I am truly sorry about the misunderstanding. I don't think it's anything I should get fired over. This is my friend Wade Cordell." She indicated Wade, who stepped forward with his hand extended.

"Apologize for the inconvenience, sir."

Vex pointedly ignored the offered hand. In the backlighting, he looked far beyond weary. His jowls sagged far more than they should for a forty-something man, and his thin brown hair fell over a deeply lined forehead.

"There *was* a communication breakdown, and I think we can blame faulty satellite service," Vanessa said, rushing to get her words out before Vex ordered them away. Or brandished a gun again. "I'm certain

Marcus would never have suggested we stay here if
he'd known you were coming down for a vacation."

He snorted softly. "This is no vacation, Ms. Porter."
He pointed at the bags. "Go."

Wade bent to scoop them, looking up at Vex.
"Would you mind if we checked to make sure there's
nothing left behind? Vanessa left her—"

"Yes, I'd mind. Get the fuck out of here."

"My other bag is in your bathroom," she said quietly, taking a step forward. "I'll get it, and we'll leave."

Vex held his hand up to halt her. "Don't come into
this house." He walked away, and Vanessa shook her
head in dismay.

"I've never seen him like this," she whispered to
Wade. "He's gruff and demanding, but I've never seen
him this nasty. I'd better call Marcus and do some
damage control ASAP."

"Can he really have you fired?"

She snorted while briskly stepping into a pair
of shorts and yanking on a tank top. "His business
outweighs my contribution tenfold—so, yeah. But
Marcus isn't unreasonable. The worst that would
happen is I just don't do any more deals with Vexell
Industries."

He appeared in the doorway with a black satin bag
in one hand, a revolver in the other, moving it with
dangerous carelessness. "Get out now." He tossed the
bag, and Wade caught it with one hand. "Too bad you
saw me here." He reached back to put his hands on
the door's shutters, eyes blazing. "You might want to
forget that you did."

The shutters met with a whoosh and the click of the lock.

"Oookay," Vanessa said. "So much for the free beach house."

Wade's expression was dark as he stared at the doors, then stepped to the left to see inside the next one just as it slammed closed, too. "Let's get out of here. There are plenty of places to stay in Nevis."

They silently walked up the boardwalk to where he'd left the Honda Element they'd picked up to replace the Jeep and climbed in.

Vanessa kept her tote on her lap, digging for her phone. "I'm going to give Marcus hell for putting me in such an awful situation. That was a nightmare."

Wade said nothing, turning north.

"Don't you think we ought to go to Charlestown?" she asked. "There are probably more hotel options in town. Up here, it's all resorts, and they're full. That's what they said at that Nisbet place."

"Those girls at the bar said their resort had vacancies. And Cliffdwellers is near Newcastle."

If the bimbettes could get them a place to sleep, fine. She was exhausted, angry, and resentful that the first amazing romantic interlude she'd had in forever was interrupted by a pissy client. She dug in the tote's side pocket for the phone, and her gut tightened when her fingers felt nothing. She bit back a curse and groped in every corner of the bag, fighting panic. Where had she put it?

Oh, oh, oh. On the bathroom counter. She'd left it there when she replaced Clive's prescription bottle and tried to reach Marcus. Vex had to have seen it when he got the cosmetics bag. She unzipped that, hope surging that it would be inside.

"Fuck a duck!"

Wade blew out a slow whistle. "Haven't heard that one in a while."

"I don't have my phone!" She reached up and hit the dome light, widening the tote and launching a full-scale search. "We have to go back."

"That'll be fun."

"I'm serious. I can't live without that phone. Everything is on it: every contact, every number, all my links. It's an iPhone, for God's sake."

"It never works. Relax. We'll get it tomorrow. Maybe he'll be in a better mood."

"I don't know Marcus's number by heart!" she exclaimed. "It's in my phone."

"We can get his number, Vanessa," he assured her.

"Not his cell."

He slid a "get real" look at her. "I can have it for you first thing in the morning."

"I want to call him now."

"What can he do now, except say he's sorry he sent us there?" He slipped his hand into hers. "Just relax tonight."

"What if Clive calls me?"

"You never have service here, Vanessa. It's late. We'll go back in the morning and ask him for the phone. Now we need to find somewhere to stay, get some food, and sleep. Tomorrow is a whole new day."

"Right." She tried to let the disappointment and

frustration fade, but it wasn't easy. "It can only get better than today."

"That last part was pretty nice." He rubbed her palm with a dead sexy look.

"It sure was," she agreed. "But he ruined it."

"Only if you let him." He lifted her hand and kissed it softly, his lips warm and soft. "Lucy's putting together as much info as she can, and she'll soon have a fix on where Clive's last message was generated. When we talk to the Bullet Catchers office tomorrow, we'll get Marcus's phone number, and you can call him. We'll be armed with information, fresh and ready to roll. Sound like a plan?"

She sighed, leaning back, letting his good sense wash over her. "You and your plans."

"I just did spontaneous back there on the beach."

She grinned. "And see how good that can be? You liked it."

"I like *you*," he corrected.

She laughed softly. "You sound surprised."

"I am."

"I am, too," she admitted. "For two people with next to nothing in common, we sure found . . . something in common."

He lifted her hand and kissed her knuckles. "That's why I call it the good thing."

Vanessa smiled. That was better than good. Way better.

The boy could boogie.

He was actually a man, but since he was about the

age of Stella's oldest grandson, she thought of him as a boy. But what a dancer!

He whisked her toward their table as "Celebration" ended, a fine sheen of perspiration under his thinning hair matching the one on her clammy neck. They'd been on that dance floor for hours.

She gulped down the glass of sparkling water she'd left waiting, catching her breath.

Jason lifted his own glass of Perrier. "To you, Stella Feldstein. You're an animal out there."

Stella winked at him and growled, just as the rising crescendo of "It's Raining Men" rocked the *Valhalla*'s packed disco lounge.

"I love this song!" She grabbed Jason's arm and headed back toward the dance floor, but he held firm.

"You're killin' me, woman!" He threw his head back, baring a beautiful set of straight white teeth. He didn't have the muscular build that Stella liked to admire, but he was tall and incredibly entertaining.

Ever since she'd practically walked right into him as she left her room on the way to dinner, he'd amused her with little digs about some of the other passengers and witty remarks about everything from fashion to food. It seemed natural to eat together since they were both alone, and then they'd meandered into the disco for an after-dinner drink. Once the DJ got rockin', so did Stella and her new friend.

"Come on," she insisted, tugging harder. "It's our last night at sea."

"Exactly why we need some salt air." He hooked his

arm through hers. "Would you care to stroll the deck with me and share a drink, madame?"

She beamed up at him. "So chivalry isn't dead. Lord, I haven't had this much fun since my last single friend left the cruise. Where were you the first half of this week, anyway? I would love to have introduced you to Vanessa."

"The slinky blonde from New York who's always in a rush?"

Stella's eyes went wide with surprise. "You know her?"

"How many Vanessas could there be on one cruise?" he asked, guiding her to an opening in the bar and signaling for a drink. "I met her on the first day, on the tender over to Anguilla. Where has she been?"

"God knows."

The bartender arrived and looked expectantly at Stella. "I don't drink because of my meds," she told Jason.

"You sure? Last night in port and all. How 'bout something light?"

"Okay. That pink wine."

"A white zinfandel for the lady," he said, "and I'll have a vodka gimlet."

Stella turned to watch the dancers, and when the bartender delivered the drinks, she picked up the tab. "I'll sign for this round. You've been a terrific partner to a talkative old lady."

"You are not talkative or old, Stella. And you do the bump! Not a single woman on this cruise can do the bump. I thank you for that, and my drink."

She giggled, letting him lead her out of the lounge and into the massive brass and blue atrium at the center of the ship. They headed to the wide stairs that led up to the main deck. All the way up, faces she recognized beamed at her.

"Hello, Stella!"

"Hi, Mrs. Feldstein."

"Saw you dance your pants off in there, Stell."

Jason sipped his drink, leading the way but not greeting the people she said hello to. He must be shy. That's why she hadn't seen him all week. She'd taken enough cruises to know the introverted passengers lay low until the very end, then they showed up and realized they'd missed the best part of the week: the other people.

When they reached the top, she lifted her glass. "You shouldn't have been so invisible this trip, Jason. I bet you would have had more fun."

"To the hottest dancer on the ship." He clinked her glass and sipped.

"I'm hot all right," she joked, fanning herself. "But you're sweet."

"What about your friend Vanessa?" he asked, looking around as if he only half cared about the answer, but so transparent she almost laughed. "Why'd she leave the ship?"

"She's looking for a friend who's somewhere in the islands."

"Have you heard from her?" He sipped and looked left, then right.

"Not a word. But her phone sucks raw eggs."

He spewed a little drink.

"That's her expression," she said. "I just liked it."

Brown eyes twinkled at her over the rim of his glass. "I do, too."

"You would have liked her."

"I did, when I met her. She was pretty." His eyes widened. "Was? We're talking about her like she's dead. She must be coming back to the ship, right? Or at least to St. Barts."

"Well, she did say she'd meet me at the dock in St. Barts tomorrow, but I don't know about that girl. I may have seen the last of her."

"Really?" He looked devastated.

"Ohhhh," she said, drawing the word out and pointing at him with a knowing finger. "Now I get it."

"Get what?"

She could have sworn color rushed into his cheeks. What a sweetie. He was actually trying to fool her—as if he could!

"You want to meet her, don't you?" she said. "That's why you're spending all this time with me. You saw me with her earlier in the week."

He opened his mouth, then closed it, fighting a smile. "Yes. I've been looking for her since I saw her on the tender in Anguilla, but I haven't caught a glimpse since . . ."

"St. Kitts. That's when she left." She grinned, so proud of her instinct. "She's a very sweet girl, under all that New York brashness. Smart as hell, too."

He smiled. "You're killin' me again, Stella. I really want to meet her."

"Find me tomorrow when we dock in St. Barts, in case she shows."

"I'll do that."

"Well, the wine went to my head for sure." She held out her glass. "Or I've just had enough fun for one night. This old bubbe has to turn in."

He took her drink and set it on a cocktail table. "Let me walk you to your room."

One floor up, on the Clipper Deck, she pulled out her card key—well, Vanessa's card key, and who could blame her for upgrading?—and reached up to give him a peck on the cheek. "Good night, Jason. Meet me on the dock tomorrow if I don't see you at breakfast."

"Count on it." He gave her a quick hug, and she slipped the key into the door, opened it to the dark cabin, and wiggled her fingers good night before she closed and locked the door.

Sweet boy. Good dancer. Not manly enough for Vanessa, though—especially after she'd met the "eleven" who was looking for the girl a few days ago. She reached for the light on the dresser, just as a massive hand clamped over her mouth.

"Go into the hall, and get him back here." The voice was so low, so close to her ear, she almost didn't know what he said.

"Mwhah?"

He jerked her toward the door, a brutally powerful man with an arm like rock and a stench like the bottom of a subway. "Go into that hall, and make him come back in here. Now. Make him." He knocked her head against the wooden door, the clunk scaring her more than the pain.

"Mwah do you meee?"

"I mean stick your ass into the hall, call your friend, and tell him you need help in this room." Something hard poked into her side. "Or you're dead."

Terror snapped through her, and she nodded furiously, seizing the door with shaking hands.

If she called Jason back in here, was she just getting him killed? And would she die anyway, too? What if she just—

"Scream and I shoot." The gun moved up to the middle of her back.

Her hands shaking so hard she could hardly turn the dead bolt, she fumbled with the latch, opened the door, and leaned out. He gripped her by the hips so she couldn't run. At the end of the hall to the right, she saw a man at the stairway.

"Jason?" She croaked.

The figure paused but didn't turn.

"Louder," the man growled.

She cleared her throat and raised her voice. "Jason?"

He half turned and looked down the hall.

"Can you come back? I . . . need to . . ." She tried to frown, willed some form of silent warning and plea. "Talk . . . to you."

"It's urgent." The words hissed in her ear. "Tell him it's urgent."

She nodded furiously. "It's urgent."

She saw Jason tense, pull back, and then run up the stairs. Before she took her next breath, he was gone.

"He . . . he ran away!"

"The fucking bastard."

The gun jammed harder, and Stella closed her eyes, muttered her mother's name and a Yiddish prayer, and waited for the shot that would end her life.

CHAPTER
SIXTEEN

"You're awake."

"Am I ever." Wade tightened his arm around Vanessa's stomach and pressed against her, his breath sending goose bumps down her back. He curled his leg over hers and tucked what was about to be yet another hard-on in the perfect curve of her backside.

Had anything ever felt this good? Yeah, that romp in the ocean was mighty sweet.

He turned her so he could see her face. He kissed her forehead, her eyes, worked his way toward her mouth, and spent a few minutes exploring her lips with his tongue and her nipple with his thumb.

"You want to know what stupid is?" he asked as he broke the kiss but still fingered the tip of her breast, making it harden the way his cock did.

She laughed. "If that's not a trick question, I don't know what is."

"Stupid is when I saw you and thought you weren't my type."

"I dropped an F-bomb, no doubt."

He kissed her. "Several."

"Types can change." She tightened her thighs and rode his growing erection once, pulling a moan of pleasure from his chest.

"No shit, as you would say." He kissed her, their bodies moving naturally against each other.

"People can change, too," she added. "So maybe I can clean up my language."

Her skin was like warm satin. "Doubtful."

"Thanks for the vote of confidence." She nuzzled into him. "Maybe you could lose that piece you pack, and I could wash my mouth out with soap, and we could see each other again when we're back on solid ground."

"Maybe."

She inched back. "You'd never live without that gun, would you?"

"I can't. It's part of who I am."

She pulled completely away, leaving him aching for what he'd just held. But he stayed still and watched her expression change.

"A gun is part of who you *are*? Why? They are instruments of death, Wade."

He'd known this was coming. He'd known that once the lust wore off, she'd realize she'd just slept with the enemy.

And she didn't even know how totally vile he was.

"Guns are designed to do nothing but kill people and commit the worst crimes in the world," she said.

It's not murder when the world is a better, safer place and thousands of people are alive because of your skills.

Somehow, he didn't think Vanessa and Lucy Sharpe would be of one mind on that point.

"Not the worst crimes," he corrected. "You don't need a gun for those." He threaded his fingers into her hair and tried to guide her toward his body. "C'mon, sweetheart. You don't want to have this conversation now."

"*You* don't want to have it."

"You got that right."

She propped herself up on her elbow, and he just knew she was about to launch into a speech that was going to kill his hard-on, wreck this middle-of-the-night sex, and make him rethink what stupid was. Stupid was getting into an ethical discussion with a boner and a beautiful woman in the same bed.

He put his hand over her mouth before the diatribe began. "Listen to me, Vanessa. When I was about three years old, my daddy put a rifle in my hand. That's just the way it is where I grew up."

"Yeah? Well, you have two hands."

"True. And Mama put a Bible in the other one, just to confuse me."

"So you shoot better than you pray."

"Oh, I pray. Right before I shoot. And . . ." Why not tell her? The mood was ruined anyway. "Whether or not you like this, I shoot very well. Real straight. Real far. Real . . . well."

"Good for you." She dropped her head onto the pillow with a puff of disgust, then looked hard at him.

"If I ask you a really personal question, will you answer with the absolute truth?"

Oh, man, he hated this. But she had the right. They'd made love, they'd trusted each other. Shouldn't she expect honesty? He might lose her forever, but he didn't want to lie. The lies were the hardest part of what he'd done. One of the hardest, anyway.

"Go right ahead and ask me," he said, expecting the worst.

"How many people have you murdered, Wade?"

He met her gaze straight. "In war, killing someone is your job, so it's not considered murder."

"How many?"

"Are you sure you want to know the truth?"

"Yes." She lifted herself higher. "One? Ten? Fifty?"

Any number he told her would make her regret having given herself to him. "You really don't—"

"How fucking many, Wade?"

"Four."

She stared at him. "You've killed four people."

He'd killed more than that during the war, but only four would be considered murder by her.

"One in Pakistan, a perfect hit to the apricot of an Al Qaeda operative. An apricot's right here." He touched the back of her skull, above the spine. "Guarantees instant death."

She twitched with revulsion, as he knew she would.

"Then I shot a warlord in Quezon City in the Philippines, from sixteen hundred yards away, freeing sixty people he'd been starving in a prison." He paused to let that sink in. "Next, I took down a dirty diamond miner in Sierra Leone who was single-handedly re- sponsible for the deaths of dozens of children."

She still hadn't blinked. "That's three."

"Well, the last one," he said, closing his eyes on a sigh of self-loathing, "was just a big, bad mess in Budapest. That's when I decided to quit consulting for the U.S. government and do some private-sector work."

"So . . . you're . . . like . . . a paid assassin?" She sounded horrified.

"Your tax dollars at work."

Seconds crawled by, marked by his steady heart- beat tracking the endless time that she looked hard at him and *judged*. She surely found him guilty and despicable.

But her expression softened. And she sighed. And, God in heaven, reached out and touched his cheek.

"You sound pretty miserable about it, Billy Wade."

His stomach dropped. "I'm not proud, if that's what you mean. I did my job. I did it right."

"But I would expect a macho military guy like you to wear those . . . kills . . . like badges of honor. All those people saved, children avenged, baddies blasted."

"I have a lot of mixed feelings," he admitted, want- ing to kiss her fingers for the comfort they offered. Did she have any idea what this meant to him?

"Maybe you're not cut out for that work."

"My aim is."

"But your heart isn't." She took her hand away, her cheek resting on her arm, her expression the exact opposite of what he expected and dreaded. "There was that other hand."

"I didn't open the Bible much."

She nodded, then grew quiet.

"You want to get out of bed, take a hot shower, and wash me off you now?" His voice sounded strained.

She shook her head. "We took a shower about two hours ago. Or did you forget?"

Forget that she got on her knees, water pouring over her head, and took him into her mouth in the most intimate way imaginable?

"I remember," he said softly, rolling onto his back to stare at the ceiling. "But I understand if you regret it now."

She shifted on the bed, and he half expected to feel her weight disappear as she got up, but instead, he felt her warmth as she pressed against him.

"You know what I think, Billy Wade? I think you hate yourself enough for both of us," she whispered.

He turned his head. "How do you know that?"

"It's coming off you in waves. Just like when I talk about the woman in jail who gave birth to me. Hatred—whether it's directed at yourself or someone else—is as real and tangible as love."

He ached to reach for her. "Sometimes I think . . ." The words stuck in his throat, very difficult to form. "About their families."

She closed her eyes as if it hurt, listening.

"Sure, they were evil. Drug lords, terrorists. A torturer. But someone, somewhere, must have loved them. Right?"

She put her hand on his cheek and stroked it with pure tenderness. "Last night, you told me it was time for me to forgive my birth mother. Maybe it's time for you to forgive yourself."

Maybe it was. He briefly closed his eyes, taking her into his arms and pulling her close.

"Vanessa, honey, you are one surprising package to unwrap. I expected a major rant on gun control, the horrors of government, and a boot to the sofa, at least. You do have a soft spot, and this is the last thing in the world I would have expected to bring it out."

She smiled. "Don't tell my clients."

He kissed her. "You don't hate me."

"It's random evilness that I hate, and the possibility of accidental deaths when people carry guns." She looked up at him, her eyes blazing with sincerity. "But I know what kind of world we live in. Sounds like you did some ugly things because you were trying to make it better."

He kissed her, pulling her silky, sexy, womanly body to his to inhale her sweet smell and warmth. Despite his erection, the kiss was simple, sweet comfort.

He stroked her hair, rocking her and being rocked, feeling the most contentment he'd known in a long time. For one crazy second, he fell a little in love with the woman in his arms.

"Now, how is it," he asked, "that you can be so reasonable about my messy past but can't let go of all that hatred you have for a woman who, in all fairness, could have just as easily had an abortion back in 1977?"

She stopped rocking. "You have no idea how hard it is for me to be affectionate. Yet you'll risk ruining this moment by bringing that up?"

"You're affectionate. You're amazing. You practically shimmer with sex appeal."

She curled a silky leg around him, then climbed on top of him.

"Sex is not affection." As if to prove that, she opened her legs and drew him to her, reaching between them to stroke him.

He instantly grew hard and achy. "It's certainly *affecting* me."

"Ha ha. It's affecting me, too," she said huskily, widening her legs. "Because you're going inside me now, and you're going to come so hard you won't remember your name—and then I'm going to do the same thing."

She arched and pushed him inside her, making his dick swell and pulling a surprised hiss from between his teeth.

"And that will be amazing and shimmering with sex appeal, or whatever you said, but it won't be affection." She pushed herself fully down on his erection. "It will be fu—"

He flipped her over so hard a shocked breath came out. He smashed his mouth onto hers, clashing teeth at the contact. "No," he said roughly, thrusting back inside her. "It isn't that. Don't say that."

She met him with so much force their hip bones smacked. He fought everything in his body that said to pump hard and prove her right. Instead, he pulled out of her, rising to separate them.

She groaned in disappointment. "What are you doing?"

Kneeling above her, he lowered his head to her breast. He licked and circled and sucked, kissing his way down her flat stomach. "Showing you affection."

She laughed a little, the movement tightening her abs and holding him there to run his tongue over each muscle. She cooed, tunneling her fingers into his hair, guiding his head as he nibbled left and right, tasting her skin, licking her navel, murmuring meaningless words of *affection* as he adored her body.

She arched her hips and pushed him lower, toward the scent and moisture that attracted him like a magnet.

"Call it whatever you like, Wade," she moaned. "Just don't stop."

He bypassed the tantalizing tuft of blond hair to work his way down the inside of her thigh. He drifted lower, filling his mouth and face and hands with her smoothness, lifting her leg to kiss the back of her knee and trail his tongue all the way down her calf.

She bunched the sheets in her fists, whimpering, shivering with each kiss, rising and rocking on the bed. When he kissed her feet, she trembled and giggled, and when he started up the other leg, she spread for him.

He wanted to show her affection. Wanted to show her how much he appreciated her response to his miserable past. Wanted to taste her come in his mouth and give her more pleasure than anything she'd ever known. He wanted to tell her all that, but her eyes were closed, her body was undulating, and she wasn't interested in conversation right now.

He'd tell her later, when he'd finished showing her what affection was. So he did this at his pace, taking his time to return to the top of her thigh, then braced her hips under his hands.

He reached up to stroke her breast and lowered his head and licked the soft, wet center of her. She rose to meet his mouth, writhing, pleading, and pushing his shoulders to encourage him to swallow her whole.

He blew on her hair and then closed his whole mouth over her, tonguing her completely, flicking the nub and sucking juice and inhaling the tangy smell of arousal. She was glistening, hot, and thrumming under his lips.

"Wade." She dug her fingers into his hair, rocking as her orgasm threatened. "I've had enough affection. Please . . . please . . . I want you inside me." She practically yanked him up, wrapping her legs around his hips. "Oh, God, *please*."

He finally climbed on top of her, blind with sweat and fueled with the rush of blood, and entered her. His whole body burned furious with need, and he grunted with the raw pleasure of being inside her.

She came instantly, biting his skin and digging her nails into his arms. He exploded with her, one long, endless, blistering orgasm, stealing every drop he had in him.

When their breathing quieted and their hearts slowed and their skin cooled, he lifted his head to look at her. Now he'd tell her all those things he wanted to say. Now he'd tell her about affection and forgiveness and the way he felt about her right now.

But the words froze as he saw the moisture on her face and in her eyes. "Why are you crying? Because of all that affection?"

"No."

"Because it was too intense?"

"No."

"Because now you know how *good* the good thing really is?"

She let out a strangled laugh, shaking her head. "I knew that down on the beach."

"Then why?"

"Because you're the kindest, sexiest, sweetest man I ever met."

"Yeah?" He fought a satisfied smile, contentment rolling over him. "Thanks."

"And you've killed four people in cold blood."

"You just forgave me that past."

"Yes. But forgiving and forgetting are two different things."

His head dropped onto the pillow again. What did he expect? All the affection in the world couldn't erase the truth.

Saturday mornings were a little different from most workdays at the Bullet Catchers headquarters. Lucy relished the atmosphere in her home on Saturdays, when as many of her staff members as possible gathered to review the status of ongoing projects and receive new assignments.

Sometimes as many as six or eight of her staff arrived in the morning, and the late afternoon often transformed into something social and fun. If Johnny Christiano was in town, he'd cook something outrageous. Dan Gallagher would invariably start a touch football game, which, if Alex Romero and Max Roper were both involved, could turn into a friendly blood-and-testosterone bath on her lawn.

Sometimes Chase Ryker would join them, as he had a few months ago, when he brought Arianna Killian into the company as their first psychic crime solver.

Earlier this morning, Lucy's former assistant Racquel had arrived, glowing from her year of travel with Grigori Nyekovic, to announce she'd become the Russian millionaire's fiancée.

Anticipating the afternoon as much as the morning's work, Lucy stepped away from the window to gather her notes for the conference call with Wade, but she stopped when a dark sedan pulled into the driveway below.

She checked her watch. Imagine that. He was on time.

Lucy curled her fingers into fists as she watched Jack Culver step out of the car, and even from there, she could see him take a slow, deep breath.

Why did the two of them always need extra oxygen when they were in the same room?

At her desk, she called up the day's agenda on her BlackBerry, just to make sure Avery had sent the memo out exactly as she'd asked. This week's agenda included a list of all attendees, so Dan wouldn't be shell-shocked by the sight of the man who'd almost killed him.

The heads-up gave him fair warning if he wanted to skip today's meeting. He was deep on a security analysis for a company in the city, which provided an easy excuse for not coming. He rarely missed a Saturday, though. In fact, he was usually the last to leave.

So maybe he would show up and take his seat at her right, reminding all of the Bullet Catchers, and *former* Bullet Catchers, of his unofficial position in the company.

She buzzed her assistant. "Jack Culver just arrived. Please take him straight to the war room. Miranda and Fletch are already in there, I believe."

"They are."

"And I probably don't need to tell you this, but—"

"Don't tell Jack anything, no matter how much he tries to con it out of me?"

Lucy laughed. "I guess I *don't* need to tell you."

"Don't worry, Luce. I have his number."

Stronger and smarter women than Avery Cole had thought they had Jack's number; then they . . . lost it. "Just be sure he doesn't leave with yours."

Avery chuckled. "Got it."

Lucy scooped up her files and breezed into the war room from her library entrance. Everyone was dressed down, but that didn't change the charged atmosphere in the room, where flat-panel monitors on every wall showed information key to every assignment.

Sage Valentine, Lucy's niece and Johnny's live-in girlfriend, ran the war room with remarkable organization, having transferred her skills as an investigative reporter into becoming an extraordinary manager of the Bullet Catchers' research and investigation department. She'd single-handedly made what was once just a computer room with a wall map into the high-tech heart of the company, including the Bullet Catchers Locator System, which fed a constant stream of information about the location and status of everyone in the company.

The only thing that looked like the old conference room was the fifteen-foot-long antique mahogany table in the center of the room, and right now, that table was covered with some newspapers, a map of the Caribbean, a picture of Vanessa Porter, several computer printouts, a few birth certificates, and . . . doughnuts.

"Hungry, Fletch?" She sat at the head of the table, her gaze flickering over the pink and white Dunkin' Donuts box, then up to meet the twinkle in his amber eyes.

"They're for Jack," Fletch said in his thick Aussie accent, his dimpled smile telling her that he was just looking to make his mate comfortable in what was surely going to be an uncomfortable situation. "They're his weakness."

"One of them," Lucy said dryly as she shifted her attention to Miranda. The fragile beauty looked stronger every day since her ordeal in California. Fletch had put a spark in her gray-blue eyes and pink in her chiseled cheekbones. "Miranda, is there any news on Eileen?"

"Some," she said, brushing back a wavy lock of auburn hair. "The doctors have agreed to forgo the heavy doses of chemo that usually precede a bone-marrow transplant. I've optimistically assured them we'd have a potential donor very soon." Her gaze shifted to the maps of the Caribbean in the center of the table. "After Vanessa takes a blood test, assuming things are positive, they can perform the procedure the moment Eileen's out of a coma. Until then . . ." She glanced at Fletch.

"They think since Eileen has responded once to Miranda's voice, she might again, so we're headed back there today."

"Take one of the Bullet Catchers planes," Lucy said. "You've gotten over your fear of flying, haven't you, Miranda?"

"She still needs some moral support," Fletch said quickly. "Which I'd like to continue to provide."

"No worries, Fletch. I'm keeping you off any assignments until Wade has returned with Vanessa and Jack Culver finds the third sister."

"Did someone say my name?" Jack strolled in, remarkably clear-eyed, clean-shaven, and . . . had he actually ironed his shirt?

For Jack, that was damn near formal.

Fletch greeted his friend with a handshake and a quick pat on the back. He was the only Bullet Catcher to stand by Jack when the shooting accident happened; their friendship was deep and solid. That's why Jack had turned to Fletch when he needed help in finding Eileen's daughters.

Miranda gave Jack a warm hug, confirming that the three of them had obviously been spending time together.

Jack turned to Lucy with a half-smile, his dark eyes hooded just enough to suggest he was hiding something. "Good morning, Ms. Sharpe."

"Jack. Have a seat. And a doughnut."

He pulled back the chair to her right. He knew damn well that Dan Gallagher usually sat there.

"You're pushing your luck," she said, softly enough that no one else heard it.

"One of my favorite pastimes," he said as he dropped into the chair and flipped open the Dunkin' Donuts lid. His fingers hovered between the chocolate and the glazed. "What do you say, Lucy? Would you like gooey or rich?"

"I don't eat sugar," she said, opening the file in front of her.

"That's right. You're sweet enough."

She splayed both hands on the pages in front of her and gave him a warning look. "We're here to launch the full-scale search for the third Stafford sister, Jack. Under your direction." She nodded a little to underscore that huge concession. "Please give us a complete status report on everything you've discovered regarding her identity to date. Sage, you probably want to join us for this."

"Be there in a second, Luce," Sage said from her terminal, fingers flying over the keyboard. "I think I've got the location on that phone call to Vanessa Porter."

"All right. Jack, what do you have?"

He placed a doughnut on a napkin in front of him. "First tell me about Vanessa. Any change in the situation down there?"

Everything in her wanted to remind him that she ran the meetings, but there were too many eyes observing this exchange, so she let it go. "She's still reluctant to leave the islands until she locates the friend she went there to find, and, to be honest, she isn't overly enthusiastic about the opportunity we've presented her."

"Euphemism alert," Jack said dryly. "So she knows and doesn't want to help. Can we force her back here somehow?"

"No." Miranda leaned forward. "I totally understand how she feels, and the decision has to be hers."

Lucy nodded. "I agree, although Wade is doing everything to help her make the right decision, and make it quickly. But now I want to talk about the third Stafford daughter." She looked pointedly at Jack. "What do you have so far?"

"Not a helluva lot, I'm afraid." He pulled out a tattered investigator's notebook.

"You really ought to try technology, mate," Fletch said, laughing.

Jack just shrugged and flipped a page. "The best lead I've had so far came from Rebecca Aubry, the nurse-midwife at Sapphire Trail who claimed to have done the tattoos. She gave me a birth cert—which was promptly stolen—with a lead on the family surname Whitaker, somewhere in Virginia. I've been sweeping the state for a female with that name or maiden name of the same age. I've found a few, but they don't check out."

"I can expand on that easily," Sage said, standing up from her computer to tighten her long honey-blond ponytail.

"Knock yourself out," he said, taking a bite. "I'll be happy to meet with anyone you find."

He looked at Lucy, his dark eyes wary and questioning. She knew that look. There was something else, and he wasn't sure he wanted to tell her.

"Come on," she said. "I want to help."

Powdered sugar rained on the napkin as he brushed his fingers. "All right. The arresting officer on the case was at the nurse's house yesterday, helping himself to papers and photos that could have been from Sapphire Trail. He's either infiltrated Rebecca's life somehow or just broke into the house—I'm not sure, but I can find out."

Lucy turned a page in her file. "You mean Willie Gilbert."

"Yes."

"I had one of my men arrange to interview him as well."

"What?" He couldn't keep the surprise out of his voice. "Why?"

"He arrested Eileen and got her signed confession. He'd be the first person I'd try to talk to."

"If you were investigating the murder, yes. *Not* if you are trying to find a child sold on the black market."

"I can't separate the two," Lucy said quietly, studying the file as she readied the bomb she was going to drop. "So it made sense for Dan to interview Willie Gilbert." She flipped a page and finally looked up to meet Jack's dark, dark gaze.

"I thought he was in New York doing a security analysis," he said.

"He had a break," Lucy replied, her tone meant to remind him that she decided who went where in this company.

"I hope he was careful," Jack said pointedly. "Because he's a mean son of a bitch. The last time I visited Willie, it ended with a threat to harm Eileen's daughter. At that point, we assumed that was Miranda, but we didn't know yet that she'd had triplets. The other two sisters could still be a target if someone is using them as blackmail to keep Eileen quiet."

"That's a good point," Lucy acknowledged. "We'll keep a close watch on Willie Gilbert."

The door to Lucy's office popped open.

"That won't be necessary." Dan Gallagher cruised into the war room with his signature smile and confident walk. Nobody said a word as he sauntered around the table, giving a wink to Sage, knuckles to Fletch, a smile to Miranda. He reached Lucy's end of the table and paused directly across from Jack.

"Doughnuts, huh? Must be a cop in the room."

Jack met his gaze. "What do they eat for breakfast in the FBI?"

"Cops." He dropped into the opposite chair, reaching over to put a hand on Lucy's. "Hey, Juice. How's tricks?"

She slid her hand out from under his. "What do you mean, it won't be necessary to keep an eye on Willie Gilbert?"

"Because there was a fire in his condo last night." Dan looked directly across the table at Jack. "I would think you would've known this, since this is your case and all."

Jack ignored the dig. "What happened?"

"Willie didn't get out in time. He's toast."

"And the contents of the condo?"

Dan grinned. "That tender side of yours always gets me, Culver. Burned to the ground and everything in it."

Jack dropped back in his chair. "Arson?"

"They don't know yet. But no one else was killed."

"He can do anything," Jack muttered under his breath.

"Excuse me?" Lucy asked.

"That's what Eileen said: 'He can do anything.' I thought she might mean Willie Gilbert, but . . ." His sigh was full of frustration. "Damn, I was sure she meant Willie Gilbert."

"Jack," she said softly, leaning close to him. "Whoever *he* is, we can find him."

"*I* can find him," he replied.

She put her hand on his arm. "*We* can find him."

"I've got Wade Cordell on the line," Sage announced.

Dan pushed back from the table, hard enough to jostle it. "You know what," he said, his casual tone belying the glint in his green eyes. "This aspect of the case doesn't concern me. I'll wait in your office." He paused and gave Lucy a meaningful look. "If that's okay with you, Juice."

The nickname, long ago derived from the term "Juicy Miss Lucy," usually made her smile. In front of Jack, it made her uncomfortable. "That's fine."

Dan left, the soft click of the door latch as effective as a slam. She refused to react, and, to his credit, so did Jack. She reached forward to touch the screen built into the table, calling up the audio. "Talk to me, Wade. We have a full house."

"Hey, Luce." The slow Southern drawl was like sunshine in the middle of the lightning storm that had just raged in the room. "Sage just gave me coordinates of the location for that cell call, and it looks like it's a fairly remote area on the eastern shore of Nevis, not far from where we are. We'll head in ASAP."

"We?" Miranda leaned in a little. "Is Vanessa with you, Wade? This is Miranda Lang."

"She's here, Miranda," Wade said.

Miranda looked at Fletch, emotions colliding over her pretty face. "Can I talk to her?"

Silence.

"Well, she's kind of busy at the moment," Wade finally said. "This isn't a good time."

Miranda nodded as though she couldn't quite speak, then said, "It's fine. I understand."

"Wade, once you find Vanessa's friend," Lucy said, "I can have a plane there in a matter of hours. There's a small airport in Nevis at the northern section of the island. The town is Newcastle."

Silence again, then, "Uh, yeah. Just a second." After another pause, Wade lowered his voice. "Listen, we're not getting on that plane until we know where Clive Easterbrook is and know that he's safe. This little gimme is a lot more complicated than you thought, Luce."

"I understand that, Wade. And you'd be doing the NYPD a big favor by finding him, too."

"How's that?" Wade asked.

"The Charlie French murder investigation is in full swing," Lucy said, opening another file in front of her. "I checked into it after we talked. Even though the official statement is that it appeared to be random violence and they're doing hard forensic investigation of her apartment, evidently some clues have them focused on an ex-boyfriend who has an airtight alibi. They're spreading out to people at her gym and work, including Clive Easterbrook, who is on an extended vacation out of the country."

"He's hiding from someone or something, I have no doubt of that," Wade said. "When we find him, I hope we'll know what it is."

"Oh, and Wade," Lucy added, pulling out the business section of that morning's *New York Times*. "Didn't you say you were staying in Nicholas Vex's house?"

"Not anymore. He showed up and kicked our butts to the curb. Why?"

"He's there? In Nevis? Interesting time for a vacation." Lucy turned the newspaper so the others at the table could see the headline. "The EPA filed a complaint yesterday charging Vexell with withholding evidence of its own health and environmental concerns about a chemical used in some of its products."

"The EPA?" Wade sounded stunned.

"That's who would investigate charges like this," Lucy said. "The impact on Vexell's stock probably cost Mr. Vex a few billion by the close of the stock market yesterday. Not to mention he's in boiling-hot water with the press and every major customer he's got. I can't believe he'd leave his company at a time like this."

"Can you find out who at the EPA is working on the complaint?" Wade asked.

Lucy frowned. "Probably. Why?"

"Remember I mentioned Russell Winslow to you? His car went over a cliff here a while ago? He worked for the EPA. It's an interesting coincidence."

Jack raised his eyebrow at Lucy and whispered, "And we all know how you feel about coincidences."

When they finished up the call, Lucy excused herself, heading into her office. Dan stood at the front window, looking outside.

"I don't think I've ever seen you angry," she said.

He didn't turn. "You've never seen me a lot of things, Luce. You've never seen me, say, working somewhere else."

She walked closer. "Is that a threat?"

When he finally turned, she froze, hit by the force of the hatred in his eyes. "I can't stay here if you bring him back."

"I'm not bringing him back, Dan. He's deeply involved in this case and has been from the start. We can solve it and close it faster with him, that's all. He's not even consulting."

"Are you paying him?"

"I'm giving him resources to find the third sister." She sat behind her desk. "Not that it's any of your business. This is my company, Dan."

He shuttered his lids and strolled over to the settee, propping his size twelves up on a table he knew she'd paid twenty-seven thousand dollars for at a Sotheby's auction last year. He'd been with her.

The move was a big *screw you*, and it hurt.

"Dan, I'm working with him for one project. I'm not forgetting the fact that he lied about the extent of his injuries and let a bullet from his gun hit you. He's never going to work for me again. We're going to find that third girl. And if anyone other than the accused is behind the murder, I'd like to find that out, too—on principle."

"That could take a while," he said, a heavy dose of sarcasm in his voice. "Might mean you and Jack Culver working all tight together. *Again*."

She kept her composure. "You are out of line."

"Not denying it, I see."

She pointed a finger at him. "Totally out of line."

"Chill, Luce. So you've got a weakness for a certain someone, and you give in to it once in a while. That makes you human. Might even put to rest those Bullet Catchers rumors that you're not." He stood and smiled that crooked grin of his, but it didn't light his eyes. "I've wondered myself, occasionally."

She just stared at him as the door to the war room

popped open. She didn't have to turn to see who it was, because there was instantly less oxygen in the room.

"I'm all set here, Luce," Jack said. "Sage was able to give me some excellent leads. I'll be in touch."

"All right," Lucy said. "And Dan will work the arson angle with the Charleston P.D."

Jack didn't look pleased, but nodded to Dan. "I'll show myself out."

"I'll come with you," Dan said, looking at Lucy. "As it turns out, I can't stay today."

Lucy sat very still for a few minutes after they were gone, staring at her desk, her antiques, her library. All perfect. Elegant. Structured. Orderly. Controlled right down to the last molecule in her world.

Weaknesses threatened that control. Was Dan right? Was she "giving in to a weakness" for Jack? She despised weakness in her company, in her life, and in herself.

She threaded her fingers through the streak of white hair, a constant reminder of the price she'd paid for losing control. She'd never make that mistake again. Ever.

Chapter
SEVENTEEN

WADE PEERED THROUGH the deluge obscuring the windshield. Parked two miles above Eden Brown Bay on the easternmost side of Nevis, all he could see was a muddy road toward the beach, almost obliterated by the rain forest. The boxy Honda Element was sturdy, but it would take a bulldozer to get through there.

He turned to Vanessa. "We're not going down there—"

"What?" Vanessa hit the dashboard in frustration. "We've come this far. We have a satellite image that shows us his location to within a quarter-mile, and you're going to let a little rain and mud stop us?"

"—in this *car*," he finished, shaking his head in disbelief. "Do you honestly think I would even suggest not going in? We go on foot. Unless you want to wait here, and I go down alone."

Behind the glasses she didn't need but insisted

on wearing, her eyes narrowed. "Like that's gonna happen."

"Okay, then. It isn't going to be easy," he warned. "Especially dressed like that." He dipped his finger into the strap of her maroon tank top, and even just that millisecond of contact with her skin warmed him.

"It wasn't raining when we left," she said. "And I wore sneakers."

And cutoff jeans so short he could see that inner thigh muscle he'd gotten so friendly with a few hours ago. "Yeah, you're dressed for boot camp, all right," he teased, then looked at the soupy sky. "This storm came out of nowhere fast, and it could clear just as quickly."

"I'm not waiting."

He laughed softly. "They'll chisel that on your gravestone, you know that?"

She grabbed the door handle. "On that lovely thought, let's go."

"Hang on a sec." He turned her face to him and slid her glasses off, folding them neatly on the console. "They'll just make it harder for you to see in the rain."

"Thank you." She threw the door open, and he did the same, getting instantly soaked in the downpour.

He locked the car and jogged around the back, coming up behind her so he could talk into her ear over the deafening pounding of the rain.

"You follow me when we're going downhill; you go first when we're uphill. Anything else, we stay side-by-side."

She gave him a salute, and they started off.

The first quarter-mile was pretty easy, a flat, muddy, narrow path with some rocks and roots hidden in the muck. They reached a small incline, slid down, and followed the path under a canopy of thick trees, protecting them from most of the rain. The air was steamy in the darkened tunnel, and staying very close to each other seemed the most natural thing in the world.

"How the hell does someone find a place like this?" she wondered. "And why?"

Wade held some palm fronds back for her so the sharp blades wouldn't slice her skin. "To hide."

"Do you think . . ." She wiped some water from her face and looked up at him. "This firm you work for . . . do you think they can help him out of whatever trouble he's in?"

"Maybe. I'm not a full-time employee, just a consultant. Couldn't say how Lucy'd handle that. She could probably help, but her price is steep." He shrugged and remembered the income reported in Vanessa's file. "You could probably afford it, though."

"Why are you just a consultant?"

He laughed. "That's what Lucy wants to know. I'm sure you'll be amused to hear that this assignment was a 'gift' to sway me to sign a full-time contract. A cushy job in the Caribbean on the tail of a pretty blonde on vacation." He snorted. "Some gift."

She gave him a friendly elbow to the ribs. "Some vacation. Seriously, tell your boss I'm sorry I made it more difficult for you. But when we find Clive, maybe . . ."

"You can try. She's as good a negotiator as you are, and she wants something from you, Vanessa."

"Yeah, I know. Marrow." She waved her hand, the way she always did when she hated a subject and wanted it changed. "Why don't you want to work full-time for her?"

"I'm considering it. Looking at all my options. I've been thinking I'd like to do something that didn't involve bullets."

She nodded, understanding. "Do you want to go back to . . . what *is* south of Alabama, anyway?"

"Ebro, Florida. I like to visit my family, but no, I'm not going back there. In the meantime, I don't actually have a job."

"After what happened to Vexell stock yesterday and our little run-in with the CEO last night, I might not, either. We can go on unemployment together."

"This news is huge for your company."

"God, yes. That stock is in every hedge fund and portfolio we manage." She shook her head. "No wonder Nicholas Vex was a total bastard when he found us at his house. He'd just lost a billion dollars. More. God, I wish I could reach Marcus." She shot him a dark look. "And I'm sorry, but your sources are wrong. That number you got from New York is not Marcus's cell phone, because he would no sooner disconnect his phone than he'd cut his arm off."

"It's the right number. Lucy's team doesn't make mistakes like that."

"They did this time. I just wish to hell I had my phone. And what if Clive tries to call me? He'll get

Vex, a pissed-off client. Former client, maybe." She wiped some wet strands from her face. "What a freaking mess."

"Don't you think it's funny that of all places on earth, Nicholas Vex would show up here?" he asked.

"Not funny to me."

"Just a few days after someone who used to work for the EPA was killed in a hit-and-run?"

She slowed at the implication. "I actually thought of that when you told me about the stock tumble."

"What about Charlie French?"

Vanessa stopped completely. "What about her?"

"You said she did a lot of deals with Vexell."

Water drizzled down her cheeks, but she didn't bother to try to wipe it away. "You think her murder is related to this, don't you?"

"I think it's possible."

She gave him a little push. "Come on. We can't waste a minute."

He broke through another deep thicket of branches, and they pushed through the last of the overgrowth, just to find that the road abruptly ended at a cliff, with a mile-wide vista of treetops that spread all the way to a deserted beach.

"Looks like mother nature is stopping us," he said.

"Shit." She kicked at mud and surveyed the view. "But we know the signal came from somewhere in this quarter-square-mile area."

"And I don't know how he'd leave, unless he has a helo or a boat." Wade walked a few steps away, testing the wet soil of the cliff. "Let's keep going this way.

There isn't a path, but we could probably slosh our way down there. You might end up on your butt, though."

"Then I'll start that way." She lowered herself to the ground, steadied her hands, and rode down the mud hill in a controlled slide, pulling an impressed smile from him.

He made it down on foot, and they went on, silent again because of the pouring rain, until they were fifty yards from the beach. Even with the rain, they could hear the surf and smell the salt.

Wade spotted a small stone structure with a thatched roof tucked into the trees. "There it is."

She followed his gaze. It took a few seconds for an untrained eye, but she found it, too. "Let's go."

"No." He snagged her arm before she got three steps.

"Okay, okay. I know," she said, ready to bolt like a racehorse at the gate. "You want to make a plan. So make it. Fast."

"You have no idea what you're walking into, what his state of mind is, if he's there alone, or if he's armed."

"Armed? Clive?" She shook her head. "Even if he was holed up with an Uzi, he wouldn't hurt me, Wade."

She knew nothing of what desperation could do to people. "You stay back here until I've cased the house and determined if he's there. After I come back, you can call out a warning to him. Got it?"

She nodded, and he inched her back into the deepest cover he could find. "Don't move, Vanessa. I mean it."

"I promise. Just come right back, no matter what you find."

"I promise."

He jogged soundlessly to the house, drawing his weapon as he came around the back, where an empty cot sat on a stone patio, a table next to it with an ashtray loaded with soaked brown cigar butts. He quietly rounded the side of the structure, glancing into a window to see a single room with a kitchenette in the corner, a sofa in the middle, and a simple wooden table with chairs.

In the front, the door was ajar.

He held his weapon with two hands at the ready and called, "Hello?"

Silence.

He shouldered the door open, getting a whiff of stale air. The room was dim, shadowed, and messy. There were dishes in the sink, clothes on the floor, and a can of mosquito repellent on the counter on top of a small piece of paper.

Wade moved toward it, sensing that no one was there, but still alert while he read the note.

Gideon—

I know this is going to make things worse, but it has to be done. I can't let what happened to Charlie happen again.

And if they kill me first, don't let V. get away.

Clive

He heard a distant thumping, and he spun around, ready to fire.

"Wade!" Vanessa came flying around the front, her

face bright. "A helicopter! It just took off about a mile from here, not far from where we left the car. I heard it, and I saw it. Was it Clive? Is he gone?"

He held the note out to her.

She seized the paper, read it, then flipped it over to see a much lighter pencil had been at work on that side. "Oh, my God."

She held it up for him to see a stick figure hanging from a hangman's noose. One word, capital letters, each underlined.

V-A-N-E-S-S-A

"So the V is for Vanessa?" She turned it over again. "That's who he doesn't want to get away?"

"There's one other V," Wade said, pulling her out of the hut. "Vex."

Vanessa put her heart and soul into digging through mud, clawing around trees, and fighting her way to the Honda as fast as possible.

Neither said a word as they heaved their way up the cliff, retraced their steps, and made it back to where they'd parked. Her lungs were aching, her legs were shaking, and her head was ready to explode.

Soaked and muddy, she slithered into the car and pressed her hands against her chest to stem the pain in her lungs. Wade threw himself behind the driver's seat, stabbed the key into the ignition, and tore the hell out of there.

He really could be fast when he wanted to, and as soon as she could talk again, she'd thank him. As her heart rate slowed, all she could think of was Clive.

And Russell Winslow. And Charlie French. And Nicholas Vex.

She looked at the waterlogged note to Gideon Bones more closely.

"Look at this paper." She lifted it up. "It's the very same notebook paper someone used to send me here in the first place."

"Are you sure that's Clive's handwriting?"

"Absolutely. Both sides."

She dove for her tote bag, finding the note she'd been given in the bathroom hallway at the Ballahoo, and held them side-by-side. "Look at this. Not the same writing but definitely from the same notebook."

Wade stayed focused on the road. "Either Clive sent you the note that said he was in Nevis to throw you off, or whoever owns that notebook was there in the house and is up in that chopper with him."

She read the note to Gideon again. "I can't believe he's involved with that big, creepy guy."

"That'll be our next stop," he said. "Right after we talk to Nicholas Vex."

"We can make the afternoon ferry back to St. Kitts," she said, closing her eyes as exhaustion hit hard. "I don't know where else to go."

"How about to the police?"

Well, yeah. There was that. Her eyes popped open. "I just remembered something: Clive had lunch with Russell Winslow the day Charlie was murdered. I remember because he invited me along, saying he might want moral support since it was the first time they'd seen each other since they split up."

"How'd that lunch go?"

"I never heard. He had a meeting with Marcus right afterward. I don't know what it was about, but I remember calling his office to hear about his lunch, and his assistant said he'd gone to see Marcus." She tried to recall exactly what had happened that afternoon. "I had a meeting with a client. Made some calls. Watched the closing bell, worked out, and went home. I never saw him again that day."

"Was that unusual? Not to see him all afternoon?"

"No, we were crazy busy with client meetings and shareholder conference calls. And the next day, the entire office was only talking about one thing: Charlie French. Except I never talked to Clive about it—not alone. We saw each other in the hall, and there were lots of people around, all kinds of tears and hugging and disbelief and speculation. Rumors were rampant. The police talked to some of the people who worked closely with her."

"Clive?"

"He never said if they'd talked to him. And he left two days later. If they wanted to talk to him, he couldn't leave, right?"

He just shrugged. "If he wasn't a suspect and wanted to get the heck out of Dodge, he might. Where was he the night Charlie was murdered?"

She closed her eyes. "I don't know. The next day, he was right there with everyone as the news went around the office. He seemed as upset as everyone else, but we never sat down and had a heart-to-heart about it.

He called me that night and told me he'd booked a cruise."

"And you didn't think that timing was odd?"

"I thought taking a vacation was odd," she said. "We had this running bet over who could go the longest without taking a vacation. So when he told me, I was surprised—but not stunned, with all that was going on. He avoids conflict and controversy, because it can send him spiraling into depression."

"So you just figured he was warding off the blues."

She nodded. "He doesn't get the blues. He gets positively black."

"So you never talked to him about Charlie? Or his lunch with Russell?"

"You know, I didn't. I never had a chance, because we just talked about the cruise. I did suggest he push it back a week so he could come to Charlie's service, but he said he couldn't get on another one for the rest of the summer because that clipper-ship cruise was so exclusive and hard to book."

"But you got on the same ship a month later."

She dropped her head against the window and let out a sigh. "He's never lied to me before."

"Desperation changes people, Vanessa," he said quietly. "I've seen it firsthand."

"I guess I'm about to, because I'm starting to feel very desperate. Can you go any faster?"

"And not go flying off a cliff or roll over one of the huge branches I've been swerving around? No." But he did kick it up a little. There was no road across the middle of Nevis, so they had to drive half the perimeter of the island to get from east to west. The rain had slowed to a steady sprinkle, and traffic was light except in the tiny towns that popped up and disappeared just as quickly. And of course, there was the occasional goat.

They arrived at the road that led to Mango Plantation in less than half an hour. Just before he turned the corner to the orchards, she reached over and put her hand on his arm.

"I owe you big, Billy Wade."

He slid her a look. "You don't owe me anything but a trip to South Carolina."

"I know. I know what we agreed on, and—"

"You're going to reneg."

Her heart swelled at the tone of resignation and expectation. "No, I'm not," she said, meaning it with every fiber of her being. "I'll go. I just meant I owe you on . . . a personal level."

He winked at her. "I'll collect. Don't worry."

He pulled into a grassy area at the edge of the property, next to the Mercedes that had been parked there when they left the night before.

Relief shot through her.

"Thank God," she said, throwing the door open and getting out. "Vex is—"

The wind gusted so hard she almost tumbled back as a sudden rhythmic pulsing shook the air. A helicopter lifted from the sand, hovering as high as the house, then soaring up, the rotors drowning out Vanessa's shout.

"Was that the one you saw before?" Wade hollered, pulling her toward the boardwalk that led to the house. "Was it a Bell?"

"I have no idea," she said, squinting up at the mighty bird. "It was a mile away, and I don't know one helicopter from another. This looks bigger, but I just don't know."

Disappointment and frustration kicked her as hard as the wind from the rotor blades. Had she just missed Clive again?

"Come on," Wade said, jogging down the wooden path to the house.

He slowed his step as they got deeper onto the property, holding her back while he pulled out his gun.

She knew better than to question that. At least two people had been murdered, and the owner of this house was armed. She let him lead the way as the last wallop of the helicopter disappeared, leaving only the soft rush of rain.

"Mr. Vex!" he called as they neared the side of the house. "Nicholas Vex!"

"Nicholas!" Vanessa yelled. "It's Vanessa Porter."

They made their way to the front of the house, where all of the shuttered doors were wide open, pools of water forming where the rain had blown into the house. The main room was empty, and Vanessa waited while Wade checked the bedroom and the bathroom.

"No one's here," he called to her.

"But his car's up there."

"He's definitely not in this house."

"Is my phone in the bathroom?"

He stepped out of the bedroom, reholstering the gun. "I didn't see it."

"Damn," she murmured, turning around to check the counters and tabletops for her phone. "Where the hell is he? His car is here, and he wouldn't go off on a helicopter ride and leave the house wide open in the pouring rain, would he?" She reached out her hand. "Can I borrow your phone? I'm going to call mine and see if I hear it ring."

He handed her the phone, and she dialed, praying for the digital jingle she'd so rarely heard since she got to the Caribbean. The ring sang in her ear, but the house was silent. She went out to the patio, listening for it. Maybe he'd thrown it out last night with the rest of their belongings, and it had landed on the grass. Of course, it would be drowned by now.

She stepped off the boardwalk, looking on the ground as she heard the click of her phone going into voice mail. Swearing softly, she touched the three button, just to hear the number of irate messages from clients she had.

Wade passed her, his eyes locked on the misty beach as he walked toward the steps.

You have twenty-six messages.

Oh, great.

Out of habit and some perverse need to hear bad news, she pressed number one, watching Wade disappear down the first steps of the beach stairs.

"Vanessa, please call me, please." She instantly recognized Clive's mother's thick Long Island accent. "It's an emergency. The police were just here. The phone won't stop ringing. They want Clive." She sobbed, out of control. "Please call me. Tell me if you found him. Please." Her voice cracked. "They think he killed that girl from your company."

She dropped her hand, and the phone hit her thigh with a thud as she stared straight ahead, stunned.

"Vanessa."

Wade's voice floated up from the bottom of the stairs, but she didn't move. Was this possible? Was this happening?

Could she be so wrong about a man she considered her close friend?

"Vanessa." He was more insistent. "Come here."

She moved like a zombie to the top of the stairs, pain and disbelief twisting her insides. "What?" she croaked.

"I found Vex."

She looked past him to the bottom of the stairs, where Nicholas Vex's dead body lay in a heap.

CHAPTER
EIGHTEEN

FOR THE FIRST time in the twenty years since Saul Feldstein had died and left her enough money to travel anywhere she wanted, Stella skipped breakfast on a cruise. Since that evil man had pushed her out of his way and run from her cabin the night before, she'd done nothing but curl in a ball on the bed and quiver.

A hundred times she had the phone in her hand, ready to call security to report the assault. And a hundred times the fine hairs on her neck rose in a warning not to do that. Saul had called it Stella's Sixth Sense, and she never, *ever* ignored it.

So she did nothing until the sun rose over morning-blue water outside the cabin window, and the sounds of the crew preparing to dock at St. Barts filled the ship. Then she forced herself to get up and pack what she'd brought into Vanessa's cabin, waiting until the last possible moment to go back to her original room. What if he was out there, ready to pounce again?

She opened the doors of the tiny closet and looked at the few pieces of clothing that Vanessa hadn't taken with her. There was more in the drawers and some stuff in the bathroom. The cruise company would probably empty the room, but who knows what would happen to Vanessa's belongings?

She found Vanessa's suitcase, flipped it open on the bed, and started throwing things in. When she stuffed some underwear into the zipper compartment, she felt a magazine and pulled it out, curious about what Vanessa had been reading.

But it wasn't a magazine. It was a glossy business brochure, the cover sleek and pale, shiny gold with black raised letters. *Razor Partners LLC. Alternative Asset Management.*

Whatever the heck that financial babble meant. Saul had kept their money in the bank, and it did just fine, thank you very much. She flipped a few pages, skimming phrases like "mezzanine funds" and "restructuring advisory partners." The last section was called "Your Partners," with a picture of a silver-haired fox, the man the company was named after.

She flipped the page to see the other photos and bios, skimming to the P's to find Vanessa.

There she was, with her long blond hair and her square black glasses. So pretty and sharp-boned, with her wide smile and fine nose. Stella had loved her instantly and sensed a kindred spirit of strength in the girl who couldn't return a hug. As she started to close the book, her gaze fell on a photo on another page.

Clive Easterbrook?

It wasn't possible. That was Jason! That was the man she'd danced with, who'd run away when she called him last night. The man someone wanted badly enough to threaten Stella with a gun.

Her instinct had been right last night: he *had* been looking for Vanessa. No wonder she'd bumped into him outside Vanessa's cabin. But if he was looking for her . . . then Vanessa certainly hadn't found *him*.

She had to be on the dock. *Had* to be. She'd promised. Stella yanked the last few items from hangers, dumped out the drawer, and swiped the items on the bathroom counter into the bag. She zipped it up, did a quick check of the room, grabbed both bags, and flung open the door.

The coast was clear.

Downstairs at her less expensive cabin, she finished packing her stuff, left another voice-mail message on Vanessa's cell phone, stuffed her unwashed hair into her sun hat, and headed out to the tender embarkation deck. Every face looked familiar and friendly; she'd spent every waking moment making friends. But Jason—Clive—wasn't there.

How had he gotten onboard? The crew would have to have known him. Of course, he'd been on this cruise before, and maybe they'd let him slip on at one of the ports.

She boarded the next tender boat, made small talk

with the other passengers, and scrutinized the decks
for his face.

After docking, she accepted help off the little boat,
gathered her bags and Vanessa's, and stood on the
wide wooden planks at the mouth of Gustavia harbor,
squinting into the sunshine bouncing off the quaint
pink and peach buildings that sloped all the way to
the top of a mountain.

She rolled the suitcases along the dock, scanning
the crowds. With two big commercial cruise ships just
emptying for an excursion, plus the arrival of the *Valhalla,* the town was jam-packed with tourists.

But no tall blonde with horn-rimmed glasses. And
no skinny, thin-haired charmer.

Sighing, she pulled out her cell phone and punched
in Vanessa's number. In the midst of all the dock's
commotion, she heard the digital melody play "Some
Enchanted Evening."

Vanessa was here! Pressing the phone to her ear,
Stella started to turn, looking for her. Vanessa had
programmed that song into her phone as Stella's private ring tone the night they'd met, because it was
Stella's favorite—

"Yes?"

Stella was startled at the man's voice in her ear.

Without thinking, she slammed the phone shut.
It must have been a mistake. She must have dialed
wrong and imagined the song played.

Taking a deep breath, she dialed again . . . and
heard the same notes. She spun toward the sound,
squinting into the crowd, praying she'd see Vanessa

answering her phone. But only a broad-shouldered man in a baseball cap happened to open a cell phone at that moment.

"Yes?"

The same voice.

Did that man have Vanessa's phone? Stella peeked around people to get a better look at him, but his back was to her.

"Who is this?" he demanded.

Who was *this*? She kept her mouth closed and waited as he turned to the side. Was he looking for Vanessa, too? He snapped the phone shut, and Stella's clicked with the sound of a dropped call.

She watched as the man turned, looking for someone.

Was he with Vanessa and maybe got separated from her?

She knew one thing: it wasn't Clive. And it wasn't that eleven who'd asked about Vanessa when they were docked in St. Kitts, the one with the Caribbean blue eyes and that Southern accent that could make a girl go *meshuga*. No, this guy had a thicker neck and meatier shoulders.

And more important, he had Vanessa's phone.

For a big guy, he slithered pretty well through the crowd, making it hard for Stella to keep up with him, lugging her suitcases. But she did, moving like a magnet to his iron, determined to find out what was going on. Maybe he could lead her to Vanessa.

He stepped into a shaded area near some street vendors, slightly away from the crowd. Stella followed, sliding her hat off. She didn't want him to notice her until she knew what the heck he was doing with Vanessa's phone.

She tried to maneuver herself to see his face, but his cap was pulled low, and he wore sunglasses, and he was deep into the shade. He propped one foot on a wooden bench, pulled out a phone, and dialed.

It wasn't Vanessa's phone. His flipped open; her little phone didn't.

Emboldened, Stella dragged her bags to the other side of the bench and sat down, earning a disinterested glance which she didn't dare return. She fanned herself with her hat and acted like the overheated grandmother she was.

He turned away to speak, but she caught the first words. "She's not here."

So, he was looking for Vanessa, too! Stella forced herself not to react but slowly leaned a little to the left to listen.

"Look, we have to stop this cat-and-mouse game right now. She could blow everything for us. Make him an offer, a million for each of them. Test the bastard to see what makes him roll—love or money. My guess is, he'll give up on love and take the offer; then he'll bring them both to my doorstep. Until we have her, and him, we're not in the clear."

Her and him? Vanessa? It had to be. He had her phone, didn't he?

Slyly, she slipped her phone from her pocket and carefully thumbed Vanessa's number.

"Some Enchanted Evening" immediately beeped

from the man two feet away. He yanked out Vanessa's phone and shut it off. Then he walked to a trash can, dropped it in, and started toward the cab stand at the end of the dock.

Meddling was a bad habit, but Stella was too old to stop now. She ignored Saul's loud voice in her head, ignored the hairs on the back of her neck, and followed him. On her way, she grabbed Vanessa's phone out of the trash can and tucked it into her bag.

Vanessa sat across from Wade at a white-linen-covered table for two, so high above the water they had to take a tram up the side of a cliff to reach the restaurant. Soft music floated on a sea breeze, stars flickered in a black-velvet sky, a half-moon hung over the Caribbean Sea, and the most gorgeous, attentive man sat across from her, offering bites of lobster that melted in her mouth.

"Pretty romantic evening, considering the day we just had," she said, passing on the next bite. "If I hadn't spent ten hours being interrogated by the police, identifying a client's body before it was whisked off to a morgue, and still trying to figure out where Clive is, I might think this was one heck of a nice date."

"There was a compliment in that mile-long sentence." Wade smiled.

"And not a dirty word in the whole thing." She tilted her head. "See? I can clean up my act, Billy Wade. When're you coming to New York next?"

"If I take the job with the Bullet Catchers, I'll be there all the time. I could, for all intents and purposes, live there."

She tried to squash the little thrill that zinged through her. If he joined the company that had the unappealing name of the Bullet Catchers, he'd still be a man who carried a gun. But at least his job would be protecting people, not the opposite.

"Think you'll take that job?"

"I don't know yet. The contract is binding. You don't just walk away from being a Bullet Catcher."

"Why not?"

"Because it's like a family. And Lucy treats her family well. No one wants to leave, so they don't unless they're fired . . . or die."

She made a face at the last word. "Razor is like that. Marcus makes it so lucrative and comfortable no one ever wants to leave."

"Unless they're fired or die."

She closed her eyes, and took a sizable sip of Grey Goose.

"You know," she said after a moment, "it's a minor miracle we weren't detained longer or put in jail ourselves, considering we found a man shot in the head, and you had a gun on you."

"Not such a miracle. That detective was smart, and he knew he was lucky to have us on the investigation. And if we hadn't seen that helicopter, I'd be inclined to agree with the police's initial take that Vex killed himself. Ballistics will probably confirm that the Glock next to him fired the shot, and the man *did* just lose more than a billion dollars in two days."

"Not to mention that his company is manufacturing a product linked to cancer," she added. "His reputation was about to go into the toilet, and the class-action lawsuits alone will shut down Vexell Industries."

"All pretty strong motivators for suicide."

"Except that Clive's prescription and my cell phone weren't in the house. And we saw the helicopter."

"There's no proof that the person in the helicopter killed Vex," Wade replied. "Heck, Vex could have taken the Zoloft before he shot himself and thrown the bottle into the sea. And your phone could be anywhere. Those guys were competent, even though they probably don't handle many cases like this. We gave them a lot of information and helped our own cause by being perfectly frank about Clive and the house we'd been to in the rain forest and giving them the note. They probably have Gideon Bones in custody over in St. Kitts right now."

"Then where did Clive go? Where could he go to 'make things worse'?"

Wade shrugged. "Maybe to kill Nicholas Vex. He could have been in that helicopter, Vanessa."

She pushed her plate away, totally disinterested in the food. "Then who was trying to set him up as the murderer of Russell Winslow, and why? We heard that guy on the phone. They may have set Clive up to take the blame for Charlie's death, too, and that's why evidence is only coming out now. It's all planted."

He looked dubious. "I told you what Lucy said, and her connections deep inside the NYPD are excellent. Clive had an argument with Charlie French the day she died. Someone saw him running in the neighborhood, about sixty blocks from his home."

She straightened her spine. "Not hard evidence of a crime."

"And yet people . . ." His voice was rich with implication. ". . . have spent thirty years in jail on little more evidence than that."

She lifted her glass. "Message received."

"The plane's in Nevis, Vanessa. We can leave tonight, or . . ." He put his hand on hers. "We can wait one more night and fly out to South Carolina tomorrow."

She gave him a look that was no doubt as miserable as she felt. "You know, you didn't meet your end of the bargain." He opened his mouth to respond, and she held up a conciliatory hand. "But you did try your damnedest. Besides, if we *had* found Clive holed up somewhere, it's not like he'd be sitting here drinking gimlets with us. He'd be under arrest and being extradited to New York."

He curled his fingers into hers. "I've met Miranda Lang."

"Have you." Her voice was flat, belying the little tingle in her tummy.

"She's a terrific lady," he continued, as if she'd asked for more details. "Very smart. And she hadn't even known she was adopted. Apparently, Adrien Fletcher had a time of it, trying to find her tattoo without telling her."

Vanessa leaned forward. "What happened?"

"A little bit of everything, to hear Fletch tell the story. But you can ask her yourself tomorrow. She'll be in South Carolina to meet you, and so will Fletch. They're inseparable now."

She said nothing, and Wade squeezed her hand. "Vanessa, I won't force you or hold you to any bargain or make you do anything at all you don't want to do. I care too much for you to do that."

"Thanks." She winked at him. "There was a compliment buried in there, too."

"At least one. I'm on your side now. If you don't want to go, for whatever reason—"

She held up her hand, stopping him. "There is a reason. Not 'whatever' reason, but it's mine."

"Tell me," he said.

For the first time in forever, she wanted to.

"Remember how you told me your defining moment was when your parents gave you a gun and a Bible? Well, I was a little older when mine took place."

He waited.

"I was almost ten," she continued. "Living in New York with my dad, who, when he was around, doted on me. And my mother, who made it fairly clear, although she was subtle about it, that she didn't love me. Then the unimaginable happened." She closed her eyes, remembering the joy on Mary Louise Porter's face, the absolute glow of victory over nature, the beam of her ultimate success. "She got pregnant."

He moved closer, surprised. "So you do have a sibling."

"No." She wetted her lips. "No. I got sick. When she was about four months pregnant, I picked up something at school, one of those violent, fevery things. My mother, my *adoptive* mother, got it."

Guilt coiled through her, as it always did when she thought about this.

"She lost the baby. I had no idea that the fever caused her to miscarry. I just thought the baby died, and I was brokenhearted because I wanted a sister to love more than anything.

"I heard her one night, one of her awful, endless crying jags. During all those horrible nights, all I wanted to do was make her feel better. Hug her, tell her it would be okay. But every time I did, she shoved me away." She cursed the crack in her voice.

Wade just listened, no expression, but completely there. Somehow that was far more comforting than if he'd patted her hand and told her it was crazy to take the blame, as others had done the few times she'd shared this story.

"I got out of bed to go to her one night, because I was convinced that I could make my mother feel better. I wanted to take away all the tears, even though it seemed to get worse when I was around. I was standing outside her bedroom door, listening to her wail to my father. And she said, 'If I hadn't nursed some baby you bought on the street, I'd have my *real* daughter.' "

"*That's* how you found out you were adopted?"

Vanessa shook her head. "I knew when I was young. My mother took every opportunity to remind me that we didn't share 'real' blood. But those words did me in. She would have had a real daughter if not for me. A girl who would have lived if not for me."

He threaded his fingers through hers. "Don't let

that be a defining moment, Vanessa. That's a bad, bad memory."

"It defined me. I killed that baby—a child who would have been a sister and a 'real' daughter for my mother. I just wanted to stay out of my mother's sight, then. Out of everyone's sight. That's when I started wearing these . . ." She touched the frames of her glasses. "And letting my hair cover my face."

"You were hiding."

"I just kind of stayed to myself until my parents finally divorced, about six years later. It was my dad's idea to try to find my birth mother. I think he hoped it would bring me out of my shell." She let out a bitter laugh. "It had just the opposite effect, though. Finding out that she'd shot a woman in cold blood in an alley in Charleston didn't exactly build my confidence. I hid even more."

"What changed? You sure seem confident to me."

She finally smiled. "I just learned my way around the world, and with my father as a role model, I entered finance and investing and excelled. I made a lot of money and a few friends. But when my dad was killed, the only family member who ever really hugged me . . . well, I just . . ." She sighed. She'd given up on the concept of family. "I've buried myself in work, doing deals."

"How is this keeping you from your birth mother and two sisters?"

"You'd never understand—you and your mama and your sisters. You would never understand what it's like to feel you don't *deserve* that connection."

"You feel like you don't deserve love?"

She picked up the glass and gave him a tight smile. "This is getting deep, Billy Wade." She blinked against the unwelcome moisture in her eyes.

"I know the feeling." He looked down. "When you've done what I've done, you fight that same battle."

"Oh! Hi!" The cheery young voice was so close Vanessa jumped, yanked from intimate to intrusion so abruptly it hurt.

"Remember me from Papaya's? Sarah?" The brunette bared snow-white teeth at Wade. "Did you find your friend?"

Vanessa put her napkin on the table, not surprised to see her hands trembling as she pushed her chair back. "Will you excuse me for a second?"

Wade gave her a wary look, ignoring the woman next to them. "Not headed for the bathroom window, are you?" he asked softly.

"No," she assured him. "I'll be right back."

She sped out to the ladies' room off the deserted entry lobby, trying to get behind a closed door before her tears spilled over.

In the empty bathroom, she whipped open a stall door for privacy and pressed her face against the cool metal. The outside door opened, but she didn't hear any heels on the floor or anyone enter another stall.

Had Wade followed her in there to see if she was okay?

Taking a few deep breaths, she dried her eyes and slid the latch open, ready to face him.

Gideon Bones leaned against the bathroom door, pointing a gun directly at her heart. "Hello again, Ms. Porter."

A little blood drained from her head, but she stared right back. "What do you want?"

"Your company. On a little trip. Let's go."

She shook her head. "I'm not leaving."

He lifted the pistol, which was smaller than the one Wade carried but certainly as deadly. "Yes, you are. You are going to do exactly as I say. We'll walk out of here side-by-side, like lovers slipping away."

She didn't move, considering her options. She could scream, fight, hide behind the stall door . . .

"As we leave, Ms. Porter, this gun will be aimed at your heart. You will follow me." He jerked the gun, indicating the door. "Go."

She did, opening the door, hesitating to look toward the restaurant. Their outdoor table was far away; Wade would never see her. How long could she stall?

The cold gun and the hot hand that held it snaked right up the back of her shirt, stopping to jab under her shoulder blade. "Move, or you're dead."

He had her out the front door in seconds, and Vanessa almost danced with joy when she saw that the tram car was at the bottom of the cliff. They'd have to wait ten minutes for it to come back up, and by then, Wade would come looking for her.

But the big man pushed her past the tram's loading deck toward the thick trees. She faked a stumble to buy some time, but Bones just yanked her to her feet.

Behind her, she heard the voices and laughter of

people leaving the restaurant. Had they seen her being kidnapped? Would they hear her if she cried out? Would that be her last sound?

What would Wade think when she didn't come back? He'd come after her. Of course he would. Unless . . . he assumed she'd run away again.

Gideon jabbed the gun, and she followed the silent order, propelled by fear and the force of his body. He muscled her deep into the trees, her breath straining with the effort, burning with the need to scream. In seconds, they were out of earshot of the restaurant and deep into the rain forest.

The ground was still muddy from the rain, reminding her of her trek that morning with Wade.

But this time, she was in the hands of a brute, and the gun he carried wasn't going to protect her. It was meant to kill her.

She slid on mud, and he yanked her up with a forceful pull, thrusting her through the pitch blackness, the only sounds her strangled gasps and her sandals sloshing in the mud. The jungle smelled earthy and wet, mixed with the lingering cigar smoke that clung to her captor.

After they'd walked for a good ten minutes, she heard the thumping of helicopter rotor blades. The trees cleared, and a wide open area appeared in the moonlight. She saw the same helicopter she'd seen near Clive's hut. But not, she decided, the one from the beach.

Gideon shoved her forward, both of them automatically ducking under the whirring blades.

"No!" she hollered, using every ounce of strength to wrest her arm from his grip. He didn't want to kill her, or he already would have, in the woods. He needed her for some reason. "I'm not going! Shoot me—I don't care!"

She tried to stomp his foot, twisting to fight him, determined as hell not to get into that helicopter with him.

Unbelievably, he released her arm. She whipped around, falling to her knees with the force of her own momentum. Mud squished between her fingers as she struggled to right herself, ready to run, just as the door popped open.

"Don't hurt her!"

Nearly inaudible over the blades and the blood rushing in her head, the words barely registered as she pushed herself up and started to run.

"Vanessa!"

She froze. Turned. And stared. The lights inside the cockpit backlit a tall, thin silhouette she knew so well.

"Get your ass in here, woman!"

She didn't know whether to laugh or cry or scream. So she just covered her mouth and whispered, "Clive."

CHAPTER
NINETEEN

It was midnight by the time Jack reached Westchester County, and he still had a good forty-minute drive into the hills above the Hudson River to get to Lucy's estate.

Not that he was worried about arriving so late in the evening. Protecting the wealthiest and most powerful people in the world was a 'round-the-clock business, and the Bullet Catchers boss was always accessible. Someone would be there to let him into Lucy's lair; it was just too bad the lackey wouldn't hand him a tumbler of scotch when he got there.

With this news, he needed some.

After he'd agreed to accept her resources, the transformation in his ability to find information, people, and documents that could help locate Eileen's third daughter had been instant and remarkable. As an investigator, he could dig up crap with the best of them.

And even before he had Lucy's stellar research and investigation team helping him out, he'd done quite a lot on his own.

But things had sped up with her impressive resources at his disposal. The price? Lucy had the right to know everything. And once he told her what he'd learned, he'd be verifying what she already suspected: something huge was at work in this case.

He can do anything.

Someone very, very powerful had put Eileen Stafford in jail and was willing to do just about anything to keep her there. Including killing innocent people. And nothing would stop Lucy from wanting total and complete involvement.

Maybe it was time he gave that to her.

He rang the buzzer at the massive wrought-iron gate, and it was instantly answered by the Bullet Catcher on duty.

"This is Donovan Rush. How can we help you?"

"It's Jack Culver. Tell Lucy I need to see her, and yes, it's an emergency that involves one of her men, one of their principals, and an open case."

While he waited, he imagined some stud named Donovan calling up to the master suite to wake her. Although company folklore said Lucy Sharpe never slept, Jack knew better.

He'd seen her sleep. In his arms, troubled, restless, fitful . . . scared, even.

And wasn't that the real reason he'd gotten the guillotine? Not a misfired bullet that hit Dan Gallagher; Bullet Catchers made mistakes. But his real mistake was seeing Lucy's vulnerabilities—not friendly fire.

"Come on in, Mr. Culver."

The gates opened, and soft lights instantly appeared along the quarter-mile-long curve that led to the main house.

Just before he parked, he glanced in the mirror. Day-old beard, too many months of thick black hair over his collar. At least his eyes were clear. It had been six months since they'd been booze-induced red. Six long, dry, miserable months.

As he walked up the stone steps to the front door, it was opened by a towering young man with dark green eyes and a mixed-race complexion. Jack resisted the urge to whistle the rock song "The Bullet Catcher's Apprentice" as Donovan greeted him and offered to take him up to Lucy's library.

"I know the way," Jack said. The new kid mustn't know all the history and dirt yet. He probably didn't realize that Jack was once an insider.

"I'll take you anyway," Donovan said, wearing that "Don't mess with me" Bullet Catchers mask they'd all perfected.

Lucy leaned against her desk, as calm and cool and, damn, beautiful as if it were one in the afternoon, not one in the morning. Her hair was clipped back, and she wore something soft and clingy and black, like yoga clothes. The only skin that showed was her hands and feet, with the ubiquitous red nails. How could bare feet be that sexy?

She didn't look the least bit sleepy. Maybe she'd been awake. Maybe she'd been working. Maybe . . .

Dan Gallagher was down the hall in the master suite waiting for her to come back to bed.

Something very dark rolled in Jack's gut.

"What is it?" she asked directly.

He crossed the Oriental carpet and sat in the chair facing her desk. "I found her."

She beamed, and even without a speck of makeup, her skin glowed with the smile that came from her heart.

"That's wonderful news, Jack." She dropped into the chair next to him, reaching out her hands. "Who is she? Where is she? Did you tell her about Eileen?"

He shook his head. "Once I ran through some of your databases, I found a child named Christine Whitaker who had originally been on that list, then removed. She'd been adopted by a Whitaker family of Virginia Beach, but they evidently died in a car accident, leaving her a ward of the state. She was sent to the foster-care system, then formally adopted by a family in Roanoke by the name of Carpenter, and the paperwork lists her only as Kristen Carpenter. Up until two months ago, she lived in Washington, D.C."

"What happened two months ago?"

"She was hit crossing a street, and killed. They never found the driver or the car. It was a hit-and-run with no witnesses." At Lucy's expression of horror and disappointment, he nodded. "I feel the same way. It sucks."

"It does. And you don't think it was an accident, do you?"

"No, I do not."

"This is going to be quite upsetting for Miranda. And Vanessa, I suppose," Lucy said.

"Not to mention Eileen," Jack said. "Listen, Vanessa and Miranda have to be absolutely vigilant. Whoever this is could very well be tracking our progress."

"Someone who cares if she gets that bone marrow?" Lucy asked.

"Someone who cares if she finally comes clean. Someone who'd be happy to see her die before that transplant takes place. Once she knows two of her daughters are safe, she might talk."

"Possibly," Lucy agreed.

"That's not all," Jack said. "Thanks to your research team, I was also able to review the records of visitors to Eileen Stafford's cell over the years. Other than Miranda, Fletch, and me, there have only been three."

"In thirty years?"

"Shocking, isn't it? First, Rebecca Aubry, many years ago. Then there was a second one a few months ago, but the name was conveniently wiped from the record—since, apparently, someone can, and will, do anything where Eileen Stafford is involved."

"And the third visitor?"

"Howard Porter."

"Vanessa's father," Lucy surmised. "She told Wade he'd gone to see her mother once."

"Did she tell him that Howard was shot in a 7-Eleven in Baltimore on his way back from visiting Eileen?"

Lucy processed that. "You don't think that was a random shooting."

"As I said, I think someone wants to be sure Eileen Stafford stays very quiet until she dies. And anyone getting close to finding out her secrets is in danger."

She reached for the phone. "I need to tell Wade immediately."

"While you have him, ask him if he's seen that tattoo yet."

"Moot point," Lucy said as she picked up the phone. "She had it lasered off."

"But has he seen the scar?"

Her look was sharp. "Why?"

"I'm curious if it's the same as Miranda's."

She pressed a speed dial but kept her dark, tilted eyes on him. "Why?" she asked again.

"I guess I've just been involved in the case too long. Details haunt me."

Her smile was slow and sly. "Have you seen the medical examiner's report for the third sister who was killed? What did her tattoo look like?"

"It wasn't on the report."

"Maybe I can get it. I know some people in Washington."

He almost smiled at the understatement. She knew the president, the speaker of the House, the directors of the CIA, the FBI, and the NSA, and a few members of the Supreme Court. She knew people—yeah.

She held up her finger and spoke into the phone. "Wade, I have to talk to you." She waited, and her expression changed as she looked across the desk and held Jack's gaze. "Are you sure?" She covered the receiver and looked at Jack. "She's gone."

Shit.

Lucy listened, wrote a note, and shook her head. "If anyone can find her, Wade, you can. And you'd better, because Jack thinks . . ." She paused, looking at Jack. Like they were in this together. "She could be in danger. And when you do, I would like a precise description of the scar where her tattoo was." She listened to his response, still holding Jack's gaze. "Because we think it could be an important clue to solving a crime."

Of course, she'd figured that out. That's what he liked best about Lucy: she was smart, she was fast, and she took shit from no one.

Especially him.

While she told Wade about the third sister and Vanessa's father, Jack got up, unable to sit for one more minute. He walked to the wall to admire an oil painting signed by Lemuel Maynard Wiles that probably earned Sotheby's or Christie's a cool twenty-five grand. The Bullet Catchers business was *very* good.

"I'm not sure that Vanessa will be arriving in Columbia to meet her birth mother and sister tomorrow," Lucy said as she hung up. "But I do trust Wade to find her. Still, that gives us some time to look into Kristen Carpenter's death more closely. And Howard Porter's," she added as her mental wheels whirred.

Jack said nothing.

"And, of course, the woman Eileen Stafford is accused of killing," she added.

"Of course."

"Donovan can put you in the guest house, Jack." She waved him off, as if inviting him to spend the night in the four-thousand-square-foot annex where only Bullet Catchers were welcome wasn't a complete sea change of attitude.

"I'm just suggesting you get some sleep," she said at his surprised look. "Honestly, you look like hell, and I already told Donovan you'd be staying."

She stood and rounded her desk, and he took one more glance at her red-tipped toes. Barefoot, instead of wearing one of about six thousand pairs of dead-sexy stilettos, she was a reasonable five-foot-eleven, giving him a chance to look down at her for a change.

He did, liking the feeling and the barely there scent of something spicy in her hair.

"Sorry I had to wake you, Luce," he said, his gaze sliding up her body as she headed out the door.

She lifted a shoulder just as she disappeared around the corner. "I wasn't really sleeping."

As he trotted down the massive curved steps he glanced behind him to a part of the house where no Bullet Catcher had ever been. Her bedroom. At least, he thought no Bullet Catcher had ever been there.

Donovan waited at the bottom. "I'll unlock the guest house for you. Although someone is staying tonight, one of the downstairs bedrooms is free."

"Fine."

He'd be a fool not to use the power and might of the Bullet Catchers on this case. He'd be a proud, stubborn, idiotic fool. So he'd use Lucy, and she'd use him.

Just as they did once before.

He followed Donovan to the guest house, turning once to see if there were any lights on in the wing where Lucy lived and slept.

It was dark. So she'd either gone to bed . . . or stood in one of those darkened windows watching him.

"Come on!" Clive hopped out of the helicopter and ran to her, reaching out. "We have to hurry, Vanessa!"

Completely confused about what was going on, unable to process the shock of seeing Clive, and with the adrenaline dump of terror after running through a jungle with a gun in her back, she remained frozen.

"Vanessa." He took her arm gently. "We can't stay here. I came all the way here to get you, to protect you, but we can't stay here. Get into the helicopter, and let's go!"

"With him?" She pointed to where Bones had disappeared into the cockpit. "You want me to get into a helicopter with the man who just kidnapped me in a restaurant at gunpoint?"

"He only did that because I can't be seen anywhere, and he knew you wouldn't believe him if he told you he was with me. He's taking us somewhere safe—this island is crawling with police and media now. He's on my side, believe me."

"Why do you *have* a side?" She shook her head as he led her to the open door. "Why didn't you just call me?"

"I have, whenever I thought I had a secure line, but your phone isn't working."

"Clive." She held back, taking his hands in hers. "Please. I need more to go on before I leave here."

"What do you need? Don't tell me you believe that shit that I killed Charlie French?" His face contorted. "I know why she was killed, but I don't know who did it. Except that it wasn't me. Don't you trust me?"

"I trust you," she yelled back, staying low. "It's just that . . . someone . . . wants me . . ."

"That guy you're with? Pretty sucky time to fall in love, Vanessa."

How did he know she was with a guy? "I'm not in love. I made a deal." She couldn't begin to explain it now. "I just can't run away. And if you're innocent, you shouldn't, either."

"This goes way past innocent. Someone wants me seriously dead, and until he's caught, I'm lying low, and so are you."

"Who?" She stayed rooted to her spot, searching his face for an answer that made sense, an answer that didn't make him a killer.

"Whoever killed Charlie." He pulled at her. "And whoever killed Russell. I swear to God, if you don't get into that helicopter and come with me, you could be next. I'm trying to keep that from happening!" His words had enough force to get her to climb into the tiny two-seat cockpit of the helicopter.

Bones's enormous girth took up almost the entire space, his stomach nearly touching the controls, and the chopper looked old and worn.

"Just sit on my lap!" Clive yelled over the roar of the blades, pulling her on top of him and yanking a seat belt over both of them. "Go, Bonesy! Fly!"

Her stomach dropped as fast as the ground below as they shot straight up, the lights of the restaurant and the hotel visible as they cleared the tops of the trees.

She leaned over far enough to see the tram, moving toward the bottom of the hillside now. Was Wade on it, looking for her? Had he checked the bathroom? Their suite? Had he just assumed she'd run again, unable to face her birth family?

"Can I make a call from up here?" she asked Clive over the engine and rotor noise.

He shook his head. "Calls aren't safe. We can be traced."

"By who?" she demanded, frustration boiling up. "What the hell is going on, Clive? Who *is* this guy? Why are we going with him? Why don't you just go to the police if you're not guilty?"

His expression darkened. "I swear on our friendship that I didn't kill Charlie or Russell. You have to believe me."

Did she?

The helicopter took a dip of turbulence, and she sucked in a breath as her knees smashed against the rusted metal. The whole thing was as flimsy as hell and felt as if it could fall out of the sky at any minute. She ventured another glance out the window. "Where are we going?"

"St. Kitts," he said. "Bones has another safe house where we can stay."

That wasn't far; she could already see the island lights. The minute they were down, she'd call Wade. She slid her gaze to Clive's face, seeing the dark shadows under his eyes, the deep lines around them.

She put her hand on his cheek. "I've been trying so hard to find you."

His look was apologetic and appreciative. "I know. And I love you for that."

She sank toward him, so many questions bouncing around that she didn't even know where to start. "Were you in that little house on the beach all this time?"

"Most of it. I've moved around. But I've been trying to find you, too. I left the beach house and got in a little freaking boat to get to St. Kitts, flew to the cruise you were on, sweet-talked the crew into letting me back onboard, and danced with an old Jewish grandmother just to find you."

"Stella? When?"

"Last night. Bones figured out where I'd gone and found me there—I'm afraid he scared your friend Stella a little, trying to get to me without being seen, but she's fine—and I agreed to come back with him, but only if he'd take me to you so we can protect you."

"I was protected," she said miserably. "I had my own bodyguard."

Clive shook his head grimly. "Not protected enough. I saw what this guy can do. I saw Charlie's body."

She jerked back. "You did?"

"When I had lunch with Russell that day, he told me the EPA was investigating Vexell's products and I knew what it would do to the stock. I knew it was huge and would cost a lot of people a lot of money. I also knew that if I did anything to stop that, I'd be trading on insider information."

"So, what *did* you do?"

"I told Charlie." Guilt and remorse pulled at his expression. "It wasn't really insider trading; I just got her to stop a deal before it happened—not dump stock. But I swear to God, Vanessa, I wouldn't have told her if I thought it would get her killed."

"You had a fight with her that day—that's what someone told the police. And then you were seen on the street in front of her apartment building in SoHo. What were you doing all the way down there?"

"It wasn't a fight, it was a loud discussion. I didn't want her to tell *anyone*—just change her buy strategy on the deal that included Vexell stock. But she was determined to tell Marcus. You know what an industrial-strength kiss-ass she was."

She could just imagine how Charlie would burn to use the Vexell leak to her advantage. "Did she tell him?"

"I don't know. He wasn't around that day. But I was really worried, mostly for Russell, who would get canned if he was identified as the leak in the EPA. So I went to her apartment that night to plead his case."

He closed his eyes. "It was unbelievable, Vanessa. She was . . . brutalized."

"Maybe it really was random violence, like the police first thought," Vanessa suggested. "If someone only wanted to shut her up, why not just shoot her?"

He shook his head. "I don't think so. Somebody left a bloody Vexell T-shirt there."

She narrowed her eyes. "Did you take it?"

"Are you fucking *nuts*? Of course not. I didn't touch a thing."

She wanted to tell him about the bloody Vexell T-shirt in the toilet tank, but something stopped her. Maybe someone had put it there to set Clive up . . . but maybe not.

"What happened after you found her?" she asked.

"I was so scared I ran my ass off," he continued. "I called Russell and told him everything. I knew he might not be safe, since he started this. So we decided to fly separately and meet down here. I went on the cruise as cover, and then Bones stayed with me like a bodyguard."

She glanced at the man flying the helicopter—big, silent, and not even bothering with headphones or the least bit of conversation with, say, air traffic control. "And you trust him?"

"I do. He's a friend of a friend of Russell's, and he's been great. A little eccentric, but he knows everybody everywhere on these islands, and people just want to help him. He's kept me safe this whole time, and when he found out about you, he—"

"Tried to freaking kill me!"

"He's very overprotective," Clive said. "He was afraid you'd find me and lead someone right to me, so he kept sending you to different places to keep you away from me."

"Did he bug a hotel room to hear me get it on with some guy?"

Clive nodded. "He's really a frustrated spy." Clive smiled and whispered close to her ear, "Plus, he's got a wicked crush on me."

"Did he send me to a racetrack on some bogus rumor that you were betting on horses?"

He smiled. "Yeah, I think so."

"Did he send some asshole in a yellow truck to run me off the road?"

"Some of his guys get a little carried away."

"Did he send somebody into your resort villa to plant evidence that you killed Russell?"

He jerked back. "No." He glanced at Bones, who shifted his massive girth in his seat, making the helicopter drop. Had he heard them?

Vanessa shot Clive a warning look. "When you were staying at the Four Seasons, that wasn't exactly in hiding."

"That's what Russell wanted to do. I told him it wasn't safe, but he didn't believe me. And sure enough, he went out and . . ." He shook his head. "I can't talk about it yet."

She still wasn't sure. Something didn't fit. "So, do you think this same person killed Nicholas Vex?"

"*What?*" Clive practically spit with shock. "Nicholas Vex is dead?"

"At his beach house in Nevis. It looked like suicide, but I'm not so sure."

Clive frowned. "Vex's house isn't in Nevis. I've been there. It's a mansion in St. Barts."

"Then he has two places, because Marcus told me—"

He shifted her from one leg to the other. "My phone is vibrating."

"Don't answer it!" Bones ordered. So, he *could* hear every word they were saying. "Even up here, someone could track you."

Clive pulled it out and looked at the caller ID, then gave her a confused smile. "Are you speed-dialing me in your pocket?"

"I don't have my phone," Vanessa said, seizing his. "I lost it at Vex's house in Nevis." But the call disappeared, the screen went blank, and she swore softly. Who had her phone?

"Like I said, he doesn't have a house in Nevis," Clive said.

She narrowed her eyes at him. "I know you've been there, Clive. I found your Zoloft bottle."

"What are you . . . do you mean Mango Plantation?"

"Yes."

"That's not Vex's house. That place belongs to Marcus."

"Marcus? He's the one who told me it was . . ."

Her voice trailed off, and she and Clive stared at each other.

Marcus?

Could he be behind all this? Charlie and Russell and Nicholas Vex?

"He has an awful lot to gain . . . or lose," Clive said quietly, reading her thoughts. "And if Charlie told him about the news that day, maybe he wanted to keep it quiet. Or use it."

"Is Marcus Razor capable of murder? Of multiple murders?"

"If so, I'm one sucky judge of character."

Maybe he was. Maybe they both were. "As soon as we get to St. Kitts, we have to notify the police. The New York police. They have to question him. I have a connection now—"

The helicopter took a quick dip, along with Vanessa's heart. Behind Clive, she could see island lights in the distance—disappearing.

"Hey!" She whipped around to Bones. "I thought we were going to St. Kitts."

His look was stony. "I'm taking a different route in case we're being followed."

Clive's gaze darted from the window to Bones and landed on Vanessa. "He's a little erratic at times."

No shit. She nudged Clive and mouthed, "Can you fly this thing?"

He just snorted.

"Where are we going?" Vanessa demanded of Bones.

He just shot a venomous look at Clive. "This is never going to work."

Chills danced down Vanessa's spine at his tone, and Clive paled as he looked at Bones. "What does that mean, Gideon?"

"I mean . . ." He moved the control stick, and the helicopter banked sharply enough to make Vanessa gasp. "That I have looked after you long enough, and now I have to look after me."

She stared out at the black sea, the sparkly island lights, and the inky sky around them, the slow burn of fear building in her gut with each question in her head.

Could anyone be trusted? Was Marcus somehow involved with all these killings? Would this helicopter ever safely touch the ground?

And the one that made her heart twist most of all . . .

Would Wade ever find her?

CHAPTER
TWENTY

WADE DIDN'T WASTE much time on a cursory search. He knew Vanessa was gone when he ran outside and heard a helicopter take off; he just didn't know where she'd gone or who had taken her there. But he was going to find out.

The first thing he did was corner Sarah and demand to know who she worked for, making sure she saw his gun and knew he wasn't afraid to use it.

"I swear to God," she half whimpered, her eyes like saucers, "I don't know what you're talking about. I don't work for anyone. I really met your friend in the bar, and we got drunk together, and he told me all that stuff Maddie and I told you . . ." Tears welled in her eyes.

"No one paid you to send us to Nisbet Plantation?"

She shook her head. "Honest."

He was back out on the tram landing when his phone rang.

"I got a reading on Vanessa's cell-phone signal," Sage said. "It's not in Nevis; it's coming from a mountain on the southeast corner of St. Barts, called Morne Rouge. Looks like pretty rough terrain on the satellite image. I can find one house with no actual address, and the owner is listed as Nicholas Vex. If you call right now, there will be a signal. I guarantee it."

But who would answer it? "Can you do me a favor and track down the owner of Mango Plantation, where Vex was shot today?"

"I did already. It's a corporation: Razor Partners."

He slammed the accelerator around a sharp curve, trying to put the pieces together. When they didn't fit, he signed off with Sage, then dialed Vanessa's phone, fully expecting voice mail.

A woman answered in a whisper. "Dolly, is that you?"

Speechless for a moment, he pressed the phone harder to his ear. "Who is this?"

"It's Stella, and God, I hope you're coming to help me."

Stella? The orange-hat woman? "How did you get Vanessa's phone?"

She was quiet for a minute, and he thought he'd lost the connection. Then he heard a man's voice in the background and a very soft whisper. "Wait."

He did, listening to soft, indecipherable sounds. A man talked mostly, but the words were impossible to make out.

Finally, she spoke again. "You have to tell Vanessa not to come here."

His heart kicked. "Where?"

"I don't know where I am. In a house. It's like suspended in air. I followed him, and he caught me. I . . . I shouldn't have, but . . ." He could hear her breathing, a soft, pitiful sound. "I think he's gonna kill me."

The clunk told him the phone had dropped, and instantly the connection was lost. His mind whirred with possibilities as he pulled into the tiny airstrip in Newcastle, where the Bullet Catchers' unmarked Gulfstream IV was already fired up and on the runway.

"We need to go to St. Barts," he told the pilot. "How far is that?"

"Fifty miles northwest," the pilot said. "Let me clear with air traffic control, and we'll be there in less than an hour."

Wade headed straight to the back conference area, where additional firepower was locked up. Only Bullet Catchers knew the safe code, and he used it, opening the door and reaching instantly for the Barrett 82A1 rifle.

He'd used this stick in Sierra Leone, and at least a dozen times in Iraq. Lifting the 50-caliber heavy from the slot, he closed his eyes.

He'd sworn to God, and himself, that he'd never take a rifle in his hands again. But some promises had to be broken.

After all the years of silent looks across a conference-room table, Vanessa and Clive were pretty damn adept at nonverbal communication. They did plenty of it while Bones swerved and dipped over strings of Caribbean islands that were only clusters of light surrounded by blackness.

Vanessa tried to track where they were going, but the darkness and turbulence disoriented her enough that she had no idea which island was which. With each foreboding second, Clive got a little more uptight, Bones got a little more nutso, and Vanessa got real scared.

They had no choice but to let him fly, even though everything had changed in the last few minutes. He muttered, threw looks at Clive, wiped a tear, and flew the shaky bird with jerky movements on the foot pedals and a trembling hand on the stick.

Gideon Bones was just crazy enough to crash this thing.

"Where are we going, Bonesy?" Clive finally asked, his voice as soft as if he were talking to a child. "Why aren't we going to St. Kitts?"

He got the evil eye in return. "You never loved me."

"No," Clive said calmly. "I like you a real lot, though."

"You loved Russell."

"Not anymore. Even before he died, I was over him."

Bones choked at what Vanessa suspected he knew was a lie. "I should have listened to Russell in the first place." He gave the stick an angry shove, making the helicopter dip and Vanessa gasp.

Clive gave her a reassuring pat. "I'm sorry. He's . . . emotional."

Great—an emotional, heartbroken, erratic, gun-carrying lunatic was flying the rickety old helicopter. She closed her hands over the seat belt that wrapped her with Clive into the seat and tried to consider her options.

Zero, at the moment.

"He has a lot more money than you do," Bones said suddenly, flinging a hand at Clive. "A lot."

"Who?" Vanessa asked.

Bones just stared straight ahead, his jowls shaking with the vibration of the helicopter. "You know," he spat out. "You just said his name."

Marcus?

"And he offered me money for you. But what did I say? 'No. I've fallen in love with Clive. I can't betray him.'" He used a singsong voice to imitate himself. "So I said no to all his money. And I was going to take you to one more hideaway, and wait one more day, one more week, one more month for you to recipro-cate my feelings. But you know what, my friend?" He snorted. "Love sucks."

They tilted suddenly, then hovered over one of the larger islands. There was a cluster of bright, citylike lights on one side and cruise ships in a harbor. Bones barreled the bird over the darkened center of the is-land and down toward the opposite coast.

Very few houses or hotels or restaurants lit this side; it was black but for an occasional glimmer as he flew them deeper and deeper into the unknown island.

Bones started to descend into what looked like a clearing, but when he turned on the headlight, she saw it was a helo pad at the top of a hill. They hit the ground with a thud, and Vanessa's stomach dropped just as hard. He shut down the engine and stared into the blackness beyond the circle of light from the front of the helicopter.

No one moved until Clive leaned forward.

"Gideon," he said gently. "I know you're upset. And I don't know where we are or why we're here, but I really think you need to leave Vanessa out of it. I'll stay here, but you need to take her back—"

"No," she interjected. "I'm getting out of this thing, and we are not separating again." She turned toward Bones, ready to negotiate for her life. "What exactly do you want from us, Bones, and how can I give it to you?"

"From you, nothing. From the man who is willing to pay the ransom on his head . . ." He pointed to Clive. "Cash."

Perfect. This she could do. This was her game. "Name your price, Mr. Bones. And I'll get you cash. It could take a few days, but you have my word: I will sign anything, and I will pay you whatever you like for our freedom. How much?"

"You can't match his offer." He glanced over her shoulder. At first, she thought he was looking at Clive, but his gaze went past both of them. Something flickered on his face. Surprise? Shock?

"I'll double the offer," she said, keeping her attention right on him. "What's your number? Ten grand? Fifty? A hundred grand?"

"He's . . . paying me a million. Two if . . . I bring you both." He still stared outside.

"Two million!" Clive choked.

"Who?" she demanded at the same time.

"Him," Bones whispered, still looking outside.

As Vanessa whipped around to see, Bones threw himself toward the door in the back. She instantly fumbled with the release of the seat belt, her fingers bashing Clive's as he did the same thing.

The door popped open, and a loud, sharp crack rocked Vanessa backward into the pilot's seat, where she watched Bones tumble out of the helicopter door, his massive body thudding to the ground.

Clive screamed, but Vanessa pulled him back before he could go after Bones.

"Get down!" She dropped as low as she could to peek out around the passenger seat to see who'd shot Bones. A shadow of a man, muscular and solid and moving with the confidence of someone armed and dangerous, emerged into the light. A silhouette of power and control, with the stance of a gunslinger.

Her heart soared as she rocketed forward, her rescuer's name on her lips. "Wa—"

Then she stopped and stared in complete disbelief.

"Clive," she whispered. "Russell's not dead."

It was too late to rent a car in St. Barts, so Wade stole one. It was an ancient Moke, a cross between a Jeep and a beach buggy, parked on a side street near a noisy bar with the keys in the ignition. He carried the rifle in a soft-sided guitar case they kept on the plane for precisely this purpose. Once he'd found a vehicle, he tossed the case in the back, and took off for Morne Rouge.

He tried Vanessa's phone again, but it went into voice mail. Sage had fed GPS into his phone, and he had a general idea of how to get to Morne Rouge, but the roads were even worse than on Nevis. Poorly paved and much more mountainous, they were so narrow at times that there was nothing on one side but cliff. And damn near pitch-black, with not a light in sight.

He wormed through the island, around hairpin turns, past gated homes and hills nestling restaurants and understated resorts. He went up one mountainside and down the other, seeing no farther than the twenty feet his headlights illuminated ahead of him.

He could still hear Stella's desperate plea: *You have to tell Vanessa not to come here.*

Would she, to save Stella? Probably. To find Clive? Definitely.

But why would she do it without telling him? She couldn't have left the restaurant voluntarily; someone took her.

A sick feeling of dread rolled through him. If something happened to her . . .

He gunned the accelerator until his phone GPS alerted him that he'd reached the address. He peered into the darkness, seeing a tall gate covered with foliage and brush. He backed up and turned to shine the headlights on the gate, looking for a keypad or a bell.

He pulled the car into the brush and climbed out, leaving the lights on to give him some path to follow, circling the perimeter of a wall that was so overgrown with shrubbery that it blended right into the trees. He dropped low, looking for an opening or a way to climb in, just as the steady thump of a helicopter filled the air.

He squinted up to where it landed, about half a mile away and up a fairly steep hill. It was a little Robinson R-22 or 44, a two-seater. Definitely not the big Bell he'd seen at the beach.

He unzipped the guitar case and grabbed his rifle, adrenaline moving through him as naturally as oxygen. He slid deeper along the perimeter of the wall and started searching for a way in.

At the crack of a gunshot, he stilled. After a few seconds of silence, he heard a loud, long wail of gut-wrenching pain.

He stopped searching for a foothold and just started climbing.

Vanessa kept her arms in up in a classic pose of surrender while Clive fell to his knees, tears rolling down his cheeks as he cradled Bones and looked incredulously at Russell Winslow.

"How could you do this?"

Russell Winslow had always looked like a textbook Navy SEAL to Vanessa—tall, wide-shouldered, with a buzz cut and a jawline that advertised steroids. Tonight, he also looked hell-bent on murder.

"Anybody stupid enough to think you're worth a million dollars deserves to die." He waved the gun. "Let's go. Both of you."

Clive held Bones tighter. Vanessa blinked, wishing she could see beyond the circle of light from the front of the helicopter. There was only enough light to see the blood oozing from Bones's stomach and the pistol lying next to him.

"Move!" Russell ordered again.

"I mourned you, you son of a bitch." Clive's voice cracked.

"Touching, dude, and I appreciate it. Move."

"But why did you make those plans—meet me in Nevis, string me along? If you want me dead because I know you leaked the information, why not just kill me?"

"I needed time, man. Needed to set you up as Charlie's killer, then get you into a place where I could get rid of you—after I'm considered dead, of course—and arrange your suicide. Which is what's about to happen."

He'd been the one in the villa when she and Wade were hiding under the bed. Why hadn't she recognized his voice? Because . . . she thought he was dead and never dreamed it could be him.

Clive stood slowly, Bones's blood on his hands and fire in his eyes. "But I *mourned* you," he repeated.

"You should have known I wouldn't die in a car over a cliff, C. I'm a fucking fish."

"You bastard!" He lunged at Russell, and the gun went off again, shattering the helo's headlight and plunging them into darkness.

Clive rolled to the ground with Russell, grunts of pain and fury coming from both men. Clive didn't stand a chance against that beast.

Vanessa dove toward Bones's gun, then hoisted it up and aimed at the rolling shadow that was Russell and Clive. Another shot came from Russell's gun, followed by an inhuman growl of pain.

If Russell was shot, Clive would find her. If it was Clive . . .

She flew over the asphalt toward a wooded area, the pistol heavy in her hand. She ran to the darkest spot she could find, slipping past trees and branches that scraped her skin, moving as fast as possible, the sound of her breath deafening her.

Her night vision improved with every step, allowing her to make out the trees and bits of moonlight and clouds above the branches, her feet going and going and going, just waiting for that shot in her back, in her head.

Then she smelled saltwater. Pausing, she clamped her mouth shut to stop the sound of her breathing and listen. Surf pounded.

Hallefreakinlujah. She was at the beach. Moving more slowly, she pushed through the foliage until it cleared at a wide strip of sand and rolling waves. She followed the beach about a quarter of a mile, to a cliffside where a huge cement deck jutted out over the sand, supported by thick, round columns that ran at angles into the side of the cliff.

Nicholas Vex's house is in St. Barts.

Was it possible? Was that where Bones had been planning to take them . . . or could the house up there be a refuge? Somewhere she could find a phone and help? What were her options? Wander through the jungle, attempt to swim around the island to safety . . .

And all the time, Russell Winslow—armed and murderously dangerous—could be ten feet away, looking for her.

She lifted the pistol that weighed her right arm down. She'd learned a little in the last few days; she could hear Wade's sweet drawl in her ears. *Move slow and smart, not fast and stupid.*

Wade would formulate a plan. Then he'd probably kill whoever got in his way. Right now, that plan made real sense.

Her plan was simply to find out who was up there. Someone she could trust or someone she might need to . . . shoot?

She scrambled through the brush to the rocky cliff, slipping in her sandals but ascending fairly rapidly, holding the gun in one hand and using her other to pull herself up the rocks until she was about ten feet from the underside of the house. Sweat rolled down her back, and her lungs felt as if they would burst, but she was finally close enough to see some light. And hear the low timbre of a man's gruff voice.

Russell?

She closed her eyes to listen, the way she'd seen Wade do, her left hand quivering with exhaustion as she gripped a gnarled root.

"Please, please. I had no idea what I was getting into." The woman's voice bounced off the concrete and echoed into the night. "I was just trying to find my friend, that's why I was outside. I swear to God!"

Stella? Vanessa's blood rushed from her head, literally making her dizzy.

Stella Feldstein was in this house?

"For the last time," a man said, "shut up, or I will shoot you."

Not *a* man. The man. Marcus Razor, sounding as exasperated as he did in a staff meeting. For an instant, Vanessa felt safe, ready to cry out for help. But why would she trust Marcus? He was deeply involved in this. No doubt in partnership with Russell, probably selling stock on EPA insider information for who knows how long.

The fact was, she couldn't trust anyone.

Except Stella, who was an innocent victim. And Wade, who couldn't possibly know where she'd been taken.

She inched the gun closer to her face to take a good look at it. How the hell did she work this thing? She ran her fingers along the grip, reading the word on the side. *Ruger.* She'd heard of that kind of gun. It felt like it sounded: chunky and mean.

There was a little latch on the side. A safety? Would it fire if she didn't switch that? Could she kill herself with it if she did?

"I want to get out of here!" Stella hollered. "I don't have anything to do with this, and I want to get out of here!"

Yes! Let the poor woman go, or I'll . . .

Kill you?

Would she? Could she? She had the means. She had the motive. And if she got lucky, she could make the opportunity. Would that make her a murderer?

Like Eileen Stafford? Like Wade Cordell?

Something scraped the concrete above her, and Vanessa looked up at the patio. She was almost close enough to pull herself under the overhang and hoist herself up. But she needed two free hands—and one of them clutched a gun.

"Helllllp—" Stella's scream was stopped midway.

Praying she wouldn't shoot herself, Vanessa gingerly slipped the gun barrel into the waistband of her skirt. She pulled herself up a few feet, grasped a rock, then shimmied closer to the cement, her bare legs scraping stones and dirt. Clenching her jaw so she wouldn't make a sound, she reached as far as she could.

Using all her strength, she managed to brace herself enough to peer over the edge of the cement. Marcus stood over Stella, who was wild-eyed and tied to a chair. Ready to rock forward and attack, Vanessa froze in mid-move as someone shoved open a sliding glass door and Russell marched onto the patio. Alone.

Oh, God, was Clive dead?

"She's out there!" he hollered, furious. "That bitch got away, and she's out there!"

She lowered herself an inch, her mind whirring. She should run. She should hide. She should scoot down the hill twice as fast as she came up it, dive into the ocean, and swim to the next freaking island.

"Please," Stella whimpered. "Please let me go. I won't tell anyone anything. I swear. I promise."

"Did she see you?" Marcus asked.

"Hell, yes," Russell replied. "She knows everything."

"You fucking idiot. Go find her," Marcus ordered.

"Find her and . . . and do whatever you have to do. Hurry up, before you make another mistake."

Was Marcus ordering her *death*? Her boss? Her mentor? Fury pushed her up again.

Russell looked daggers at Marcus. "The only mistake I made was going into business with you."

"I'm done now. This is out of control. *You* are out of control. This started as a good scheme, dropping hints about EPA tests on products, then reaping the benefits when the stock fell. But Christ, no one should have *died*. Now look where we are."

Russell lifted an enormous shoulder. "I'm dead, have a new ID and shitloads of money. I don't know where you are."

"Running a company into the ground."

"Hey, shit happens," Russell said. "I didn't think Clive would tell Charlie. He was just supposed to be a conduit to you and take the rap if we got caught. But Charlie was one loose cannon. Nasty little bitch, that one."

"Well, you took care of her, didn't you? Took all your miserable anger out on that poor woman."

Russell's face reddened. "She shouldn't have fought me. She shouldn't have pissed me off."

"She didn't even know that much," Marcus shot back. "She knew a sliver of what was going on, just enough to make her dangerous. And why the fuck did you have to drag Clive into it? God, you slept with the guy. You know he's not made like that."

Russell snorted with disgust. "Well, now I'm dead, and I don't care."

"How long do you think it'll take them to figure out that you're not really dead? They don't have a body yet, just an ID and a car you rented. You're leaving a trail of dead bodies a mile long, and someone is going to figure it out."

"Don't worry. I know how to get rid of those bodies, how to fly that chopper, and how to get myself lost in Indonesia. I only have to get rid of some evidence—starting with Vanessa Porter."

"You're going to kill one person too many," Marcus spat. "Do whatever you need to do, Winslow. I'll keep your dirty secret, but I'm out of here."

He turned and started toward the house, and Russell lifted the gun and aimed at his back.

"No!" Vanessa shouted as the shot exploded. Marcus fell, Stella screamed, and Russell whipped around to where Vanessa hung, the gun aimed directly at her.

She fell a few feet, making a noisy landslide. The gun loosened from her waistband, and she managed to yank it out with one hand and stop her fall by grabbing a branch with the other. She could hear Russell's footsteps as he bounded over the concrete toward her.

There was no cover, nowhere to hide, so she just leaned back, raised the gun, and prayed to God it would fire. Because the second his face came over the edge, she'd pull the trigger. His head popped over the edge of the patio, looking too high to see her.

Her hand quivering so hard she could hardly aim, she put her finger on the trigger. *This is murder. This is murder.*

He saw her.

She clenched her entire body and squeezed.

And nothing happened. A second later, a bullet whizzed past her ear with a jaw-cracking noise. She threw herself farther under the overhang but was still an easy target.

He aimed again, and she stared at the barrel of the gun and the eyes of the killer behind it. This was it. She was dead.

She closed her eyes . . . and heard the shot.

But there was no pain, no darkness, no . . .

Above her, his body thumped. She opened her eyes and saw Russell's gun tumble as he fell to the edge, blood dribbling out of a small red dot in the back of his head—the apricot.

She dropped her useless weapon, squinting into the darkness of the mountain, disbelieving but knowing exactly who had saved her.

He appeared out of the darkness, the rifle in his hands as natural as a mother carrying a baby. His eyes were trained directly on her, his expression all business.

"Wade!" She reached for him, aching to hold him. He pulled her up, easily supporting her with his free arm, his gun pressed against her as firmly as his body. She lifted her face to plaster him with kisses and gratitude, but he quieted her with one finger to her lips.

"I have to tell you something," he said.

"Just tell me you love me right now as much as I love you. That's all that matters." She kissed his cheeks, his mouth, his wonderful, brilliant, slow, and deliberate self. "Because I do," she said. "I love you. I *love* you."

He didn't smile or react. "You need to listen to me." His voice was far too ominous for his message to be anything she wanted to hear. "Your father was not a victim of random violence."

She just blinked at him, her mind blank.

"He was murdered by someone who followed him from the jail where Eileen Stafford is. He was killed because she told him something. Probably the real identity of the killer."

"Oh, my God."

"And Vanessa . . ." His expression softened as he touched her face gently. "There's more. It's about . . . your sister."

CHAPTER
TWENTY-ONE

THE AFTERMATH HAD taken six endless, miserable days. Six days of interrogations and interviews, meetings with the police and the SEC, briefings with the EPA, depositions with the cruise-line owners who'd inexplicably let Clive and Bones board a ship though they weren't passengers. Six days of compiling answers to questions Vanessa didn't even know to ask.

Slowly, the truth emerged, and Vanessa and Wade pieced together what they'd been through. While Bones was trying to send them away from Clive, Marcus and Russell wanted her to find him so that they could, too. As a safety net, Russell started planting clues to make Clive look guilty of the murder. When the scandal broke, Vex figured out enough to fly down to the islands and confront Marcus, but Russell swooped in and ended that meeting before it started.

The packs of hungry reporters who'd descended on St. Barts and Nevis were starved for news about the EPA-Vexell scandal, but the only news Vanessa wanted to hear was about Clive, recuperating in a hospital in San Juan with Gideon Bones, and Marcus Razor, who was paralyzed for life but able to fill in all the holes before he spent the rest of his life in jail. Stella was doing interviews on the cable channels, gaining a million new fans and friends in the process.

But six days of hell also meant six nights in the arms of the only man Vanessa could imagine next to her during this nightmare.

Finally, after the authorities had every morsel of information they could eke out of Vanessa and Wade and had pieced together the scheme of insider trading Marcus and Russell had devised, they were free to leave.

And there was only one place Vanessa could go. After all, she'd made a deal.

After having been searched and interrogated yet again, Vanessa waited on a wooden bench in a windowless room in the bowels of the Camille Griffin Graham Correctional Institute.

Waiting to meet the woman who'd given birth to her.

The guard said she'd be right back to take her to Wade, who presumably endured his own search, along with the man who'd picked them up when the plane landed, Jack Culver.

The door creaked open, and she looked up, expecting the guard.

"Hi. Are you Vanessa?" A woman stepped into the room, the fluorescent lights picking up gold in her long auburn hair and casting a shadow over her delicate features. The eyes that met hers were sky-blue and wide, and the skin glowed with the look of someone happy, healthy, and well loved.

She opened her mouth to speak but just stood instead, slowly taking in every detail and feature, aware that the woman was doing the same.

They exhaled softly at the same time.

"Miranda." Vanessa took a step forward, the unfamiliar instinct to reach out and hug a perfect stranger actually making her arms ache. But she didn't.

The woman nodded, as tentative as she, her eyes a little moist. "Yes. I'm Miranda Lang. I'm your sister."

They both stared, tears and smiles at war. Then Miranda stepped forward with extended arms, and Vanessa returned the embrace with a force Stella would have been proud of.

This was how they were born, Vanessa thought, a lump making it hard for her to swallow. Next to each other.

But something was missing. *Someone* was missing.

Miranda eased back, tears trickling down her cheeks. "It feels incomplete, doesn't it?"

Vanessa nodded quickly. "Silly, since I didn't even know you—or she—existed."

Miranda gave her a squeeze and held tight. "I don't know if you feel the way I do, but ever since I found out we were triplets, I had this . . . this fantasy. That the three of us would be reunited, and I don't know . . ." She swiped the tears that flowed freely now. "Act like sisters."

Vanessa smiled. "We *are* sisters. We don't have to act."

There was a tap on the door, and Wade's smile greeted her, next to him a strapping man with the golden eyes of a lion and a mane to match.

"Vanessa," Wade said. "This is Adrien Fletcher, the man who found Miranda."

"Pleasure's mine." His smile was warm and genuine. "Call me Fletch."

"Before I go in," Vanessa said, taking Wade's hand and instinctively pulling him closer, "I'd like Miranda to see what's left of the tattoo since I had it lasered off."

"I'm rather adept at finding them," Fletch said with a quick smile at Miranda. "Let's have a look-see."

She turned her back to them, lifting her hair.

"Here," Wade said, his familiar fingers slipping into her nape to part her hair.

"It's not quite in the center," she said, tapping a little to the left. "There's no pigment where the tattoo was. According to the dermatologist, she used India ink. I could have had the skin removed completely, and there wouldn't have been a scar, but . . . I didn't."

"Look at that," Miranda said. "Totally different from mine."

"Like two little squiggles, right?" Her mother had told her when she was young that it was the mark of an adopted child, and she'd always hated it.

"It's hard to tell," Fletch said, "but it looks like two sixes or curled ribbons."

"Here, look at mine." Miranda stepped around and turned her back to Vanessa.

"Hi," Vanessa read as Fletch revealed the spot. "Someone with a very strange sense of humor."

The door opened, and Jack stepped in. "Ladies. We can go see Eileen now. But they'll only let three people in."

"I'm sure Vanessa would like to go with Wade and her sister," Fletch suggested.

The term curled through Vanessa, foreign and scary and a little wonderful, too. "I'd like that." She reached for Miranda's hand and smiled. She still had issues with Eileen Stafford but not with Miranda.

Wade kept his arm around her as they walked down a hallway, went outside, and followed a concrete path to the medical eval unit.

"Ready?" he asked, tightening his arm protectively.

She nodded, and the three of them entered, and followed one more hallway, stopping outside an open door.

"I know she's in a coma," Miranda said, taking Vanessa's hand in her slender fingers. "But I think she can hear us. So you can talk to her."

Vanessa nodded, squared her shoulders, and stepped into the room. One bed was empty, and for a moment, she thought the other was, too. Then she saw a bald, shriveled woman with IVs connected to her arms and an oxygen tube up her nose. She was as pale as the sheets and impossibly small.

Miranda's grip tightened in empathy with the emotional waterfall cascading through Vanessa.

"Eileen," Miranda said loudly as though a slightly deaf but wide-awake old woman lay in the bed. "This is Vanessa Porter. Your other daughter."

Not the slightest response.

Vanessa's throat went bone-dry, and her palms did the opposite.

"Go ahead," Miranda said with the tiniest nudge. "Talk to her."

"Hello, Eileen," she said, clearing her voice. "I . . . we . . ."

Miranda smiled encouragingly, as though she expected Vanessa to shed tears and fall to her knees and somehow thank the fates for bringing them all together. But all she wanted to do was run.

She took one step closer, memorized Eileen's face, and nodded. "All right. I've met her. Do the blood test, and let me out of here."

She turned and walked out of the room.

When Vanessa heard the soft vibration of Wade's cell phone on the nightstand, she opened her eyes to look at the clock. No good news got delivered at 4:07 A.M. Instinctively, she tightened her legs around him and held his arm where her face pressed against his shoulder. But he sat straight up.

She propped herself up on her elbow as he lifted the phone from next to his gun.

"It's Jack," he said as he flipped it open. "Yeah?" He was still for a moment, then reached to touch her bare shoulder, running his hand slowly down her arm and closing his fingers over hers.

Eileen was dead—Vanessa just knew it. She never came out of the coma, so she couldn't get the transplant of Vanessa's bone marrow, and she was dead.

"She's awake," he whispered. "She's awake, talking, and getting the transplant procedure later today."

Vanessa fell back onto the pillows with a thud. Confusion, the only word she could use to describe her emotions where Eileen Stafford was concerned, burned her gut.

"What?" Wade asked, his voice as sharp as the look he gave Vanessa. "No. That's ridiculous. She's not going up there, and she's not going to South Carolina." He listened, then said, "She doesn't need to explain it to you, Jack. She's talked to Miranda, and frankly, that's the only person in the mix who matters."

Well, Eileen mattered. Vanessa pushed that thought away, concentrating on how beautifully Wade defended her position.

"That's not good enough," Wade said in response to something that obviously riled a man who didn't rile easily. "She's given plenty to your cause, Jack. Bone-marrow cells, for one thing. Good—" He hesitated, narrowing his eyes. "Are you *kidding* me?"

Vanessa sat up. "What?" she asked.

He held up a finger for her to wait. "Listen," he said, his voice softer now. "I'll tell her, but don't hold your breath." He shut the phone, put it back, then settled down next to her, maddeningly silent.

"What is it?" she demanded again. "She's awake.

She's getting the transplant. What else did he say, Wade?"

He repositioned himself on the pillow, then tugged her down to his chest, even though she resisted the pull.

"Don't go all Southern slow on me, dammit! I want to know what the *hell* that call was about."

"He wants you to go up to Lucy's today and let him examine your tattoo scar again."

"Oh, please. Take a picture, and e-mail it to him."

"That would probably work."

"Why does he need it?"

"Because," he said, drawing the word out, "when Eileen learned that two of her three daughters had been located, she said the tattoos had the answer Jack wants. The killer."

Vanessa practically choked. "Why is she being so damn coy about it? Why has she sat in jail for thirty years if she knows who the killer is? This is just *bullshit*!" She punched the pillow with the last exclamation, but he grabbed her wrist and pulled her to him.

"What if there is a connection to your father's death? And your sister's?"

She was silent.

"Lucy's calling an all-staff meeting for the Bullet Catchers who are in driving distance today. That's very rare; it means the assignment is massive and urgent."

"Are you going up?"

He shrugged a shoulder. "I told her I'd come up

this week anyway and make a decision on her offer. I might as well make it today."

"Have you made a decision?"

He turned to her, his eyes clear and blue and cutting right through her. "I've thought about it."

"And what do you think?"

"That it could take me away from you. A lot."

She released the breath she didn't know she was holding. "Work takes me away from you a lot," she said. "Especially now that Clive is back and we're starting this firm together. Anyway," she said, forcing the words out, "you shouldn't make lifelong decisions based on your feelings for someone you've known for a month."

His laugh was dry. "Says the woman who moves like a bullet out of a forty-five."

"Not about love."

He blew out a breath. "I need to know where you stand, Vanessa. I need to know if you love me."

"I told you—up on that mountain in St. Barts. I told you I loved you then."

"I'd just saved your life. It doesn't count. You've never said it since."

She reached for him, pulled him toward her bare body, and curled a leg around his. "I'll *make love* to you, how's that?"

He resisted the kiss. "That's not what I mean."

"C'mon, Wade. This is good enough, isn't it? We're together. We're a team. We do the good thing and have fun." She added a deep kiss, reaching down to stroke the erection he always had when he awoke.

"We'll do it your way, Billy Wade. Slow and sweet and easy."

His hands closed over her breasts as he returned the kiss, sliding on top of her in that familiar, exciting, perfect place. She spread her legs, closing her eyes to block out everything but his achingly hard body and the pleasure of him inside her.

But he didn't go inside her. Instead, he lifted his body and looked down with something tough in his eyes.

"Come on, Wade," she urged gently.

"No." He flipped off her, stealing her heaven and all that warmth and hardness. "I can't."

She circled the smooth head of his manhood, certain she could distract him from this conversation, the way she had a hundred times already. "Feels like you can."

He faced the ceiling and closed his eyes. "I won't. How's that?"

Vanessa shot up. "Why? Because I don't want you to make lifelong decisions based on a sexual relationship?"

He snorted softly, then faced her, his eyes fierce. "I can't, because until you give up all that hate you carry around, Vanessa, you *can't* make love. You can't *love*. You can fuck, and you can play, and you can have 'a sexual relationship.' But you can't make love. And call me an old-fashioned Southern boy, but that's what I want."

He whipped himself out of bed and strode into the bathroom, closed the door, and turned on the shower.

She wanted to follow him. Wanted to climb into that shower and show him just how well she'd learned to . . . love. But she closed her eyes and finally gave in to the tears she'd waited a month to shed.

Bitter, hot tears of anger and regret and grief. They flowed as long as his shower did, feeling like a lifetime of crying, probably because it was.

When he came out of the bathroom, she reached for her glasses to hide her tear-reddened eyes but stopped. Instead, she hooked her hair behind her ears and looked right at him. "Are you going up to Lucy's?"

"Yes. You wanna come with me? Just for the ride?"

She sighed. "I have to work. The new offices are still a wreck, and Clive needs me to be there."

"Of course he does."

Her heart tumbled. "When will you be back?"

He was silent long enough for her to know that was the wrong question.

Will you be back?

But she couldn't bring herself to ask.

The receptionist in the tiny lobby of the yet undecorated and unpacked offices of Porter and Easterbrook LLC gave Wade a surprised look when he stepped in from the street. "She's gone," she said, accurately assuming that Wade was there to see Vanessa. "She popped in to get some files this morning, then left with luggage."

Luggage? "Any idea where she was going?"

"No, I'm sorry, but she was in a real hurry."

Something new and different. He returned to the

crowded streets of lower Manhattan, flipping his phone open. He had so much to tell her about his day at Lucy's, and it had to be told in person. Even as he dialed, he shooed away any doubts. He knew where she'd gone. He *knew* it.

"I need a plane," he said when the call was answered on the second ring.

Lucy laughed. "You're a full-time employee for what, an hour, and you want one of my jets?"

"My principal is on the move, and I have to get her."

"Where are you going?"

"Columbia, South Carolina."

"You're in luck. Get to JFK, and meet Fletch and Miranda. They're about to take off. I'll have them wait for you."

"Great. Any progress on the investigation since I left?"

"A few of us are brainstorming. I'm bringing in a specialty team to step up the investigation. I've promised Miranda she'll be the first to know our progress, and you can tell Vanessa she's next in line."

"Great. Thanks, Luce."

"And Wade, thank you again. I'm so happy to have you onboard." Lucy's voice was warm. "You seem much more . . . content than before."

"I'm gettin' there, Luce."

Fletch didn't seem thrilled to have company on the flight, but Miranda welcomed him with a genuine hug. That affection never wavered. In fact, she never once took her hand out of Fletch's, especially during takeoff and landing. The entire time, Wade watched her interact with the man she obviously loved, and the three of them discussed the investigation Lucy had decided to undertake.

In addition to Eileen's ramblings, they had some solid clues—the tattoos, some missing transcripts from the trial, lists of people who had enough pull for media silence on the case.

Lucy could figure it out with the help of the Bullet Catchers. And, Fletch added with a bit of Aussie smugness, ex-Bullet Catchers. It would be interesting to see who Lucy picked to be on her team for this one. But Wade's job was to protect Vanessa, and that's where he planned to put one hundred percent of his efforts.

When the plane landed, they took a cab to the hospital where Eileen had had the transplant procedure done. Once they were cleared, they took an elevator to the second floor, then followed a long hallway to reach a nurses' station, where they were told to wait. As they turned into the waiting area, Wade balled his hands into fists, certain that Vanessa would be right there.

The room was empty.

He stood for a moment, disappointment punching his chest. He'd been so *sure* she'd be there. So sure she'd let go of that hate, so she could love.

Was he just kidding himself?

"Wade." Miranda put her hand on his arm, pulling him back to the moment. "Fletch and I are going in to see her now."

"Okay," he said, dropping onto the closest seat. "I'll be here." He leaned his head back against the wall and closed his eyes, trying to imagine all the places where Vanessa might run and hide from life and love, and all the affection he could give her that she didn't want.

"You really *are* good at finding people."

For a moment, he thought he was dreaming. But then he opened his eyes and saw her sitting next to him, her eyes as red as when he'd caught her crying that morning.

He touched her cheek, noticing she wasn't wearing her glasses and her hair was pulled off her face. "You're not very good at hiding."

She turned her face and kissed his palm. "I'm not hiding from you. Or from my past. Or from my murky gene pool anymore."

"Did you talk to her?"

She nodded. "A little. She was really out of it. I'm not sure she knew who I was."

"Lucy is certain she's innocent, Vanessa. And that the killer is still very much a threat. I'm not going to let you out of my sight until that person is caught, convicted, and put away."

She smiled. "Or you've taken him down."

"Some other Bullet Catcher gets that job. Mine is to protect you."

"You signed the contract?"

He nodded with pride. "I did. With the caveat that I had first dibs on all jobs in New York City, starting with protecting you." He closed his hand around hers. "I can't think of anyone I'd rather have on my radar."

"Yeah? Me, too."

He rubbed her knuckles. "I guess that's the closest thing to 'I love you' that I'm going to get from you, unless you're hanging off a mountain, waving a Ruger with the safety on."

She laughed softly. "I still can't believe I did that."

"I can," he said seriously. "It shows what you're capable of."

"Murder?"

"Love. For a woman you barely knew."

"Stella is like a mother to me." She rolled her eyes. "As if I didn't have enough of those."

He lifted her face to his. "I was thinking about this on the plane down here. You know, you've never really been taught to love. Everything that happened made you tough and strong and able to handle anything. Anything but . . ." He gently rubbed her lower lip. "Love."

She cupped his face, her fingers warm and steady. "I've been thinking about it, too. And talking to . . ." Her eyes filled. "My mother."

"What did she say?"

"Not much, but I said plenty."

He waited, holding his breath.

"I told her that of all the people in the world, you made me figure out why I am . . . lovable."

So, so lovable. Still, he waited.

"And worthy," she continued softly, a tear falling. "Of your affection . . . and your love."

Finally, he exhaled.

She smiled. "I'm just sorry it took me forever to catch on. I'm usually much quicker on the uptake."

Inhaling her sweet scent, he closed his arms around her. Lucy had said he seemed content; that was an understatement. This was so much more than content. This was bliss.

"You know, Vanessa, taking forever is not a bad thing," he said. "Forever . . . could be really nice."

She leaned closer and kissed him. The kind of kiss he liked the best—long and slow and sweet like a summer evening. When she pulled away, her face was wet with tears. "I could do forever."

He couldn't stop the smile that came from deep inside. "If those aren't the sweetest damn words I ever heard, I don't know what is."

"You watch your mouth, Billy Wade. There are ladies around."

"Don't I know it." He closed his eyes and kissed her hair. "*My* lady."

His tarty, speedy, stubborn, brilliant, sexy, amazing lady.

Turn the page for a sneak peek at

NOW YOU DIE

BY ROXANNE ST. CLAIRE

The stunning conclusion to the Bullet Catchers trilogy!
Available from Pocket Star Books
in September 2008.

CHAPTER
ONE

LUCY SHARPE WOKE to the sound of gunfire. Distant, steady, and infuriating.

She rolled out of bed and strode to the window, totally naked, completely awake, and royally pissed. Who the hell was taking target practice at three in the morning?

She peered at the training compound a half mile away, a few security lights casting yellow circles around the perimeter, but otherwise dark. Only one man had the nerve to do something like this.

Jack Culver. A master at worming his way into places he didn't belong.

She resisted looking at the empty bed behind her. Instead, she scooped up her satin drawstring pajama pants and stepped into them, then yanked the matching camisole over her head.

As she flipped her hair out from underneath the thin fabric, she snagged her G23, checked the magazine, then headed out of her room. Barefoot, armed, and riled enough to scare the crap out of that son of a bitch, she padded down the long, dark hallway that separated her private living quarters from the rest of the ten-thousand-square-foot mansion.

Another gunshot echoed.

He wasn't even *allowed* to fire a gun. Downstairs, she stabbed at the alarm pad in the kitchen and stepped outside into the night air. The stone path was cool under her feet as she moved soundlessly, passing the guesthouse. This smaller version of her own Tudor mansion was dark for the night, the bodyguards and security specialists who were at headquarters for training or for assignment briefings all asleep now.

Another round popped. *Not all of them.*

The shots were slower now, as if he'd switched to a .45 and the recoil and that wounded trigger finger had changed his rhythm. And the echo told her he was out on the straight range, behind the two-story building they used for training.

Breaking every rule and pissing her off: that would definitely be Jack.

When she reached the classroom and simulation facility, she stealthily moved around the building.

She saw the target silhouettes, five of them static, others moving on a cable between them. She heard him rack the semiautomatic he had no right carrying, let alone firing, and then the shuffle of his foot as he took his stance.

She inched out and lifted her Glock, her eyes on the central moving target. When she smacked that silhouette right in the heart, he'd get the message to stop. She slipped her finger over the trigger just as the moon came from behind a cloud, spilling silver light all over the range . . . and over Jack.

She couldn't look away. She could barely breathe.

His dark hair tumbled down to broad, bare shoulders, the carved angles of his back shadowed and smooth. He aimed his gun with steady, tensed arms, his legs in a wide stance. He wore only jeans that were slung low on his narrow hips and fitted over his hard, curved backside.

She closed her eyes, leaning her warm face against the cool cement wall, the image vivid in her mind.

But wait a second. Something was wrong with that picture . . .

Jack was shooting left-handed.

She popped around the corner again to make sure. Of all the arrogant, stubborn, stupid things to try. Did he think she'd change her mind and let him carry if he fired with his other—

The shot cracked and the moving target stopped dead on its cable, shot to the heart.

All right; everyone got lucky sometimes. Especially Jack. She waited, her weapon down as she watched.

He fired. Hit the head. Fired again. Hit the heart. Fired again. Hit the kidney. Fired again. Right between the eyes.

He lowered the gun, and his black hair caught the moonlight as he gave a hoot of victory. The sound reached into Lucy's gut and twisted something she did not want to have twisted.

Not by a man she loathed, blamed for almost killing one of her best men, and had fired because of it. Still, as much as she hated him, as much as she vowed he'd never be a Bullet Catcher again, as much as she regretted the long-ago night she'd actually allowed him near her body—she couldn't fight the tendril of respect that curled around her heart.

He'd taught himself to shoot left-handed—and damn straight, too.

Did he really think that would change her mind? Earn his old job back?

Get real, Jack.

The only reason he was allowed here was because he had information that could help her on a case, and the briefing was early tomorrow morning. *Very* early.

Once more, she drank in the vision of his half-dressed body in the moonlight, then started home, moving as silently as she had on her way there.

Forget sleep. *That* was a lost cause.

She followed alongside the building, thinking about tomorrow's meeting and how Jack would undoubtedly—

A hand clamped over her face and she bucked backward, instantly raising her weapon only to have it knocked right out of her hands. She whipped her elbow around, aiming for the throat, but her attacker ducked at exactly the right instant.

She coiled to throw a kick, but he twirled her effortlessly and pressed her flat against the wall, pushing a shocked breath from her lungs.

Firm, confident hands pinned her against the wall. "Leaving so soon, Ms. Sharpe?"

"You bastard."

"Love you, too, darlin'."

He was six-two and a hundred eighty pounds of solid attitude, but she could have fought him. "I have ten different moves that could fold you in half."

He laughed softly. "Sweetheart, you fold me in half by standing still."

Of course he'd turn it into a sexual tease. "If you don't get your goddamn hands off me, Jack, I'm going to kick you so hard, you'll still be limping tomorrow."

His expression was pure sin, white teeth gleaming, midnight eyes mocking. He took that same wide stance he'd had at the range, offering her direct access to his crotch. The move brushed his hips against her satin PJs, the contact branding her.

"Go ahead. Gimme your best knee."

Her body betrayed her with a white-hot crackle of response.

"You are seriously pushing your luck, Culver."

His eyes narrowed and he pinned her, his chest against hers, his hips dangerously close. "Actually, I'm pushing you against the wall. Like it?"

"Unless you want me to hurt something you value, let me go."

"It's so damn hard . . ." He paused, dropped his

gaze to her mouth, and leaned in an inch, as if he might show her exactly *how* hard it was. ". . . to get your attention around here."

"That's because I'm working. I have a company to run, and you're interrupting the sleep I need to do that." She pressed harder against the building, determined not to give in to the impulse to press against him.

Just once. Here in the dark, alone. Just one more time.

"We'll talk in the morning, Jack. You'll have my attention at the meeting."

"But I have it now."

She shook some hair off her face so she could look right into his eyes. "You've got five seconds to back off."

"Then I'm gonna use them—"

"Four."

He stared at her, his eyes smoky and heavy lidded. "To ask a favor."

"Three."

"You know I'll go right down to the wire."

"You know I'll break your balls, just like that drug addict broke your trigger finger."

His look grew dangerously dark. "My *old* trigger finger."

"Yeah, I saw your new trick. Not impressed. As far as I'm concerned, your *only* trigger finger is injured for life. Regardless of the fact that you managed to get that expunged from your NYPD record, and lied about it to me."

His fingertip grazed the skin under her earlobe, sending a shiver from her neck to her toes.

"My trigger finger works just fine." He dropped his gaze, looking right at the one place where she couldn't hide her response. Her nipples pressed against the thin satin, twin peaks of reaction. "It's firing you up."

She gave him a solid push. "Stop it."

He backed up with a smile, keeping one hand on her shoulder. "Since you're here, let's talk."

"I'm going back to bed."

"I'll go with you." At her look, he grinned. "Up the path, I mean."

That's how Jack always operated. He inched his way into places, eased himself where he shouldn't be, and the next thing she knew, wham—he was taking matters into his own hands. "No."

"Then how about a little friendly competition?" He turned to pick up her gun. Handing it to her, he let their fingers brush. "My left hand against your right?"

He never took no for an answer. "I can't take advantage of you like that, Jack."

"Sure you can. Come on." He notched his head toward the range. "It'll be fun."

Actually, it probably would be. Wrong on every level, but fun. "No."

"You're worried I'll beat you."

She snorted softly.

He leaned closer. "You'll like the prize."

Something unholy and unwanted rolled through her at the rumble in his voice. "Which is?"

"Oh, let's see. Let's make it interesting, but . . . safe."

Nothing was safe with him.

"How about . . ." He was already leading her toward the firing range. "The winner gets to do anything they want to the loser . . . above the neck."

She laughed. "Above the neck."

"Yeah." He guided her to the shooting position. "You win, you can do anything you want to me above the neck. You can box my ears. You can pull my hair. You can—"

"I get the idea."

"Kiss me with tongue."

"We can't—"

"We could."

"—*can't* set up a Tyro course, because I only have one round."

He turned toward a prep area where he'd laid out several different weapons and magazines. "Got a Glock mag right here."

So he'd been planning this all along.

"I'll set up the Tyro," he said. "Three stages, three targets, twenty four shots, ten yards."

"Fine." She slipped the extra ammo in the elastic waistband of her sleep pants and got into position. "I'm going to kick your injured ass and then slap your arrogant face. And then I'm going to bed." Alone.

At the opposite end of the range, the circular markers thunked into place. Without taking a breath, she stood, aimed, and fired eight times. She missed the third shot by a millimeter, but made the rest.

He fired eight times. And missed nothing.

Neither said a word.

She shook her hand, shot until she had emptied the clip, reloaded, racked, and finished the next eight. She missed nothing.

He did the same, missing one.

"Tie game," he said. "Together, this time."

Her eyes locked on the target; she aimed the Glock. Next to her, he did the same.

"Shoot," he ordered.

They fired simultaneously, each shot echoing over the hills and disappearing into the night.

She missed one. He drilled a three-inch hole in the bullseye.

She lowered her weapon. "Nice work."

He shoved his weapon into the waistband of his jeans, then took her Glock, setting it with the others.

"Time to pay the piper," he said softly, turning back to her.

Anticipation rolled over her skin, leaving chills and making her take a half step backward as he lifted his hands to her face.

She couldn't really say no if she wanted to.

"Above the neck, one can find . . ." Strong, warm fingers cupped her face, lifting it toward his. The twinkle in his eyes was the only evidence of humor; otherwise his expression was purely serious. Purely hot. "Many attractive things."

Against her will, she parted her lips. She could do this. She could kiss Jack Culver, take his tongue, feel his body, and walk away. She had control over everything—including her libido.

No one was *that* irresistible.

Her eyes drifted closed as he lowered his face, his breath on her mouth, his fingers just skimming her hairline. He didn't kiss her. Instead, he threaded his hands in her hair and slowly, gently combed through, sliding his fingers all the way to the ends with a sigh of raw appreciation.

"Are you done now?"

"Mmmm. No." He cupped her chin and turned her face, his lips brushing her cheek. A stroke of her hair and a kiss on the cheek? Surely Jack wouldn't settle for that.

Disappointment, cold and sudden, dropped through her.

She stiffened and started to pull back as he placed his lips over her ear.

"All I want above your neck, Lucinda Sharpe, is your brain. That incredible, wicked, keen mind that puts others to shame."

She stayed very still, the sensations of his words in her ears whirling down to her toes.

"Do you know what I love most about your mind?"

The word *love* delivered a little jolt through her, but she didn't move. "I can't imagine."

"That it's open." He punctuated that with the tiniest flick of his tongue against her lobe, firing a few more sparks and deadening any common sense.

"Open?"

"Open to every possibility, no matter how outrageous or unbelievable or impossible it might seem when you first hear about it."

She inched around to face him, close enough to count every lash and every unshaved whisker, but far enough away to lessen his magnetic pull.

"What are you talking about?"

"I need you to have an open mind tomorrow when I present the evidence in the Stafford case." He paused, then leaned a little closer to whisper the rest. "No matter what I say."

"I always have an open mind."

"I'm going to be testing it."

She pulled away completely. "How?"

"You'll see."

All her synapses were firing now, her mind firmly back in focus.

"That's why you did this? You made all this noise, which you knew would get me down here, just to ask me to have an open mind?" She didn't believe it, not for a minute.

"Yep. Unless you want to go into the woods and make out."

"What do I have to have an open mind about? You have a theory about the murder?"

He stepped away to get her gun. "Here you go, Luce." He handed it to her, letting their fingers touch again. "You better get some sleep now. Be careful on your way back to the house. There are wolves all over this place." He winked and walked away, disappearing into the darkness.

Three hours later, Lucy was still at her desk poring over files and thirty-year-old transcripts from Eileen Stafford's trial, when her breath was stolen for the second time in one night.

She blinked at the picture, turned it upside down, and slid her gaze over to the list of names she'd been jotting down on a yellow pad.

"No damn wonder he wanted me to have an open mind." A wry smile pulled at her lips.

Jack was a lot of things: a tease, a flirt, an unrelenting, shameless, fearless smart-ass who had his finger on all her hot buttons and loved to press them. He was also a brilliant investigator, and he could solve crime puzzles like no one she'd ever met.

But more than anything, Jack had a vigilante streak that had gotten him in a lot of trouble.

If he was right about this . . . what would he do about it?

She shuddered to think of the ramifications.

She wanted the truth, and then justice. Jack wanted retribution—period. That was the fundamental difference between them.

She flipped the picture again, looking at the names she'd written, especially at one she'd originally discarded.

Jack wanted much more than an open mind. He wanted access. And she was one of the few people in the world with the connections to investigate something of this magnitude.

Jack knew that, and he was using her.

Which made them even. Because that night a little

over a year ago, when he'd made her forget every pain and every injustice ever inflicted on her . . . she'd been using him.

So she owed him one. And if he was right, this would make history. No, this would *change* history.

Jack knew all too well what she found irresistible.

Sexy suspense that sizzles

FROM POCKET BOOKS!

Laura Griffin
THREAD OF FEAR
She says this will be her last case.
A killer plans to make sure it is.

———◆———

**Don't miss the electrifying trilogy from
New York Times bestselling author Cindy Gerard!**

SHOW NO MERCY
The sultry heat hides the deadliest threats—
and exposes the deepest desires.

TAKE NO PRISONERS
A dangerous attraction—spurred by revenge—
reveals a savage threat that can't be ignored.

WHISPER NO LIES
An indecent proposal reveals a simmering desire—
with deadly consequences.

Available wherever books are sold or at www.simonandschuster.com

Love a good story?
So do we!

Don't miss any of these bestselling romance
titles from Pocket Books.

The
New York Times
Bestseller!

One Last Look • Linda Lael Miller
Someone wants her next breath to be her last...

Alone in the Dark • Elaine Coffman
A woman discovers she has a long-lost twin...and is plagued by
recurring nightmares of her own death.
Is she...**Alone in the Dark**?

Priceless • Mariah Stewart
A man and woman discover that love is the most precious
treasure of all.

Paradise • Judith McNaught
Escape to passion. Escape to desire. Escape to...Paradise.

FINALLY A WEBSITE YOU CAN GET PASSIONATE ABOUT...

Visit
www.SimonSaysLove.com
for the latest information
about Romance from Pocket Books!

READING SUGGESTIONS
LATEST RELEASES
AUTHOR APPEARANCES
ONLINE CHATS WITH YOUR
FAVORITE WRITERS
SPECIAL OFFERS
ORDER BOOKS ONLINE
AND MUCH, MUCH MORE!

POCKET BOOKS
A Division of Simon & Schuster
A CBS COMPANY

POCKET STAR BOOKS
A Division of Simon & Schuster
A CBS COMPANY

16035